the
Hunger

A native of Devon, David Rees is the author of many novels, including some for young people, and of several works of literary criticism. In 1978 he won the Carnegie Medal for *The Exeter Blitz*, and in 1980 The Other Award for *The Green Bough of Liberty*.

the Hunger

DAVID REES

First published in April 1986 by GMP Publishers Ltd
PO Box 247, London N15 6RW, England

British Library Cataloguing in Publication Data

Rees, David, *1936–*
   The hunger.
   I. Title
   823'.914 [F]   PR6068.E368

   ISBN 0–85449–008–6

Typeset by Wilmaset, Birkenhead, Wirral
Printed by the Guernsey Press Company Ltd
P.O. Box 57, Braye Road, Vale, Guernsey, C.I.

Acknowledgment

I am indebted to many books for the background information in this novel, in particular to *The Great Hunger* by Cecil Woodham-Smith, which still remains the classic work on events in Ireland in the eighteen-forties.

for David Grosvenor

CHAPTER ONE

NEVERTHELESS, there is something odd about the man, Mrs Peacock said to herself. Her inability to define what that peculiarity was annoyed her; she was so proud of being able to summarise people in a few well-chosen words. Her eyes darted shiftily back and forth as always when she was nervous, or irritated, or trying to think. She voiced her doubts aloud to her husband. "There is something . . . queer about him," she said.

Reverend Peacock sighed and put down his pen. He was writing a sermon based on the parable of the loaves and the fishes; apt, he thought, considering the rumours concerning the failure of the potato crop and the possibility of a famine more severe than normal. In Ireland at this time – the year was 1845 – starvation occurred to some extent every winter, but reports that in some districts the potato had been destroyed by a hitherto unknown blight suggested that what was merely an annual scourge, usually borne with Christian fortitude and endurance, could turn out to be a catastrophe.

Not that Mr Peacock had a great deal of sympathy for the improvident poor: what might one expect from people so thoughtless that they relied on a single food for sustenance? Which showed his grasp of the history of his own country to be almost wilfully deficient. He was not an evil man, however. He was the Church of Ireland minister of the parish of Clasheen, and of impeccably Anglo-Norman origins. The poverty-stricken Catholic peasantry who lived on nothing but potatoes did not form any part of his congregation. He was afraid of them, he admitted in rare, candid moments: that dark, sullen, brooding mass, secretive and discontented, that bred like rabbits. There were so *many* of them.

"What do you mean, queer?" he said to his wife. The implications of that word have altered, of course, with time, though the Irish still use it to mean "strange". Certainly to neither of the Peacocks did it suggest what it hints to us: probably no word in its vernacular usage had ever conveyed to either the Reverend or his wife the idea of attraction to a person of one's own sex. But he was aware, through his scanty reading of the literature of the Ancient Greeks in translation, that in some far- off, flawed society in the distant past such errors occurred. Also, quite remarkably, in the Ireland of his day, there had been the extremely distressing case of the Bishop of Clogher.

"He has never set foot in a church," said Mrs Peacock. "Neither ours, nor Father Quinlan's."

Mr Peacock sighed again. "We have discussed this before," he said. "That is neither here nor there." More charitable than his wife, he considered non-attendance at church something to be regretted rather than a matter for instant damnation. The Church of Ireland, even in the nineteenth century, was a more liberal and more elastic institution than its Roman counterpart.

"I must beg to differ," Mrs Peacock said. "I, for one . . . well, to other things: you have to agree that his house is run in a most peculiar manner. No servants! It is *most* extraordinary. Neither cook nor bailiff . . . nor gardener . . . just that boy."

"Not exactly a boy: he is a young man in his twenties. I imagine he is cook, bailiff *and* gardener. Perhaps Altarnun is hard up. Many landlords are these days, you know; mortgaged to the hilt, and tenants not paying their rents on time."

"Hard up, my foot! The family owns *two* estates, one of them in England."

"We are not privy to the Altarnuns' bank accounts, my dear."

Mrs Peacock pulled her shawl tightly about herself. "When I arrived at the house," she said, "I rang the bell. No one answered it. I rang again, then discovered that the bell was broken; it came away in my hand. The door was ajar, and so . . . it was perhaps indiscreet of me, even, you may say, unseemly — but I was there on important business: *you* had sent me. I went inside. I could hear Mr Altarnun in the parlour; he was not so much speaking as . . . reciting. I called out 'Is anyone at home?' My voice was evidently not loud enough, for the recitation continued. I knocked on the parlour door, but, again, the monologue went on. So I opened the door, and . . . I'm not sure how to put this . . ."

Mr Peacock, until this speech, had paid attention to his wife with only half his mind; the other half was on the loaves and the fishes. He felt a little annoyed that she had come into his study to prattle about the neighbours, thus interrupting him in work of high seriousness. But now the sermon was forgotten. "Put it how you will," he said impatiently. "What was Altarnun reciting? And to whom?"

"Shakespeare."

"Shakespeare!" Mr Peacock frowned. It seemed a remarkable thing for a landlord to be doing at eleven o'clock in the morning, even if this one had only three hundred acres. Why was he not out of doors shooting, fishing, or galloping his horses?

"The person to whom he was reciting, if you can call him a person, was that *boy*. The servant-of-all-work. Who was lounging, I may add, on the sofa with his feet up on a table."

"Good Heavens!" Mr Peacock stood up, looked out of the window, then paced about the room for a few moments. He stopped in front of his wife. "Now that *is* queer," he said.

"I told you so. What do you make of it?"

"Make of it? Why, I make nothing of it. Nothing." He picked a book off a shelf, blew the dust from it, and replaced it. "It is not our business," he said.

"Of course not." Mrs Peacock stared down at her feet. Large ungainly feet encased in sensible walking shoes.

"I think you should not discuss this with your friends."

"Naturally." There was the tiniest hint of sarcasm in the way she said the word, for Mrs Peacock had virtually no friends, at least not in the immediate environs of the rectory. Clasheen was a small town in the wilds of County Galway, not far from the sea. The countryside was some of the most ruggedly beautiful in the world, a landscape of soaring mountains and rocky inlets of the Atlantic. Mrs Peacock often enjoyed herself walking for miles along the beaches or up the paths in the glens, but for civilised, human society she often thought she could have been better served in Tibet or Mongolia.

The west of Ireland in the 1840s had little communication with the outside world; no railways, almost no decent shops, and certainly nothing of a social life for the "better" class of person – no commercial entertainment in the way of theatres or concerts, few private parties or balls. The people with whom she might have been on visiting terms often lived vast distances from each other over roads that were pot-holed, boggy tracks. The peasantry, in her opinion, had much more fun than she did, dancing and drinking at their eternal round of fairs and wakes.

Galway City was fifteen miles off. Clasheen was nothing, a parish of some five thousand people, the town itself a straggle of dull houses inhabited by the slightly more prosperous Catholics – the doctor, the blacksmith, the small shopkeepers. The Protestant congregation numbered only thirty souls – widows, a schoolmaster and his family, drunken squireens. Mrs Peacock's friends were the wives of such squireens, and she did not consider them bosom companions but persons she was obliged, occasionally, to ask to dinner. She had no children. Her real friends were her two sisters who lived in Dublin, so the pleasures of human intimacy in her case were mostly conducted by post.

She was not, let it be said, completely depressed by her situation. She was a voracious reader and letter-writer, devoted to her husband, and she loved the surrounding landscape.

"Did you recognize the play Altarnun was reciting from?" Mr Peacock asked.

"It was not a play; it was one of the sonnets. I know it well: I had to learn it at school –

> All days are nights to see till I see thee,
> And nights bright days when dreams do show thee me."

"Lord bless us! How *odd*! And . . . what happened when you appeared?"

"The boy jumped to his feet and immediately left the room. The expression on his face was, I thought, somewhat insolent. Mr Altarnun was clearly embarrassed. But he recovered himself – snapped his Shakespeare shut, apologised for not being in the hall to greet me and then asked, with perfect politeness, what he could do for me. I told him I had come on your behalf, that you were busy, and that you had received a letter from the authorities in Dublin."

The letter to which Mrs Peacock was referring came from a civil servant in the British administration in Dublin Castle, and announced details of the relief plan which the Government had devised should a disastrous famine result from the failure of the potato. ("Thank God Sir Robert Peel is our prime minister," Mr Peacock said, more than once. "And a *Tory*!") The Relief Commissioners, the letter said, were asking the more influential residents such as landowners, their agents, the clergy and the magistrates, to form committees which would raise subscriptions to buy food for distributing to those who in the coming months might suffer from starvation.

Mr Peacock had experienced a big puff of self-importance that the letter had been addressed to him rather than Altarnun, Father Quinlan, or any other of the "influential residents". He had spent more time that week with those residents and his fellow pastor of souls than he would have done if the letter had been sent elsewhere. For Father Quinlan he had a grudging respect; the Catholic priest was tough, intelligent, and persuasive. He reminded Mr Peacock of the blocks of granite that protruded in immense quantities through the soil in the coastal areas of County Galway; earth might be eroded by rain and wind, but granite endured.

A sermon, however, on charity during times of famine and pestilence was needed for the Sunday services. Today was Saturday; the sermon was not even started, and Altarnun and two or three others had not yet been told about the letter. Which was why he had deputed Mrs Peacock to make the necessary calls.

"What did Altarnun have to say?" Mr Peacock asked.

"Oh, he was very helpful. If famine does occur, he would be pleased to sit on any committee you wish to form. He would, he said, be the first to give a large donation."

"So he is not poor."

"It seems not."

"Hmmm. I think he is a good man. He is kind to his tenants, one hears. Which cannot be said of most landlords."

"Tut! Do not forget my father has an estate."

"My dear, you cannot think I impugn *him*! It is a fact, however, that there are a considerable number of landlords, absentee mostly, who grind their heels in the faces of the poor. When rents cannot be paid, they throw the defaulters out, pull down their cabins, and turn them loose on the highways to beg – men, women, children and little babies. Property is sacrosanct, but such behaviour is not Christian."

"No, indeed. Are you quoting from your sermon?" Mrs Peacock stood up and smoothed her skirts. "I had better find out from Bridget why lunch is so late."

WHAT ugly specimens they are, Anthony Altarnun said to himself after Mrs Peacock had left his house. Physically ugly, he meant, not morally. She with her darting, inquisitive eyes and hair cut any-old-how, sitting on her skull like an upturned bird's nest; wisps of facial hair, and her purposeful, bandy-legged walk! The rector was even more unprepossessing. Dumpy, with a head much too big for his body, an untidy mop of grey hair, and a squint: it was disturbing to look at him, for his thick-lensed spectacles made his eyes misty, and you could never tell when he would change the focus on you from one eye to the other. And their clothes – so dowdy, so shabby. Anthony put a high premium on an attractive appearance. It was a weakness.

The boy – who was twenty-seven, the same age as Anthony – came back into the parlour. They smiled at each other, silent for a moment. Then Michael said "In the words of the Iron Duke – a damned close-run thing!"

"Yes. We must be more vigilant."

"I will ask my father to repair the bell." Eugene Tangney was a blacksmith, a profession that was not just confined to the shoeing of horses; he was frequently called upon to repair every sort of ironmongery – farm implements, carriages, kitchen utensils, even door-bells. In the rebellion of 1798 – the Year of Liberty, the Year of the French – Michael's grandfather had worked in the forge all the hours God could give him, repairing pikes to stick in the guts of English soldiers.

"You should be gone," Anthony said, looking at the clock. "You know your mother detests unpunctuality."

"And what will your honour be doing while I'm out?"

"Me? I shall inspect the potatoes."

"Ah. This talk of blight."

"Yes, this talk of blight." Anthony sounded a little irritated. "I want to reassure the tenants. If that is possible."

"*We* shall come to no harm, I am thinking."

Anthony scowled. A blacksmith, and therefore the son of a blacksmith, was at this time in Ireland thought to be middle class. Except for owning a large shop, teaching, or the priesthood, it was almost as high as a Catholic could rise, socially and financially. The equivalent today – the proprietor of a garage – is perhaps lower down the scale. Because of their physical toughness, the roar and glow of their fires, the darkness in which they worked, the secrecy in which they wrapped their talents, they commanded respect, indeed awe; many were thought to possess magical powers.

The Tangneys, as far as it was possible for Catholics to be in backward, distressed Ireland, were upwardly mobile. Like Mr Peacock, they had a poor understanding of the tenant-at-will who lived on five acres and sold his oats, butter, eggs and milk to pay the rent, and who was forced in consequence to live on a diet of potatoes. "Bog-trotters," Mr Tangney said of them, though not to their faces. He was only too glad to have left that sort of existence behind; his grandparents had been cottiers in the penal days. He had once heard Michael, as a child, talking in Irish to a friend: "Why are you after speaking Irish?" he had said scornfully. "The language of peasants, beggars, and workhouse paupers! Think *English*! Talk *English*!"

Anthony disliked the Tangney snobbery, the tendency in Michael to be uncaring and dismissive. To some extent he had opened Michael's eyes, but still on occasion the patterns of thought which upbringing had fashioned came out. "I shall not allow the tenants to starve," he said.

Michael looked embarrassed. "I'm sorry," he answered. "I did not think." He moved uneasily from one foot to the other.

"They are no more and no less human than we are. Made in God's image."

Michael lifted his head, and dared a smile. "That from you, who says there is no God!"

Anthony laughed. "You'll be late."

It was a mild, blustery morning in October; huge white clouds scudded towards the Atlantic, like so many boats departing for the United States, Michael said to himself. He swished his stick at the hedge nettles and blackberries as he walked the three miles to Clasheen, and sang: "I met her in the garden where the praties grow!" He had a good singing voice, and could play the piano quite well. Anthony liked to listen to him in the evenings, though Michael pretended to be shy of an audience, and would not usually perform until he had drunk several whiskeys. I'm happy, he said to himself: it was an emotion he had only begun to experience recently. Perhaps it was something to do with the weather, he thought – the sudden warmth and sunshine after weeks of fog and drenching rain that chilled to the bone.

The reason why he was twenty-seven before he had permitted himself to be happy was that he had considered that his way of life – in part carefully and deliberately chosen, in part the consequence of intense feelings – would lead his soul to be damned for all Eternity. He went to Mass every Sunday, but had not received Holy Communion for four years, not since he had moved in with Anthony at Eagle Lodge.

The traditions of Roman Catholicism in Ireland are penitential, puritanical and monastic, their spirit much influenced by the French Jansenists of the seventeenth century. There is conflict between agape and eros: sex is strictly for procreative purposes within marriage, and is not, even in that area, to be enjoyed. Man is essentially a feeble, sinful creature, and requires constant acts of self-denial and contrition. Life is a vale of tears to be got through as best we may. The body must not be seen, must not be a source of pleasure. Such thinking is older than the Jansenist heresy, which merely reinforced what was already engrained in the character of Irish Catholicism. Even Saint Patrick is said to have been alarmed by his converts taking so easily to ascetic celibacy in such numbers.

Michael was not, by nature, inclined to be celibate or ascetic, but he might, all other things being equal, have managed to conform. His sexual experiences, however, were not procreative, and he had learned to enjoy them; nor did he think – now – that his body should be unseen and untouched. But he knew he could burn in Hell for this. It was the influence of Anthony who had altered "would burn" to the more comfortable "could burn"; without this change Michael might have suffered a complete mental and emotional breakdown.

He had discovered that his body was not vile; sometimes he even thought it beautiful. Which it was. He was tall, slender, and graceful, which had caused his father – who was short, stout, and thick-set – to look at him on one occasion and say, with a certain disgust: "girlish!" Mr Tangney was not alluding to sexual orientation, which he would have assumed in any man was the same as his own, but to Michael's apparent want of strength. Though Michael would never have made a blacksmith, Mr Tangney was wrong; there was plenty of muscle on his son's frame. He had not seen it since Michael was a young boy. Maybe Eugene was also referring to the face, which matched the gracefulness of the body – a fine skin drawn taut over prominent cheekbones, full lips, soulful, dreamy eyes, and a mass of dark curls that fell to his shoulders. Mr Tangney's own face was florid, coarse-skinned, and inclined to fat, and his hair was lank and lifeless.

Father and son had an uneasy relationship. Eugene was glad that Michael was bookish, "learned" as he proudly told neighbours, and that he had a secure job at Eagle Lodge, even if Anthony Altarnun – here he would not have argued with Mrs Peacock – was a bit queer, and that that queerness was something more than being good to the tenants and living a bachelor existence with only one servant. But Eugene had hoped Michael would follow him in his own craft. It was customary for a forge to be handed on from father to son; the smith's secrets were family secrets. Five more children had followed the birth of Michael. Three of them had died in infancy: the two survivors were girls. One day the forge would have to be sold to a stranger.

Michael's decision to work elsewhere was not because he wanted to quarrel with his father; on the contrary, he was saddened that he had turned out to be such a disappointment. He suffered in childhood and adolescence from what would nowadays be recognized as an allergy to horses, but at this time the condition was totally mysterious. Was it a punishment, Mr Tangney asked himself, for his family's climb up the social scale? Or a mark of the fairies, his wife wondered? Doctor Lenehan was baffled.

It is a rare allergy, and no one in Clasheen had ever seen anything like it. If Michael came too near a horse, he broke out in hives, his face swelled, and an hour or so afterwards he would suffer from a terrible fit of asthma. His parents constantly feared for his life when he was young. It is difficult to be the son of a blacksmith and not be close to horses; indeed in the Victorian age it would have been impossible for anybody to avoid some proximity. Michael knew that one day he would have to leave home to find work.

For some years he was employed as a servant on Lord Smithers' estate at Coolcaslig, twelve miles from Clasheen. Then he met Anthony Altarnun, who possessed only three horses and who did not ask Michael to have much to do with them. Michael, in any case, had grown out of his allergy in his early twenties, but, nevertheless, he felt that his father never quite forgave him for something that was entirely outside his control.

"Michael Tangney!" he said aloud, which made a bullock look up from the field it was chewing and stare at him. He laughed, and childishly yelled "Moo! Moo! Moo!" The bullock, perhaps thinking he was mad, plodded slowly away. "Tangney!" he repeated. His mother's maiden name was Polyphant. "Elephant! Elephant!" kids had called after her when she was at school, though nothing less like an elephant than Michael's mother could be imagined.

The name was not Irish. In the multitude of Reillys, Healys, Kearneys, Kennedys, Maloneys and Macarthys, related and unrelated, it stood out like a sore thumb and was another factor contributing to Michael's family thinking they were not of the bog-trotting Irish. No Polyphants existed in Ireland, his mother told him, other than those who were cousins, second cousins, third cousins of the same clan. Polyphant is a village in Cornwall, and from there, generations back, their ancestor had originated; a sailor, shipwrecked off the Galway coast, who had decided not to go home. Cornish Celts they might once have been, but Mrs Tangney was as Catholic and Irish a Celt as the Maloneys and the Macarthys. Altarnun is also a village in Cornwall. "That's about the only thing you and I have in common," Michael had said rather sourly to Anthony on one occasion.

His high spirits soon left him. As he approached Clasheen he saw an astonishing amount of activity in the potato gardens, a great crowd of men, women and children milling about. Women were throwing their aprons over their faces and shrieking dementedly. What on earth was the matter? Then he detected a smell more disgusting than any he had ever experienced, worse than muck-heaps outside peasants' cabins, animals wallowing in their own filth, or fish stinking on Galway quay. It was like nothing he could describe, and it seemed to be drifting towards him from the potato gardens. The potatoes! What had happened to them? Where there should have been lines of green-leafed plants, there was a blackened mass of foliage and stalks as if a fire had blasted them. He stood, amazed, then ran towards the crowd.

Father Quinlan, who was trying to restore some sort of order, stopped what he was doing when Michael appeared and said "This is calamity. Calamity. We have the blight." He was as Mr Peacock said, a tall rock of a man, his face as grey as his hair, lined, weather-beaten. His nose was a round knob of stone that had been stuck on the rest of him as if it was an afterthought. Michael was more afraid of him than any other man in the world. He had not received Holy Communion because he had not confessed his sins; if he did, Father Quinlan would know what caused his fear of damnation and be appalled. The priest would never look him in the eye again without squirming.

"Calamity," Father Quinlan repeated. "If the Government does not bail us out we shall all starve. May God have mercy on us."

"Mrs Peacock spoke of Relief Committees," Michael said.

The priest raised his hands in a gesture of despair. "That will be a drop in an ocean," he said.

Michael hurried away from the revolting stench and the slimy, black caricatures of potatoes to his father's house. He went in by the side door to avoid the forge. Though he had not been laid out with asthma for years, he hated the forge, the reminder.

MICHAEL saw his parents every weekend, even though he sometimes found he had little to say to them. These visits did not often make a complete gathering of the family as the second daughter, Noreen, was married and lived in Galway City. Not a brilliant marriage, in Eugene's opinion, for the husband she had chosen was a grocer. It was a step down the ladder, even though this man kept a good shop and was relatively prosperous. Noreen had produced a baby, a boy, "but," Mr Tangney had said to Michael, "he does not bear *our* surname." Michael had taken this as a hint that he should look about him for a wife; he had not answered his father's comment, however, so uncomfortable did it make him feel. The first daughter, Madge, was single. She helped her mother in the house, "until," she said, "the Lord is willing and the right man finds me." She and her sister were copies of Margaret, their mother, as was Michael — the same high cheekbones, dark curly hair and dark eyes, though Mrs Tangney's hair had long ago turned grey.

When he arrived, his parents and Madge were in the best room of the house drinking tea. He slipped in quietly, his "God bless all here" a murmur, for Mrs Tangney was telling a story and she did not like to be interrupted. He sat down by the piano.

"This old woman," his mother was saying, "is a hundred years old and sick unto death with a mortal sickness. But she cannot die. The priest comes to give her the last sacraments, and she confesses a terrible sin she has never told in all her life." Michael shifted uneasily; Mrs Tangney glanced at him, then continued: "It was nearly a century since and she a little girl that the sacred host dropped from her tongue at Communion and hit the floor. She left it there. That is a fearful thing to do, of course, but her punishment is even more fearful: though suffering in her sickness all the pains of our Lord on the cross, she cannot die. The host, do you see, has to be found.

"So the priest gallops off on his horse, and comes to the church which he finds in ruins, plundered I don't doubt by Cromwell. Among the stones is a beautiful tree in full blossom and in its roots is the host — the body and blood of our Saviour. The priest digs it out and takes it to the old woman and puts it on her tongue with the words from the Mass — *corpus Domini nostri Jesu Christi custodiat animam tuam in vitam aeternam. Amen.* The old woman dies, and her soul flies up to Heaven at last."

Madge seemed thoughtful, but Mr Tangney said "Prut, Margaret, have you nothing better to do than tell old women's tales? Fiddle-faddle church stuff!"

"It is only a story, sure," Mrs Tangney agreed. "But it is important the way you receive the Blessed Sacrament." She looked at her son. "It is important to receive it at all."

"Michael, these women will unman us and I the only male in the house now."

"I will play the piano for you," he answered, wishing to change the subject. He turned in his seat and struck out a ringing arpeggio in F major.

"When we have eaten!" his mother cried. "We haven't eaten! First things first." She went out to the kitchen.

"How are you, Michael?" Madge asked. "You *look* fine!"

"I *am* fine, praise God."

"Any girl would turn her head to see you. But you don't see them."

He smiled, and said "I'm waiting for the one who is as beautiful as you."

"You always say that," she answered, laughing. "Don't wait too long. It's as easy for a man to end up on a shelf as it is for a woman."

"Let the boy alone," her father said.

"Do you have enough to eat up at Eagle Lodge?" Madge asked, a little anxiously. It was difficult for her to imagine that two males could between them cobble together a dinner that was fit for human consumption.

Michael smiled again. "We eat like lords," he said. "Don't fret yourself. It's a grand life there, with a view of the bay from the rooms at the front of the house and the mountains at the back. I'm busy with work I enjoy, out of doors hoeing and trenching and weeding the garden, and that improves my muscles, do you see?"

He flexed his right arm; she felt his bicep and said "Oooh!"

"Then indoors I'm cooking and dusting and polishing. At night I improve my mind, for himself lets me read his books. It's Shakespeare I'm onto now. And he pays me handsomely for my work."

"Isn't it a lonely life you are leading?"

"Not so."

"It isn't good for a man to stay single," said his father. "It is unnatural."

Madge sighed. "And for a woman. I don't like it one bit. Brother, you should come down to Clasheen one evening, a Saturday, and take me out dancing."

"I will. Yes, I promise you that. But I warn you I'll look at *all* the girls."

She laughed, content with him now. "You're a terrible man, Michael Tangney. Wicked."

How exhausting it is to lead this double life, he thought to himself. The secrecy. Being constantly on edge.

Mrs Tangney returned, pushing a trolley on which were plates of salad, cold meat, bread and butter, and another pot of tea. "We don't dine like cottiers yet," she said. "Come all of you, sit at the table."

"What news do you have, Michael?" Eugene asked, as he helped himself to enormous quantities of ham and bread.

"You have not heard? I would have told you, but I did not wish to spoil my mother's story. The blight is upon us."

Mr Tangney dropped his fork. "Potato blight? Where? I was not in the forge these two hours, and I miss all the chatter."

A loud knock on the door startled them. "Lord save us, who can it be?" said Madge, getting up to answer it.

It was Father Quinlan and the Reverend Peacock. The Tangneys looked at them, astonished. Never before had the Protestant minister been inside their house, though he had taken his mare to the forge more than once. But most remarkable was the presence of the two men of religion together. Something extraordinary must have occurred. They were soon told what it was; the entire potato crop had been destroyed in every field within a two-mile radius of the town. Beyond that the potatoes seemed, for the moment, to be in excellent condition.

Mr Tangney got up and rushed into his garden. He did not grow many potatoes for he had money to buy them: he had a mere two or three lines, and he found them, as Mr Peacock said he would, in a state of stinking black decomposition. He stared in bewilderment, then checked the other vegetables – turnips, cabbages, onions, carrots. They all looked perfectly healthy.

He went back indoors. Father Quinlan was underlining the significance of the event. Many families now had nothing to eat until the next crop was ready for digging, which would not be till the following autumn: a year without food. Some people might want to eke out their existence on the corn and dairy produce of their holdings, but that was a temptation to be resisted; corn and dairy produce were the rent money. Eviction was inevitable if it was not paid.

"What has happened to the potatoes already dug?" Michael asked. "Surely the crop has been lifted in many fields?"

"They are destroyed too," Father Quinlan said. "Destroyed utterly." The usual method of storing potatoes in Ireland was to keep them in a pit covered with turf sods; the blight had been just as successful at getting inside these pits as it had been in decimating the living plants and their tubers.

"What is the cause of it?" Mrs Tangney asked. "An act of God to punish us?"

"I do not think it is God's handiwork," Mr Peacock said.

There were many arguments in Clasheen that day as to whether the disease floated, invisibly, through the air, or whether it was some kind of poison in the soil. Nobody at this date had heard of the fungus *phytophthora infestans*, which arrived in Europe in the 1830s, probably in a diseased potato from North America. "If a man," writes E. C. Large in *The Advance of the Fungi*, "could imagine his own plight, with growths of some weird and colourless seaweed issuing from his mouth and nostrils, from roots which were destroying and choking both his digestive system and his lungs, he would then have a very crude and fabulous, but perhaps an instructive, idea of the condition of the potato plant." The people of Clasheen had no knowledge of this; all they understood was what they could see and smell: ruin.

The potato is an extraordinary vegetable. Great quantities can be grown for a minute financial outlay; an acre and a half will feed a large family for a year. Pigs and cattle can also be reared on it. As a diet it is probably the most useful food known to man: no other gives so much varied nourishment, and its taste does not pall. It is perhaps for these reasons that the population of Ireland grew far more rapidly than that of any other European country in the late eighteenth and the early nineteenth centuries.

Before the Famine emigration from Ireland was virtually unknown, so that by 1845 the country was almost literally swarming with people, most of whom were so poor that they had to live on a single food. For a nation to be forced to rely on one food is extremely dangerous; if it fails, what then? The potato was vulnerable because it could not be stored for long. It couldn't then be pickled or preserved or frozen, and the Irish had nothing at all to replace it.

"We are forming a Relief Committee," said Mr Peacock, assuming his most pompous voice, "under the joint chairmanship of Father Quinlan and myself. Its purpose is to consider ways and means of helping those who may otherwise starve. We would be delighted, Mr Tangney, if you will serve on it."

"I would think it an honour," said the blacksmith.

"Dr Lenehan," Father Quinlan said, "will serve too, and, we would hope, Mr Altarnun. But he was not at Eagle Lodge when we called, so, Michael, would you ask him on our behalf?"

"Certainly," Michael replied.

"We are meeting at Dr Lenehan's house at ten o'clock on Monday morning."

The two clergymen departed. "I must go too," Michael said, when he had finished his dinner. "If the potatoes at Eagle Lodge have rotted, himself will be needing me."

"But you haven't played the piano!" Margaret Tangney protested. "Why . . . you've not been with us two hours!"

"Mother . . . go out and see what has happened. There are whole families left with nothing." At the door he stopped, turned, and looked at his parents and sister. "I promise that no one in this house will go hungry," he said.

"What talk is this?" his father answered. "We do not live on potatoes here!"

24

CHAPTER TWO

THE English reader who has the stereotypical notion of the Irishman as suited only to navvy's work, fighting, and getting drunk, may think it odd that an Irish blacksmith in 1845 should own a piano, serve on a committee, and have a son who read Shakespeare. But the English have never known much about their western neighbour. "The moment the very name of Ireland is mentioned," said Sydney Smith, "the English seem to bid adieu to common feeling, common prudence and common sense, and to act with the barbarity of tyrants and the fatuity of idiots."

Another stereotypical idea has to be knocked on the head, this time from the other party: that all Anglo-Irish landlords were monsters and tyrants, concerned only with collecting rents. Most of them, it is true, fitted this description, but there were others – the Marquess of Sligo, the Duke of Leinster, Arthur Lee Guinness, Lord Courtown and Colonel Vaughan Jackson are examples – who, during the Famine, gave generously of their own money to feed their tenants; they served indefatigably on relief committees, fever committees and Boards of Guardians; they employed the destitute to drain land and to build roads and houses. Such a person was Anthony Altarnun, though his finances and the estate he managed were nowhere near the size of the Duke of Leinster's or indeed those of any of the people mentioned above.

Eagle Lodge and its three hundred acres belonged, in fact, to his elder brother Richard. The Altarnuns also had an estate in Cornwall, which was owned by the second brother, Charles. Anthony, the youngest, had inherited no property. He had decided on a career in the army and served as a lieutenant in a regiment in India, where Richard also lived, working for the East India Company. Eagle Lodge had been run for years by an agent, with the result that the Altarnuns had a generally bad reputation for absenteeism, a reputation that changed when Anthony came to live there.

After only two years with his regiment, Anthony had abruptly resigned his commission and announced to an astonished Richard that he would like to manage the Clasheen estate. Richard had tried to dissuade him – he could not understand why anyone in their right senses should want to give up the officers' mess for a solitary existence in a backward, primitive, barbaric country. However, he had eventually agreed, though he neither liked nor approved of Anthony. Richard was a conventional product of his period and class: cautious, prim, genteel, a Victorian paterfamilias and a devout Christian of the high Anglican persuasion.

His brother, in his opinion, was rakish, restless, and reckless; Anthony thought Richard profoundly dull. Other people saw Anthony as intelligent, free thinking, an attractive breaker of orthodoxy. He wanted to go to Ireland, he said, to do something more useful with his life than taking potshots at Afghan bandits and getting drunk. He would stay there only a year or so, for he would not be happy for long in isolation; but his relationship with Michael was to change that.

Anthony had always been a confident man, sure of his own capacities, though he had not yet found the right slot in the world; Ireland, maybe, would show him what that was. Self-confidence had led him at the age of twenty to a position where he felt it quite easy to abandon his religious faith – well before the publication of *The Origin of Species* might have influenced his thinking, as it did many later Victorian agnostics. He loved reading anything that came to hand – novels, plays, philosophy, mathematics, scientific books, poetry. He was a more voracious reader than Mrs Peacock (whom he detested: a nasty-minded busybody) though not so discriminating. She never opened a book she thought might be the least improper. Unlike her, he loathed writing letters, particularly to Richard, who was always anxious to know if the rents, down to the last penny, had been collected, and to hear of the minutest details of expenditure:

repairs, paint, seed, even how much had been spent on nails and screws. Michael wrote these letters for him.

He was physically confident, too, good at all games and an expert horseman. The word that summed him up best was enthusiast – in his appetite for whatever he was doing: reading, eating, drinking, talking, listening; even stillness. Energy is eternal delight; the spell he cast over Michael was total. His tenants, suspicious at first, were rapidly won over. His body was the opposite of Michael's; a big man, over six foot, big-boned, with a tough, well co-ordinated sportsman's physique. In middle age he would grow fat, whereas Michael would always be lean. He had a pale skin, hair the colour of straw, and brilliant blue eyes: despite his Cornish origins, his face and build were as Saxon as Michael's were Celt.

He was in his element that afternoon with the tenants. The news from Clasheen had reached both him and them. Every man, woman and child was out of doors, anxiously inspecting the plants still in the fields and prodding the potatoes that had already been dug and stored in pits. Not a trace of blight was to be found on any of them. "I shall not see you starve," he said to the Widow O'Gorman. "If it does fail and you cannot pay the rent," he told Mr and Mrs Keliher and the ten young Kelihers – the most fragile family on the estate; they had only three acres and lived in a one-roomed cabin with a pig and six chickens – "well, you cannot pay the rent. The crop next year will be good, and then you can pay." (My brother be damned, he said to himself.)

"God's blessings on you, your honour," said Keliher, going down on his knees. "May the Lord and the Holy Virgin herself see you in Heaven."

"Get up, man! Get up!" Anthony replied, acutely embarrassed. "I will not have people kneeling in front of me. Who do you think I am? Prince Albert? Chance, fate – call it what you will – has put you there and me here. It could easily have been the other way round."

"May God spare your health," Keliher said, not understanding more than a word or two of this line of argument. He shuffled himself into an upright position.

"Dig up all your potatoes now and keep them indoors. That is

27

my advice," he said as he rode away. He gave similar advice to the Scannells, the Sullivans, the Leahys, the O'Learys, the Cronins, everyone. His last visit was to Patrick O'Callaghan, the oldest tenant, and in his opinion the wisest and most sensible.

"What do you think?" he asked the old man, unable to conceal the worry in his voice.

O'Callaghan took off his cap and scratched his skull. He was bald; his brown skin was leathery, like the binding of an ancient book, and his voice creaked with age. "The crop was scarce in the Thirties three years running; that was the curl and the dry rot. In 1807 praties were after being ruined by frost; I remember it well. But this – this, I have seen nothing like it. Never."

He shook his head.

"Did you notice, your honour, in the fields in Clasheen this morning before they went black, a kind of whitish dust? Dust, but not dust. It settled on the plants. A seed, maybe."

"I have not been in town today."

"It's a seed I'm thinking, blown on the air. A monstrous, evil thing of a seed. It does not come out of the earth. The earth is good; it is rich – we have all been fed by this land and our fathers and our grandfathers before us."

"Do you think the crop will fail here?"

"Why, if the wind blows this way, it surely must!"

Anthony thought for a while. "I have an idea," he said. "And I'd like your opinion of it. If the blight is airborne, then the safest place for the crop is indoors – in a cellar that has no windows and no vents. I have such a cellar at Eagle Lodge, and it's free of damp. If everyone on the estate brought their potatoes up to the house while we still have time, well then, the crop might be rescued."

The old man was silent. He stared at the sun, in and out of clouds. "Saving your presence, your honour, it will not do."

"Why not?"

"Your honour . . . no one will know whose praties are which."

"Does that matter, man? We are facing starvation, disease and death!"

"The Sullivans will think the O'Learys are taking more than their own. The O'Learys will not trust the Kelihers. Everyone says the Widow O'Gorman is as greedy as a pig. The Cronins will not care to traipse in and out of the Lodge; they think they are too grand to ask favours. The Scannells will say their pit is as sound as your cellar."

"This is childish. Absurd!"

"It is." The old man sighed, and replaced his cap. "It is so, surely."

"Will you ask them? See what they think."

Some hours later, when Michael had returned from Clasheen and he and Anthony were exchanging the afternoon's gossip over a meal — roast lamb cooked by Michael, and a bottle of red wine — Patrick O'Callaghan came to the back door of Eagle Lodge. Not one of the tenants liked the Altarnun's idea, he said to Anthony, who answered his knock. Ah, sure, they were the soul of politeness; it was kind, it was generous, and they were grateful they were in the Altarnun's thoughts, but for the present they would look to themselves, thank you all the same.

Ireland in 1845 was clearly not ready for an experiment in socialist co-operatives.

Four days afterwards the entire potato crop at Eagle Lodge — except for Anthony's and Michael's, which they dug that Saturday evening and put in the cellar — was a dark, evil-smelling, pulpy mass of putrefaction.

IMAGINE that same Saturday in Clasheen at — roughly — half past eleven at night. It is pitch dark, for the moon has been obscured by thickening cloud. There is a lamp or a candle burning in a bedroom here and there, for not everyone is asleep. Anthony and Michael are two who are very much awake. The only noises are those of animals — the clop of a horse's hoof, two cats fighting, the howl of Mrs O'Leary's dog — and the wind, which is growing restless.

Mrs Peacock, disturbed by her husband's snores, opens one eye but she soon falls asleep again. Eugene Tangney is sleeping the sleep of the just and righteous, but Margaret is awake, praying that the Lord will listen to her and avert all catastrophes to come, particularly starvation. Madge Tangney did not drop off as easily as usual; she, too, was thinking disquieting thoughts on the subject of potatoes, though she is sleeping now. Dan Leahy is doing nice things with her in her dreams.

Father Quinlan is dreaming of brimstone and rotten potatoes; he will soon sit up in bed with a shout, then light his candle and read Cornelius Jansen's *Augustinus* for an hour to solace himself. He is a little unusual among Irish priests, for he is not the twinkling curmudgeon of American films or the type who enjoys kicking a football with the lads; he is rather a thirsty idealist, a Victorian Reverend Hale – that seventeenth-century connoisseur of Massachusetts witchcraft. His background is educated intelligentsia and comfortable living for more than twenty years in England, where he lost his Irish speech rhythms and some of the accent, though not the peculiar brand of Catholicism of his heritage. He would make an intrepid hunter of witches.

In cabins and hovels there are many people lying awake – those whose entire means of feeding themselves has vanished in a single day: distraught women, unquiet men tossing fretfully, husbands and wives staring at the future, at hunger and workhouses, at fever and begging. A few couples are making love. Despite the Irish detestation of the body, there are those in Clasheen who at this moment are enjoying – up to a point – the pleasures of the flesh. The teeming millions of the country bear witness to that fact.

In the master bedroom at Eagle Lodge two people of the same sex are making love; Anthony, having penetrated Michael fifteen minutes ago, is very near climax. It is a scenario that has been repeated almost every night these past four years, with Anthony invariably taking the "active" role. Their orgasms come at more or less the same moment, for they have long since perfected their technique. Anthony then stays inside Michael for a while, and whispers "I love you. I don't think I could go on living without you." He withdraws, and Michael turns over, so that he is facing his lover, who enfolds him in his arms. "I love you too," Michael says. They fall asleep like two adjacent question marks, Anthony's breath moist on Michael's skin.

Anthony sleeps first because he has an untroubled conscience; Michael, for a few minutes, thinks of what he has done and what it means. I was expressing my love, he says to himself; how can that be wicked, filthy, deserving of hell-fire? He pushes thoughts of Sodom and Gomorrah out of his mind (he can quote those bits of Genesis by heart) and searches instead for more reassuring texts. His mind picks on a verse from the New Testament – "The Father himself loveth you, as you have loved me." God is love. Sometimes he has felt that making love with Anthony has brought him nearer to God than he has ever been. Anthony just looked bewildered when Michael once told him. "The Father himself loveth you, as you have loved me." He sleeps, profoundly, without dreams.

Just as there are no registers that spell out the names of the Famine dead, so there are no documents to read on the subject of Irish gay life in the mid-nineteenth century. Anthony's and Michael's behaviour was probably very unusual, but homosexuals there surely were, though they would not have known that word or used it to describe themselves. Considering Irish attitudes to the body, the majority of them would have repressed their tendencies, particularly in the rural west; quite possibly they would have married. But, if you recognized you were of that inclination, had to some extent given it room inside yourself, had met another such, and you fell deeply in love: what then?

You would, most likely, have stayed with him/her for life. Or tried to. Where would you find another? They would certainly have tried to be very discreet, to merge into the indistinct background. But Anthony and Michael were not as discreet as they could have been. Anthony had already caused some eyebrows to be raised by employing just one "servant," and Mrs Peacock this morning had found that "servant" lolling on the sofa with his feet up on a table, while his boss read a Shakespeare sonnet to him. (One of the sonnets that refers to a male lover, but Mrs Peacock didn't know that.)

Such carelessness in the 1980s would have led outsiders to put two and two together and arrive at the correct answer, but in 1845 it would not have done. Mrs Peacock, like many respectable – and indeed not so respectable – men and women of that time wouldn't have imagined in a million years that people of the same sex screwed with each other. Her attitude, if such things had been suggested to her, would have been like Queen Victoria's when she struck from the infamous Labouchère amendment of 1885 the clause that proposed fines or imprisonment for women who indulged in lesbian activities;

or perhaps Judge Brack's remark when he heard that Hedda Gabler had committed suicide – "People don't do that sort of thing." Or maybe what it is rumoured that King George the Fifth said when he was told an acquaintance of his was homosexual: "Good God, I thought men like that shot themselves!"

Anthony and Michael had both been, when they found each other, lonely almost to the point of desperation. Anthony had had an easier life coming to terms with himself; after the age of seventeen he had had no worries about why he preferred men, nor any wish to straighten himself out – he simply wanted to meet homosexual men. He was educated at an English public school, an institution in which it was not difficult to find other males to have sex with – and his teenage years were over before Dr Arnold's reforms infused the public schools with the spirit of muscular Christianity. Nor was it a problem in London or the big cities of India. There was always a supply of young men willing to offer their bodies for a few coins; but it was not so easy to meet someone he could love.

Michael, when he had met Anthony, had had no sexual experience at all. He recognized the nature of his desires, however – at seventeen he had fallen madly in love with Joseph Lenehan, the doctor's son, a year older than he was. This boy, like Anthony, was fair-haired and blue-eyed. They rarely spoke; Michael's feelings made him stammer and go red with blushes. Joseph, as a result, thought him a little stupid. To love this boy was extremely painful: he haunted every hour of Michael's life, and to say one word about the situation to anyone at all, let alone to his beloved, was obviously out of the question. Should he confess to Father Quinlan? He was on the point of doing so more than once, but he did not. It wasn't a sin. It became a sin if they touched, if they kissed, but that, clearly, would never happen. There was no need, therefore, to confess. So Michael argued with himself.

And it was not a sin to walk past Dr Lenehan's house at night, hoping Joseph would look out of the window; nor a sin to be in a street, accidentally on purpose, where he knew the object of his affections would be strolling by. But loving weighed on him as heavily and as wearily as the sailor on Sinbad's back, and his prayers before he slept were the same as Christ's in the Garden of Gethsemane: that this cup might be taken from him.

32

It was taken from him. But only because he fell for another boy, Dan, the eldest son of the Leahys, a hefty, tough, good-looking peasant and Clasheen's hurling champion. It was the same thing all over again – affections bottled up, not a word said to anyone. Michael was twenty-three when he met Anthony, and by then he had learned to live, sulkily and unwillingly, with this aspect of himself. Though he had never felt the slightest prick of desire for a girl, he was at ease in female company – he had grown up with two sisters – and thought that one day he might get married. To be alone all his life was pointless, absurd; he was fond of children, liked the idea of having his own, and marriage might "cure" him – the pleasures of sex with his wife might push these devils of other men from his thoughts.

But when he imagined himself making love with a woman he shuddered. Why am I like this, he asked frequently. Am I really "girlish" as my father once said? Is there something about my body that is different from the bodies of other men? I'm less hairy, perhaps. Is that a sign? Is it an affliction of unknown cause, like a cleft palate, a club foot? An indication that God is displeased with me? But I've done nothing to displease Him so much that He'd give me this as a penance. Michael felt he was unique. What other men were like him? The last of them were destroyed in Sodom and Gomorrah, or were found only in the pages of books written long ago.

His parents worried about his taciturnity, his withdrawal into literature, his withdrawal from the company of other young people. "I admire his learning," his father said, "but he should go to Flanagan's Bar on a Saturday night and get himself drunk!"

"Is that a sign of being a man?" Mrs Tangney asked, sarcastically.

"Well . . ." Eugene relapsed into silence. Michael, in fact, did sometimes get drunk, but his parents did not know it.

"He has the mind of a priest," Margaret Tangney said. "It would give me great joy if he entered the Church."

She had said this on one occasion to Michael, who was incredulous. "Me? In a soutane?" He laughed. "God is not mocked, Mother."

"What does that mean?"

"It means I am not worthy. *Domine non sum dignus ut intres sub tectum meum.*"

"If all Irishmen spoke so we wouldn't have a Church at all! And you are not finishing the prayer: *sed tantum dic verbo et sanabitur anima mea* — say but the word and my soul shall be healed. Is something troubling you, Michael?"

"No." He stared, feigning surprise. "Should there be?"

HE had met Anthony on a hot Sunday afternoon when he was trespassing on the Eagle Lodge estate. He had heard of the agent's departure and that no one else had yet arrived; it was an excellent opportunity to explore. Michael had lived near Eagle Lodge all his life but never seen it — he had not previously risked entering the grounds as the agent had a reputation for shooting accurately at poachers. The house was not as large as some country houses in Ireland. It had been built in the 1780s as a summer residence for the Marquess of Letterfrack, who, at the turn of the century, had got heavily into debt and sold the house with the surrounding three hundred acres of land to Anthony's grandfather.

Michael, watching from a clump of rhododendrons, saw at the end of a neglected, gravelled drive an attractive brick Georgian villa, a window on either side of the porch and three above. In the middle of the lawn was a group of larch trees. He loved larches: the tiny buds in spring like green dust, the pale feathery needles in autumn. He walked boldly up the drive, round the house — there was no sign of anyone indoors — and found himself in a huge, wildly overgrown garden. The grass came up to his knees; summer flowers blossomed in great profusion, enswathed in thistles, docks, dandelions, buttercups. The agent had evidently been much more interested in poachers than in gardeners.

At the bottom of the garden, beyond a hedge, was a patch where vegetables had once been grown, but it was derelict now. There were trees laden with ripening apples, plums, pears; soft fruit bushes, the crop unpicked or fallen to the ground. He helped himself to some raspberries — delicious, sweet — and wiped his brow. It was a sultry July day. The vegetable garden petered out in a tangle of bushes, but someone, he noticed, had once made a path that was not yet quite impenetrably dense with brambles. The path led into a small wood – unusual in treeless Galway – and the land sloped sharply downwards. He could hear a stream. He walked on, and the noise of the stream became a roar: he could now see a waterfall cascading over rocks into a pool of some size. Stretched out by the pool was a man. He had no clothes on.

Michael was acutely embarrassed. He had never confronted a naked adult body before apart from his own; what kind of person was this who dared to reveal himself so brazenly? Was he someone in authority at Eagle Lodge? But . . . he was asleep. And beautiful.

A lazy, drawling, English voice said "Are you going to stand there the whole day? Come down here."

Michael turned on his heel and made to run off, but the other called "Don't go! There's no harm done." The voice was not angry, Michael realized; it was gentle and . . . almost pleading. He walked slowly down to the pool. "You thought I was asleep, but I wasn't. I saw you before you saw me. You look hot."

"It's hot weather, surely," Michael said.

"Why don't you strip too, and swim?"

At that moment there was nothing he wanted to do more. He was prickly with sweat – the heat of the day, his struggle with the overgrown garden, the tension of this meeting. Who was this man? Presumably the owner, but English landlords were not in the habit of taking all their clothes off and talking to Irish natives as equals. Why don't I swim, Michael thought, but the idea of his naked body being scrutinized made him feel very uncomfortable. Then . . . to hell with it. Let him stare if he wants to; I'm not so ugly. He undressed and ran into the pool.

It was superbly cold. He splashed about, then swam, ducked his head under the waterfall. The tension drained away.

"Here, you may have my towel," Anthony said.

As he dried himself Michael was aware of the eyes looking at his face, then at his legs, his arms, elsewhere. *He is as I am!* He turned and gazed at Anthony, astonished. There is someone else in the world. *I am not alone.*

Anthony was smiling, Michael solemn.

"When you're dressed," Anthony said, "and it's time I got dressed too, we'll go back to the house and I'll make tea. There are no servants yet; I've been here only one day. And you can tell me who you are and what you're doing here – your whole life story. Then I'll tell you mine. Why are you looking at me like that? I'm not a ghost!"

Three hours later Michael was walking back to his parents' house, seeing little of the familiar landscape; his mind was in turmoil. Heavy, bruised clouds gathered over the mountains and lightning flickered. The air was muggy, still. He would probably not reach home before the storm began, but he was oblivious to the weather. He did not even notice the first heavy drops, and was amazed to find, when he opened the door of the forge, that he was wet right through.

What had been left unsaid was as important as what was said. There had been no instant invitation, as might happen nowadays, to go upstairs and fuck; and neither of them mentioned past sexual histories and non-histories, or present desires. Michael felt certain of one thing, however: he wants me as much as I want him. But . . . there is danger of hell-fire.

What was said, as Anthony had intimated, was biographical, though Michael did most of the listening. Anthony's world was a revelation. Michael knew of it, of course, from books, newspapers, and people talking, but he had never conversed with an Englishman in this way, and had never met anyone who had been to India. Places that were abstractions, coloured by his own mental images, suddenly became alive, no longer figments of his dreaming. He felt he could really see London now.

And there was the sheer niceness of this man, too, his charm and exuberance, and the way he sat in his parlour drinking tea with the son of an Irish blacksmith as if it was the most common everyday occurrence. Books: "Have you read. . . ?" Anthony asked, several times, and on the whole Michael had not. "It's in the house," Anthony said; "borrow it if you want."

Was this love? Did it happen so quickly? Yes, it did: one day he had not noticed Joseph Lenehan or Dan Leahy, the next he had, and he could not take his eyes off them or get them out of his thoughts.

If he didn't want me, I wouldn't have been sitting on that sofa drinking tea. He'd have accused me of trespassing, ordered me out of the grounds, probably handed me over to the peelers. Is it love with him, or does he just want my body? Not that in either case Michael was at all ready to hand himself over, but he would soon find out. Anthony had offered him employment and he had unhesitatingly accepted, even though the idea of quitting his present situation had not previously occurred to him. The job was that of general factotum: the garden needed attention, and Michael could perhaps help in the house until Anthony hired a cook and maybe a couple of other servants.

A month went by, and Anthony made no attempt to find other servants. He did the work himself, or shared it with Michael — directing operations in the garden, cooking some of the meals, even cleaning the rooms. Michael was surprised, but said nothing. He was given a free run of the house as if they were partners, ate his meals with Anthony, sat with him in the evenings, reading, talking.

There were few visitors — Mrs Peacock had been an early caller — and when they were present, Michael made himself scarce or acted up the servant role. He did this without being asked, but Anthony said "If you didn't do so, I would tell you to." Anthony knew no one in the neighbourhood, and seemed disinclined to form any acquaintanceships. It is because of me, Michael said to himself, as they swam together in the pool; it has to be that — there is no other reason.

But still nothing was said. His bedroom was across the passage from Anthony's, and he would lie awake at night, wishing he could sleep, listening to Anthony turn over, or snore, or get up to shut a window. This love was far more painful than the previous two, for he *knew* this man, spoke to him, shared the same space all day, every day. And yet . . . we have not touched; I have not sinned.

He was on the point of giving in his notice. He couldn't stand the strain any longer; it would surely be easier to be apart from him, not see him again. Not see him again? He couldn't live with that either.

He lay in bed staring at the moonlight. He heard Anthony's footsteps: the door opened. "I wanted . . . that first afternoon!"

Anthony said. "I've watched you . . . how you walk, your eyes. Your body. I had to be sure. I had to wait. I love your gentle, sweet character . . . I love you."

Michael lay there a moment, then got out of bed; touched Anthony's skin, shoulders, arms. Anthony took his hand and led him into his own room. The first real kisses of Michael's adult life. The first hands stroking his body.

Afterwards, drifting towards sleep, he thought: I have sinned now. But was Sodom and Gomorrah as this was? "But the men of Sodom were wicked and sinners before the Lord exceedingly . . . Then the Lord rained upon Sodom and upon Gomorrah brimstone and fire from the Lord out of Heaven; and overthrew those cities with all the plain, and all the inhabitants of the cities, and that which grew upon the ground." There were no wicked men in this bed, he told himself, no one who has sinned exceedingly. It was love. But the Lord rained down brimstone and fire. God is love.

CHAPTER THREE

"THAT man should be in the army, not in the church," said Mrs Peacock. "He would make an excellent sergeant-major." She was referring to Father Quinlan.

"Nevertheless, my dear," Mr Peacock replied, "without him this morning the mob would have been uncontrollable. We would have had a riot on our hands."

The Relief Committee had held its first meeting, but so great was the crowd who wanted to hear its deliberations that it had adjourned from Dr Lenehan's house to the bigger premises of Flanagan's Bar. Nearly everyone whose entire subsistence was the potato tried to cram in, demanding immediate solutions to their problems. When the committee had no immediate solutions to offer, the scene grew ugly; Mr Peacock could not make himself heard above the noise, and Keliher, enraged because he had the impression he and his family were to be allowed to starve, threw a glass of porter at the Protestant clergyman. Anthony leaped into action and bundled him outside; "I expect the highest standards from my tenants!" he shouted. "You will set an example!"

"You won't go hungry!" Keliher shouted back. "You'll see to yourself first!"

"If you had brought your potatoes up to the house on Saturday," Anthony said, "you'd have no worries now!"

When he returned inside, Father Quinlan was imposing order on the chaos, yelling out instructions left, right and centre. Only one representative of each family was to stay in the bar. If there were any further disturbances, he would send for the peelers. Mr Peacock, Anthony noticed, had a very disagreeable expression on his face, as if he had stuck his head near some disgusting smell. His hair was wet with porter.

"The police are of no use," said Mrs Peacock, in a tone of voice that sounded as if she'd like to see blood flowing. "Soldiers are required when peasants run amok! A few shots would have scattered them like sheep!"

What slaughter might have ensued had soldiers opened fire in a crowded bar did not enter Mrs Peacock's head, but her husband, knowing she would not understand – or did not want to – merely said "They *did* scatter like sheep. We had no trouble after Father Quinlan spoke to them." He sighed. "He certainly knows how to lead his flock."

"It is still no way for a man of the cloth to behave," Mrs Peacock sniffed.

Dr Lenehan was listened to in silence. He was a short, peppery, red-faced man, extrovert and not without a sense of humour. The committee, he said, had no power to distribute relief in the form of money – many people were suffering under the misapprehension that they would be given cash or tickets they could exchange for food – and in any case it had, as yet, very little money: when more subscriptions came in, members would buy food and store it for distribution when there was nothing left to eat.

"We *have* nothing left to eat," an old woman said.

"You must all have a few coins, surely," the doctor answered. "Or goods to pawn."

"So the gombeen man becomes rich? Never!"

The doctor was incorrect in assuming that everyone possessed a few coins. Some people had no money at all. They did not go into a shop from one year to another; they grew their potatoes and survived: they did not need to buy anything.

Mr Peacock read aloud the letter sent from Dublin Castle. As well as suggesting that committees be formed to collect food, the Government had other schemes in mind. Landlords were asked to give increased employment on their estates. The Irish Board of Works would create jobs by building new roads, and relief committees were being asked to submit plans for this, with estimates of costs and how many men could be used. If there was any likelihood of fever resulting from starvation, new hospitals would be erected. And lastly, the Government itself would buy quantities of Indian corn from the United States which it would sell so cheaply that the price of food in general would be kept down.

"It is an extraordinary scheme," Mrs Peacock said. "Grossly extravagant! We shall have all the beggars of the nation on our backs in no time! That will be the consequence, mark my words!"

"I completely agree with you, my dear." Mr Peacock had not ventured this opinion to anyone else. "Who is to foot the bill for it all? We, the taxpayers!" He was not wholly wrong: it was a more generous and far-reaching scheme for famine relief than any government had ever devised, and it was to cost Sir Robert Peel the premiership.

"If women had the vote," Mrs Peacock said, "I would vote for Lord John Russell."

"My dear! You could not do that. You were brought up a Tory!"

"It is nothing to do with upbringing, sir; it is a matter of common sense. No more Orange Peel for me!"

Mrs Peacock may have been in an uncommonly bad temper as she thought of what the Government might do with her husband's taxes, but Mr Peacock was more concerned with his role as the co-chairman of the Relief Committee. "The letter was very respectfully received," he said. "I think perhaps I read it quite well." Here he adjusted his collar, as he had done during the reading. "At the end, everyone applauded."

"Applauded! I should think they *would* applaud!"

The idea of new roads created much interest; all of the subsequent discussion at the meeting was concerned with this. "The road past Eagle Lodge is in a very bad state of repair," Anthony said. "There are so many ruts and pot-holes that carts regularly break axles and lose wheels; and there is no proper drainage, so for half the year it is flooded in several places."

"I am bound to point out," said Mr Peacock, stiffly, "that this letter expressly says that no works may be carried out for the benefit of any one man in particular."

"I am not merely thinking of myself," Anthony said. He felt quite angry. "The road past Eagle Lodge is the main highway to Clifden. To repair it – indeed to macadamise it – would benefit the whole community. If there was a good road through

Clasheen from Galway to Clifden commerce would improve. Meat and fish would not rot before they arrive at their destinations and travellers' time would be reduced considerably."

"We cannot build a road to Clifden, nor even to Galway. Whole tracts of it would be in other parishes, quite outside our jurisdiction."

"Nevertheless, Mr Altarnun has a point," Father Quinlan said. Dr Lenehan and Mr Tangney agreed, as did everyone else. Mr Peacock was annoyed to find himself in a minority of one, and even more annoyed that Anthony had brought it about.

"You will have to draw up plans, estimate costs, and work out the number of men required," Mr Tangney said.

"I have no ability in this," Anthony answered, but the doctor and the Catholic priest persuaded him to try. The meeting then broke up in a very orderly fashion. The crowd was mollified: the Government was doing something. Clasheen's peasants were, for the moment, almost converted to Peelism; their votes might even have helped the Tory candidate at the next election despite Daniel O'Connell and the Repeal party. But, being peasants, tenants-at-will, the vote was one of the many basic necessities of life that was denied them.

"Doctor Lenehan, what do you think is the cause of this rot?" Anthony asked, as they went out into the street with Father Quinlan and Mr Peacock.

"I have no idea," the doctor answered. "A kind of dropsy? There has been so much rain this year . . . A sort of wet corruption?"

"A letter in the paper two days ago," Mr Peacock said, "suggested the cause was the smoke and steam issuing from railway locomotives."

The doctor laughed. "A new invention is always blamed as the origin of every inexplicable ailment," he said. He twirled his walking-stick vigorously. "That has been so since inventions were invented. It is absurd – we have no railways here, not for a hundred miles."

"Mortiferous vapours belching out of the centre of the earth," said Father Quinlan. "That is what the Widow O'Gorman believes. Mortiferous: I like the word. I have never come across it."

"I think it is some air-borne parasite," Anthony said. "A fungus. It has to be."

"Gentlemen, I must leave you." The doctor pulled his watch out of his waistcoat pocket and looked at it short-sightedly. "I have calls to make on the sick. Not to mention the deaf, the blind, the halt and the dumb." They raised their hats to each other.

He went off with Mr Peacock; Father Quinlan and Anthony walked up the road in the opposite direction. "Now we are by ourselves," the priest said, "there is a little something I should like to discuss with you. It concerns Michael."

"Yes?" Anthony was on his guard at once, and hoped he was betraying no interest that might be construed as out of the ordinary.

"I was talking to his mother last week. Ladies, as I'm sure you're aware, often fuss about details that do not worry you and me; I listen in my confession box to many sins that are not sins at all." He laughed his most man-of-the-world laugh, thinking of Mrs Tangney who often wasted his time on a Saturday morning whispering peccadilloes that were not errors of taste, let alone sins even of the venial kind. "This is not, however, a secret of the confessional. No, she is bothered about her son. He attends Mass as punctiliously as she does, knows his Bible better, and, once upon a time she thought, might have considered entering the priesthood. But he has not received Holy Communion in four years, which is, I have to say it, a very long while. I wondered if you could throw any light on the matter."

"The religious practices and beliefs of my servants," Anthony said, "are none of my business."

"There are people, however, who think the health of the souls they employ as much their business as the health of the bodies."

"I am not one of them."

"I see. But . . . perhaps you could find out? Tactfully, of course. His mother, you understand, is worried."

And you are an interfering busybody, Anthony said to himself. "I would consider it an impertinence," he said.

"Oh." The priest rubbed his stone knob of a nose. "Good-day to you, sir. I have a call to make here on the Kearneys; old Mrs Kearney is dying."

Anthony returned to Eagle Lodge, unaware that two people who didn't like him very much – the clergymen of both persuasions – after this morning's events liked him even less.

MICHAEL sang as he cleared away the remains of their evening meal:

> "'Tis the last rose of summer, left blooming alone;
> All her lovely companions are faded and gone;
> No flower of her kindred, no rose-bud is nigh,
> To reflect back her blushes, or give sigh for sigh."

Anthony looked up from the table where he was working, and said "Why are all Irish songs so sad?"

"It is a sad country," Michael answered. "Our only songs are of martyrs and death in battle and broken lovers' vows. 'For they're hanging men and women for a-wearing of the green.' "

"That's right. That's right. They did." Anthony bent over his work: the table was covered in paper, pencils, compasses, rulers, protractors. "You were singing one of Tom Moore's Irish Melodies. He also wrote 'There's nothing half so sweet in life as love's young dream.' "

"Your people would hang us still, given the chance. I heard in town today that some Irishmen would prefer armed rebellion to hunger."

"Talk."

"Yes, we are fond of talk. My father spends his day gossiping in that forge of his; business is bad since the praties rotted." He took his empty wine glass out to the kitchen.

"Is that so?"

"If a man cannot buy a loaf of bread he cannot have his horse shod."

"Before we leave the subject of hanging, I have told all our tenants that I'll waive half the year's rent. Let it hang; isn't that the phrase you use? So they can eat till the next year's potato crop is dug."

Michael came back from the kitchen and stared at him. "You've done that? What will your brother say?"

"He won't know." Anthony drew some lines on his map,

slowly and carefully. "I was awake last night, worrying about it. I shall have to pay him out of my own pocket."

"I thought you were restless." He went up behind Anthony's chair and put his arms around his lover. "You are a good man," he said, softly. "I will compose a false set of figures and put it in the mail to India."

Anthony laughed. "You're devious."

"We're devious and secretive; we're liars and dissemblers. Isn't that what is said of us? The English made us so; it was how we survived the penal days."

"That is not *my* fault."

"True for you. But the sins of the fathers are inflicted on the children, even unto the seventh generation." He kissed Anthony on the top of his head and stroked his arms. "You know what is best about yourself? Your hair. That straw colour drives me wild. I never see wheat growing without your image in my eyes."

"My hair?" Anthony laughed again. "Not my goodness of character?"

"I said you are a good man." The expression on Michael's face was serious, almost doleful. "We have each other. That is all that counts."

"Yes. Love's young dream."

"It is not a dream! Though I've fallen asleep five nights now without you. I woke last night and still you had not come to bed; I thought for a minute I was back in my father's house, a young lad and a virgin. What is this marriage when one of us stays up poring over plans and maps and calculations? It is no marriage at all."

"I'm sorry. Another two hours and I think I'll be done with it."

"In that case," Michael said, "I will wash the dishes, sweep the room, bolt the doors, and sew the missing button on your shirt. And wait up for you: it's freezing out – there's frost on the grass already. I don't fancy the cold white sheets of the bed without a body to keep me warm."

"I'll finish as soon as I can. And be your bed-warmer. I promise."

"My obedient servant."

"Tomorrow," Anthony said, "I think I shall visit the Kelihers.

I haven't seen him since our altercation at Flanagan's last week. It was his wife I spoke to about hanging the rent. Will you come with me?"

"If I must."

"Now, may I work?"

"Sir." Michael bowed to him mockingly, then left him alone and started on some of the chores. When he had finished, he sat by the fire and read. Midnight struck; he glanced at Anthony who was still adding up columns of figures. He returned to his book, *The Rights of Man*. "Every generation is equal in rights to the generation which preceded it, by the same rule that every individual is born equal in rights with his contemporary . . . All men are born equal." Powerful, seditious stuff, he thought; Mr Peacock would certainly not approve, and even Father Quinlan would be lukewarm.

It was also difficult to read . . . not perhaps relevant, or only in part. Relevant to what, he wondered, surprised that he had fished up the word from the recesses of his mind. To himself, perhaps: and it occurred to him that when he read these days he was always looking for something – an authority that would give him blessing, a licence to be Michael. Thomas Paine, however libertarian and correct in his argument, was not that authority. Some weeks later he mentioned this to Anthony, who said "I have just the books for you" and gave him copies of Blake's *Songs of Experience* and *The Marriage of Heaven and Hell*.

Michael loved Eagle Lodge, more than Anthony did. A house to Anthony was a place where one slept, ate, talked, put things; though, when Michael protested at such an attitude, he said "If I owned it I might feel differently." He then unpacked his Indian souvenirs, which had been lying in boxes in a spare room for months – paintings, sculptures, rugs, animal skins – and let Michael transform the parlour. Grandfather Altarnun's hunting prints, faded and dispiriting, were banished to the cellar. The Indian effect, Mrs Peacock said on one of her visits, was "most unusual", though, later, to her husband, she described it as "foreign", "savage", and "not at all the kind of taste one expects in a gentleman."

In fact the parlour was pleasant, comfortable, lived in, as were the other areas Michael and Anthony inhabited – the kitchen, the main bedroom. The size of the house was obviously excessive for just two people. The dining room was never used, nor were most of the bedrooms and the servants' quarters. Here furniture gathered dust; wallpaper unstuck itself, and spiders and wood-worm enjoyed a field day. Michael fantasized new colour schemes, curtains, carpets, furniture, and often said it was a great pity they did not own Eagle Lodge. "And if we did," Anthony said, "where would the money come from to carry out such plans?"

"There is no harm, surely, in dreaming."

"One day we will buy a house of our own. Smaller than this."

"There is a beautiful house for sale in Coolcaslig. It has pink walls, bow windows, and it overlooks the sea."

"Yes. I know it, and I'd love it too. But the price is out of this world."

Musing over the pink house and the life they would have in it, Michael fell asleep, *The Rights of Man* on his lap. Anthony, at two o'clock in the morning, lifted him out of the chair and carried him upstairs; when Michael woke he discovered himself in bed in the pitch dark, warm from Anthony's skin touching his. The only sound was Anthony's deep, even breathing. He searched for his lover's hand, felt it close round his, then slept again.

The tenants' cabins, particularly the Kelihers', were disgusting, a moral blot on his family's name, Anthony thought. They should be pulled to the ground and new houses built, but he had neither the authority nor the means to do this. His brother owned them. He had already written twice to Richard in some indignation about the way the Kelihers in particular were forced to live, but Richard felt the matter was of little importance. "They are no worse off than many Irish," he wrote in reply. "Indeed, I imagine better off, for you say every one of the children is healthy. I have not the money to dash around rebuilding cabins. You tell me the rents barely cover the costs of running the estate and your own expenses and needs; so how should I find the wherewithal? My salary would not run to it, and asking the East India Company for a loan would be laughed at."

At least the Kelihers had windows, which half the population of rural Ireland did not, but that was their only advantage. Ten children, ranging in age from a girl three months old to a lad of fifteen, who, it was said, was a bit simple-minded, lived in one room that contained almost no furniture; they had no beds, no table, only two chairs, and almost no cooking utensils. Their clothes were rags, and they did not possess a single shoe. In this cabin a pig slept, and outside the door was a muckheap as high as the house. There were of course no toilet facilities, nor any way they could wash themselves or their rags. They drew water from the stream or the Widow O'Gorman's well, both of which were half a mile off.

Yet, until the potato failed, they were happy enough. The pig and growing a little oats paid the rent, and they kept warm – throughout the winter they huddled around a peat fire which, even on the coldest days, stopped them from shivering. They were sociable people and enjoyed the company of their neighbours, spending a great deal of their time just talking, telling stories, or joining the throng at the cross-roads that danced to Patrick O'Callaghan's fiddle. They liked markets, fairs and horse races, and would often travel great distances to attend such functions. Work did not tire them out: cultivating potatoes and looking after a pig took very little of their time. Most of rural Ireland, until the Famine, lived existences like the Kelihers'.

Anthony walked up to the cabin, the smell of the muck-heap making him choke. Michael stood fifty yards off: he had no urge to chat with tenants-at-will. Anthony's influence during the past four years may have changed some of his attitudes to those at the foot of the ladder, but Michael still felt uneasy in the proximity of Sullivans, Cronins, Kelihers, Scannells, Leahys and O'Learys. Once he had loved Dan Leahy – or, at any rate, lusted after him, dressing desire in romantic clothes so that it was made to look permissible – but Dan, he thought, like Mr and Mrs Keliher, would never think of him as other than the blacksmith's educated boy, above them, nose in the air, a snob. Michael may have shifted a little; they had not. So he kept his distance.

Keliher, surrounded by his entire family, fell to his knees the moment Anthony appeared (like an inverse jack-in-the-box, Anthony thought) and no amount of protest or command could get him up again until he had finished his speech: a torrent of gratitude for your honour allowing the rent to hang, and a score of invocations to the Blessed Virgin and various saints in Heaven to protect your honour's soul and remember your honour's goodness when your honour would be dying. Anthony laughed.

Keliher stood up and said "What in the Devil's name are you laughing at?"

"Because I'm pleased," Anthony replied. Which wasn't true; the grotesquery he had just been forced to witness had made him laugh. "Pleased that you bear no ill will for what occurred at Flanagan's."

"It was the drink in him, your honour," said Mrs Keliher. "It was unpardonable, shouting at yourself and yourself so good to us and ten hungry little children at home."

They didn't look, Anthony thought, as if they were hungry — yet. The eldest was an albino, a tall, slim boy with a shock of white hair that flopped over his forehead. In a few years' time he would be beautiful. If there were enough potatoes between now and then.

"She beat me for it," Keliher said, almost proudly.

"I did so," his wife confessed.

"But my father is nimble and dashed out of the cabin," the albino said. Keliher aimed a swipe at him, but the boy was nimble too and ran off, gurgling with laughter.

"Here's a shilling for you," Anthony said. "Spend it on the children."

Keliher stared at it on his outstretched palm, and the whole family crowded round to look. Some of them had never seen a silver coin before. "How do we ... spend it?" one of the younger girls asked.

"You take it into a shop and buy things."

"It's a few years since I did that," said Mrs Keliher. "But I'll make sure, your honour, it is not given over to Mrs Flanagan. It will not cause liquid to pour down Mr Keliher's throat. Not that he often has the means to do it; drunk he is not since my brother's wake, and that was, let me see, seven years last March. I will buy things for the little ones, and may the saints preserve you."

Anthony rejoined Michael, and when they were out of sight of the Kelihers, they walked hand in hand. In the wood just above the waterfall, Anthony pushed Michael against a tree-trunk and kissed him passionately.

"Hey, hey!" Michael said, after he had regained his breath. "What is this, then?"

"You were grumbling yesterday that your conjugal rights had been neglected."

"Do you want me to prance about naked here? On a frosty November morning? I would freeze to death and the whole process watched and listened to, no doubt, by the peeping eyes and flapping ears of little Kelihers."

Anthony looked round. "I see no Kelihers. Hear no Kelihers. But, I thought, back at the house . . ."

Michael's eyes lit up. "Back at the house," he said, tracing a finger along Anthony's eyebrows, "You may do with me as you please."

"I may? You are an abandoned sinner."

" 'Necessity knows no laws,' Saint Augustine says."

"This is necessity?"

"It is. I love you."

But, though not heard, they had been seen. Timothy, the eldest Keliher – Ty he was nicknamed – had tracked them, just for fun, for something to do to pass the time: he was imagining he was a king in ancient Ireland, stalking two prehistoric elks. Bare feet gave him the advantage of silence. What he observed he could make nothing of: he had never been told of such things – not as a warning or a joke or a simple fact. Fifteen he might be, but his ignorance was as total as Mrs Peacock's though a lot more innocent. He simply saw what he saw, and had no attitudes to it. The picture was filed away in his head, and there it remained, for the time being.

IRELAND struggled through the winter of 1845 and the spring of 1846 as best it could. The failure of the potato had been patchy; there were many parts of the country unaffected by the blight. This, and the Government's relief schemes, staved off a widespread famine. Though distress and poverty were much more acute than usual, not many people actually died of hunger. There were cases of severe hardship in Clasheen, but no deaths.

Anthony's plans for the new road were passed by the Board of Works, and employment for eightpence a day was given to people who would have otherwise found themselves totally destitute. The subscriptions collected by Mr Peacock's and Father Quinlan's committee did not amount to a great deal, but they helped to buy some essential food. The Government's Indian corn was distributed: those who ate it loathed it. It was so hard it was nearly inedible, and it sometimes caused vomiting and internal bleeding. The trouble was that there were no mills in Ireland that could grind it properly and, even if there had been, the peasant women, used for a lifetime to cooking nothing but potatoes, did not know how to prepare it. Peel's brimstone it was called. Anthony and Michael tried it on one occasion, and pronounced it revolting.

Other places with leadership less able than that of Dr Lenehan, Mr Peacock, Father Quinlan and Anthony Altarnun, fared much worse. An example of the horrifying reality experienced elsewhere came to Clasheen's attention at the beginning of April. Mrs Peacock, out walking along the strand near Eagle Lodge, saw a boat making for the shore; there were half a dozen people on board who waved "frantically" (she said later), "with gesticulations of despair", though she did not interpret their behaviour as such at the time. She thought it had something to do with the weather. A breeze was blowing up strongly and dark clouds were building on the horizon; she was on the point of turning for home as she feared it would snow. It was certainly cold enough.

The boat people, she assumed, wished to land before the storm caught them. Maybe they wanted to find out where they were and if the mooring was adequate. As she approached she saw that this was not the case. She was confronted with a crew of skeletons dressed in rags, six emaciated men who were nothing but bones and skin, their eyeballs bulging and wild. "They looked," she said, "as if they had just stepped out of their coffins." They begged her for food. A seventh man, near death, lay in the bottom of the boat; he was calm, just able to breathe, but already unaware of what was going on around him.

"Follow me," she said, but pushing the boat ashore was the last act the crew was, for the moment, capable of doing. Three of the men found they could not walk at all; the others tottered a few steps, then collapsed on the beach. Mrs Peacock hurried away, indeed almost ran, to Eagle Lodge, where she poured out her tale to Anthony. (Michael's father had repaired the bell months ago.)

Anthony told Michael to make a cauldron of soup, then he went out to fetch the nearest tenants, the Sullivans and the O'Learys. It was snowing; the rising wind was hurling the flakes into their faces, but the adults of the two families did not pause. They rushed down to the beach, picked up the skeletons and carried them to Eagle Lodge. The man in the bottom of the boat they left where he was. He was dead. He was buried, a few days later, in Clasheen cemetery.

The kitchen of Eagle Lodge was packed. Inside it were the entire Sullivan and O'Leary clans, agog with curiosity and amazement; Anthony, frowning; Michael at the stove ladling out soup while Mrs Peacock instructed him in recipes superior and less expensive, to her mind, than the one he had prepared; and the six skeletons at the table eating so voraciously "you would think," Mrs Peacock said to her husband that evening, "that they had never seen a bowl of soup in their lives before." They had come from an island some way up the coast; there was no food left there – even the stinging nettles and the sea-weed had all gone. To stay was certain death. They had rowed to the mainland in desperation; with a little food inside them they could probably walk to the nearest workhouse. But there was no food. The villages towards Clifden, they found, were starving; people were grubbing for berries, roots, moss. The Sullivans and the O'Learys marvelled, and blessed their good fortune. To be tenants-at-will at Eagle Lodge was luck indeed.

The six men went on their way. They were polite, very grateful, and would not think, they said, of putting people to any further trouble. They could walk now, and the snow had stopped. Barefoot they might be, but it was only twelve miles to the workhouse at Coolcaslig.

Anthony, eventually alone with Michael, was still frowning. "What is the matter?" Michael asked.

"We shall have many unexpected visitors before things improve; we must watch ourselves and be on our guard. Keep the bed in your room made up, though I don't want you to sleep in it."

Their life-style changed. It had to, with Anthony allowing the rent to hang. Roast meat dinners with bottles of wine were now an infrequent luxury. Repairs to the house – replacing a cracked window, mending broken gutters, papering the dining room, carpentry on the staircase (some of the wood was rotten) – were left indefinitely.

They were not the only ones to feel the pinch. Father Quinlan gave food to many families. As a result his own diet, much to his housekeeper's concern, had become little more than that of the most distressed people in the parish. "I miss my cheese," he said to Mrs Tangney. "I am exceedingly fond of cheese!" The Lenehans' dinner table was spartan too; the doctor worked for nothing when his patients could not pay. Shopkeepers tightened their belts – few of their customers had anything to spend, yet prices were tumbling. The fire in Mr Tangney's forge was allowed to go out, and he dipped into his savings. But the Peacocks, though their contribution to the Relief Fund was generous, continued to live as they had always lived.

Michael kept his promise to his sister and took her out dancing on one of the few warm nights that spring. His parents didn't approve of their children attending cross-road assemblies; "you don't know who will be there," Margaret Tangney sniffed.

"Only the people I've known all my life," Madge said.

"Every Tom, Dick and Harry!"

Several girls had eyes for Michael, which made him uneasy. He enjoyed dancing – he had a natural sense for it, rhythm and gracefulness; but, during the first hour or so, he would only dance with Madge. Eventually she wanted to be with others, in particular with Dan Leahy. Dan was still very attractive, an adult now, looking for a wife. Michael felt jealous.

"What is it with you and Leahy?" he asked.

"Should I tell you?" Madge said. "Or not? I . . . love him."

Michael drew in his breath. "And he?"

"He loves me too." Michael stared at her, amazed. "You will not utter a word of this to a living soul! My father would kill me if he knew . . . Dan Leahy, a barefoot, ragged peasant!"

"This is not good, Madge."

"It is not your business."

"Are you thinking he'll marry you?"

"Yes."

He was silent for a while, then said "If he does, you will need me at the wedding to give you away. I doubt our father will want to do this."

"Michael!" She was grateful, beyond words for a moment. All she could say was "Thank you." Then "He's handsome, isn't he?"

"Oh, yes, he's handsome all right!"

He turned to poteen after that for Dutch courage, then found he was able to dance with Nora O'Donovan, a red-haired girl who had been looking at him the whole evening. It was dark now. She led him away, into the trees at the road-side. He held her in his arms for some time, and kissed her.

"Did you enjoy it?" Anthony asked, when Michael told him.

"I . . . don't think so."

"Then why do it?"

He wasn't sure. "It excited me," he said. "A little. It was the drink. You have nothing to fear."

"I know that."

"Well . . . the reputation it may give me could do us some good."

Anthony nodded, then said "That's true."

AS people expected and feared, evictions in many parts of the country followed non-payment of the rent. Families were thrown out of their cabins by force, and then the cabin itself was destroyed – the thatch set on fire, the walls pulled down. The worst kind of landlord used the current distress as an excuse to get rid of unwanted tenants even when they could afford to pay – at Tullala, not far from Clasheen, seventy-two families, ready with their rent, were evicted because the proprietor wanted the land for cattle to graze. These people had no one to turn to; they dug holes in the ground which they roofed with sticks or reeds and lived like that: thousands of Irish people did so.

Anthony, when he heard what had happened at Tullala, wrote indignantly to the owner, and persuaded nearly everyone at Clasheen who could write his or her name to sign the letter. The owner did not reply. Charles Trevelyan, the British civil servant in charge of relief plans, thought from the safe distance of London that no real hardship existed yet. "Dependence on charity is not to be made an agreeable mode of life," he said. Like most Britons, he knew more of the realities of Hong Kong (recently acquired for the British Empire) than he did of the realities of Ireland.

Everything now depended on the potato crop of 1846. The spring had been mostly wet and cold, but the summer was warm; the plants were scrutinized as frequently and with as much care as sick children watched by anxious mothers. "They have never looked better," Patrick O'Callaghan said to Anthony. "It will be a grand harvest! A vintage! See the leaves, how green! How strong the growth!"

"Luxuriant," Anthony said.

"Plenty follows scarcity," said Michael, and he smiled. He was thinking it would not be long now before they could eat roast beef and drink wine again. Living with Anthony had given him expensive tastes, which was dangerous: his position in the house was so ill-defined. Anthony's lover he might be, but he had no share of ownership in anything. Anthony fed him, bought him clothes, paid him for his work. Decisions and orders, in the last analysis, were not Michael's, and he resented this at times. Only in their thoughts and feelings for each other was there equality. It was a relationship of unequal dependencies, therefore easy to walk away from. They both knew that, and, paradoxically, it made them closer; they were held by each other's vulnerabilities.

Patrick O'Callaghan's next words reminded Michael of that. "There is a problem," the old man said, "and few have thought of it. If the crop is good, and surely to God it is, it will not feed us all. The hunger next year will be worse."

"How is that?" Michael asked.

"Not enough has been planted. So many have eaten the *seed* potatoes. They had no choice: do that or starve."

The moment of shock in Anthony's eyes made Michael say to himself: I could never leave him. Even if I wanted to. Which I don't.

"The Government should have given us seed," Anthony said. "Not Indian corn."

But the Government was busy with a particularly difficult

problem – its own survival. The prime minister, one of the few people in Britain to understand the extent and consequences of the potato failure, decided to repeal the Corn Laws – the statutes which protected home-grown produce from foreign competition – in an attempt to bring food prices down. His own party was split on the issue, and though the repeal measure was forced through, the Government lost its majority. Peel resigned; the Tories went into opposition, and the Whigs formed the new administration with Lord John Russell as prime minister. "Rotten potatoes have done it all!" the Duke of Wellington complained.

Irish policies altered immediately. Everything was to be left to private enterprise – there was to be no more distribution of Indian corn except in the worst-hit places in the rural west, and the public works would be stopped. The outcry against the latter was so great that Russell changed his mind. Road-building was allowed to continue, but the expense would not be borne by the taxpayer: it would fall on the local property-owners. The Whig government's treatment of Ireland turned out to be mean, short-sighted and cruel, incomprehensible by any standards. It virtually left the country to starve.

In July there were reports of disease in the potatoes. During the first week of August the crop failed entirely. From Kerry to Antrim, from Donegal to Cork, all was lost: the leaves were scorched black; whole counties looked as if burned by fire. The stench of rotting vegetation was universal from one end of Ireland to the other. It was a week of tremendous storms: lightning flashed over the blackened potato patches; dense, chill fogs followed the thunder, and rain fell in walls.

By the end of the month people were walking for miles in search of food; in some towns there was nothing to be obtained, not even a loaf of bread. The new Government was deaf to appeals for help, which were regarded merely as entreaties from beggars who had begged once too often, even though the catastrophe was fully known. A "total annihilation" *The Times* called it, a disaster without parallel in modern history.

CHAPTER FOUR

ANTHONY was faced with a very difficult choice – let the rents hang again, or evict the tenants. He could not, from his own pocket, make up a second time the deficit in the money coming in. He had little left: barely enough to feed himself and Michael for twelve months. If he waived the entire rent, it would be impossible to buy sufficient seed, do even emergency repairs to the house, and generally run the estate – everything would collapse.

His brother urged eviction. "If what I hear of conditions in Ireland is true," Richard wrote, "it cannot be that any significant rent will be collected in 1847. In that eventuality, we will need to get rid of delinquent tenants. I would like to see the whole estate cleared of small-holdings; a grazing farm would be much more profitable. Income from cattle should be our future, and if all the land were put to grass I could furnish you with the wherewithal to buy a considerable quantity of heifers and steers. You are *in medias res* so to speak and I am not, so you must judge for yourself. It would of course be an act of charity not to press the most unfortunate cases just yet, but we have to look to our own interests. The harvest is poor this year the world over."

He added, in a postscript, that he would probably be returning to London for a long leave next spring, and that he might visit Ireland to see for himself how the situation was progressing.

"What do you think?" Anthony said. He passed the letter to Michael, who read it through twice.

"I cannot say, surely! It is nothing to do with me."

"But how would you act in my position?"

Michael was silent for a long time. "You ask a hard question," he said.

"And I need a hard answer."

"Whatever your decision I will accept it."

"You don't say what you would do!" Anthony sounded impatient.

"How can I know what I would do? What *you* will do is more to the point."

"There is no choice." Anthony took the letter back and tore it to bits. His face was creased with worry; the blue eyes were angry, and frightened. "I cannot evict the tenants," he said, pacing up and down the room. "If they die – if some die – I can pull down their cabins and put the land to grass. Not otherwise. You realize what this means? When Richard comes here, *we* will be evicted. It's his estate; he'll say I have grossly mismanaged it. And he will be right."

"What will you do then?"

"I don't know. I wouldn't expect you to burden yourself with the hardship of it."

"Why not?" Michael suddenly blazed with fury. "How dare you say that! I would go with you anywhere, whatever our fortunes! How dare you!"

Anthony stopped pacing. He touched Michael's cheek, but Michael pushed his hand off. "I'm sorry," he said. "I put it badly."

Michael averted his eyes; he did not want Anthony to see tears. "I consider myself as married to you as my father is to my mother. In sickness and in health. For better for worse. There is no exception for the subject of failed potatoes."

Anthony stood looking at him for some while, then kneeled beside him, holding his hands. "I was not sure," he said. "That was wrong of me . . . You are . . . a marvel. A revelation. But we'll go hungry."

Michael smiled, then leaned forward and kissed him. "Then we'll go hungry together."

AS they did not have to pay the rent, Anthony's tenants were able to eat their pigs and their dairy produce, and sell their oats to buy food – when they could find it. There was little for sale in

Clasheen; they often had to go as far as Galway to obtain anything. Anthony, deciding to stock up on his own supplies, went to Dublin to see what was available. He found, unlike in the west, that trade was brisk, and though there was not plenty, there was some variety.

But the cost of everything had risen since the new Government came to power, thanks to the private enterprise in which Lord John and his ministers so fervently believed. Rapacious little dealers – the gombeen men – were buying up everything they could, Indian corn in particular, then selling it in minute quantities at vastly inflated prices. Though food existed, many starved because they could not afford to buy. In the west, the gombeen man was not so much in evidence: almost nobody there could afford to buy.

Anthony returned, having spent more money on fewer goods than he had calculated beforehand. Last year he had been able to eke things out with potatoes; but this August his own crop, like everyone else's, had been destroyed.

His tenants, because they could eat, were not popular with the less fortunate; the Keliher children, for instance, had stones thrown at them one afternoon. So the families stuck together: the Eagle Lodge estate became a sanctuary in a hostile land, though Clasheen was faring better than any other district nearby.

It was when they ventured further away, to Coolcaslig or Clifden, that they witnessed horrifying sights they could scarcely put in words, so moved, or so angry, did they feel – miserable, ragged, evicted men and women, their children shrieking with hunger; once respectable elderly widows who had nothing left; men still able-bodied but who had no work; half-naked women with crying babies; all scratching at plots that had been scoured again and again for one small potato, only half-diseased, that somebody might have overlooked. Families of ten or twelve dined on a turnip or three or four cabbage leaves, or stinging nettles. People lay dead on the roads or in ditches where they had crawled, in such numbers it was not possible to bury them quickly enough, and their bodies were sometimes mutilated or half eaten by starving dogs.

The Sullivans found in one derelict, rat-infested hovel seven corpses, grey, ashen, and naked except for a few filthy rags about their waists. Dan Leahy was accosted by a woman wearing nothing but an old sack, a baby just born in her arms, screaming at him for food, anything, anything she could eat. The O'Learys found that the dying in cabins lay beside the dead: no one had the strength to lift the bodies.

Coolcaslig Workhouse was besieged by hordes of living scarecrows, yelling to be allowed inside, women demanding that at least their children be taken as it was impossible to feed them. The homes of people who still had food were often surrounded by the famished poor, staring in through the windows at dinner on the table, groaning, weeping, pointing fingers at their mouths. Mrs Peacock, as a result, kept her curtains permanently shut.

Animals had almost totally disappeared; in vast tracts of the country not a pig, a sheep, a cow, a chicken, even a cat or a dog could be found: they had all been eaten. Weeds, berries, roots, even limpets and mussels became luxuries. The landscape began to look more and more like a desert. Yet Charles Trevelyan, still directing Relief operations from Whitehall, and aware of all this, said in December 1846 "The great evil with which we have to contend is not the physical evil of the famine, but the moral evil of the selfish, perverse and turbulent character of the people."

Inertia, that lack of will to eat, to do anything, is a late stage in the starvation syndrome. At the onset, the body eats its own carbohydrates and fat; in the middle period it digests its own protein, the liver swells and the pain is at its worst; then people run about searching for food, screaming with the torment of hunger. To starve to death is a slow process. It is like being on the rack, every raw nerve tingling with agony, and it goes on for weeks, even months if there is water to stave off thirst, and the odd nut or edible leaf to swallow. That is the pain of starvation.

In 1846 and 1847, the conscience of the British public was troubled; immense sums of money and whole mountains of clothing were gathered and sent to Ireland. It proved – as Father Quinlan had forecast – to be a drop in an ocean.

To add to the problem, the winter of 1846–1847 was, all over Europe, one of the worst of the century. In London, just before Christmas, ice-floes appeared on the Thames. In Ireland, snow began to fall in November and continued to fall, nearly every day, till the following March. Freezing east winds blew, and there was continual frost, hail and sleet. Drifts of snow blocked highways, and traffic was at a standstill. The man who cultivated potatoes would, if such weather occurred in normal times, have stayed indoors by his peat fire, but now he had to go out, ragged and starving, to report at the road-building site – even if the weather prevented him from working – or he would not get paid. Many, weakened by hunger, died from exposure to the arctic temperatures.

Michael and Anthony huddled over their fire, or sometimes when blizzards went on for hours they stayed in bed, clinging to each other for warmth. Whole days passed when they did not go outside and nobody came to the house. Michael, looking at the bleak, white landscape, the dead larch trees, the black etchings of hedgerow twigs, saw no sign of life anywhere, not even the prints of a bird in the snow. "We are two sailors marooned on a desert island," he said. It was the same for the Peacocks, the Kelihers, the Lenehans, the Widow O'Gorman; everyone.

"I fear for the seed you planted," Anthony said. He had brought back from Dublin a quantity of vegetable seed – carrots, turnips, cabbage, onions, kail, lettuce, radish, and so on. Michael had dug over the kitchen garden and sown what was suitable for winter cultivation.

"It will be safe," he said. "The white blanket keeps it warm."

No work could be done on Clasheen's contribution to the new, macadamized Galway-Clifden road. Six-foot snowdrifts covered the site of operations, which, as it happened, had just reached the gates of Eagle Lodge. All very well for the Altarnun, people said. A rumour had gone around that the Government would once again order the public works to stop. Himself had a fine new road to drive on from Eagle Lodge to Clasheen, but no others would benefit.

On New Year's Day 1847 a man called at the house with a letter from Michael's parents. "Come and see us," Eugene Tangney wrote. "We must have your help. We have nothing to eat."

MICHAEL struggled through the snow to Clasheen. At least I have boots, he said to himself; how do the poor wretches who have no shoes fare in this weather? But the snow was so deep in places that it came half-way up his thighs, and when he reached his father's house his legs were dripping wet. He dried out in the forge; he had not expected to find the fire lit and his father working. "Not horseshoes," Mr Tangney said. "I am beginning to think the horses are all eaten."

"Dr Lenehan has his mare," Michael answered. "I saw him on my way now, riding to Coolcaslig."

"This work is for the doctor. He once told me he fancied a wrought iron gate for his front garden. Well, I have nothing better to do."

"I doubt he could pay for such a thing."

Eugene sighed. "Go indoors and talk to your mother," he said. Michael went, bare-legged; his trousers and boots he left steaming by the fire.

Madge was in the parlour, alone. "Now there is a pair of legs," she said, laughing, "that would delight any girl who clapped eyes on them!"

"No girl has ever clapped eyes on them," Michael answered, "except my inquisitive sisters." He surveyed himself. "You think they look good? Not too skinny?"

"It is a crying shame no girl has yet had the pleasure! You are wasting the seed of the Tangneys by keeping yourself unwed."

Michael thought of Onan who spilled his seed on the ground, which displeased the Lord: wherefore the Lord slew him. But God has slain no one else for doing that, he said to himself. "Why this desire that everyone should marry? Is it the be-all and end-all of life to procreate? I don't want a herd of squawling babies. What future can there be in it? They would only starve to death."

"Brother, I have such news for you." Madge's eyes shone with excitement, but she heard her mother approaching. "I will tell you later," she said, and composed herself.

Mrs Tangney was thinner, her face more lined. "There is nothing left to eat!" she said, dramatically.

"Nobody in this house seems hungry," Michael replied. His mother looked pained. "But it's true," he added.

"You know how your father is." She could not stop fidgeting with her fingers, pulling her wedding ring up and down. She sat at the table, then burst into tears. "I don't know what will become of us!" she sobbed. "God must help!"

"Mother – "

"We are not hungry today," Madge said, quietly. "Nor shall we be tomorrow. We have a sack of meal, a chicken, and a few vegetables. We can still get milk, and there is tea in the caddy. But that is all. We have no money to buy anything else."

"It's your father's doing," Mrs Tangney said, drying her eyes. "Every day for months I am telling him we should not eat so much. With care, with real care, we could have disciplined ourselves and lived through till summer. He is an enormous man, you know that; a hill of flesh. He needs more food than others, and he could not get himself to cut down. He took a little of this and a little of that, and now it is nearly all gone. He has had no work. No money is coming into the house, and the better part of our savings spent in the hunger last year. The rest is spent now. We have nothing. Nothing!"

"We have been most improvident," Madge said.

"Father is on the Relief Committee," said Michael. "Why does he not ask the other members for help?"

"The shame of it!" Mrs Tangney answered. "To go to Mr Peacock or Dr Lenehan for assistance! As if we were evicted squatters in some scalpeen, who at best only knew a one-roomed mud cabin!"

"Mother, you have to ask yourself which is more important: your snobbery or your survival." He felt very impatient.

"You promised you would not see us starve," she said, bitterly.

"And I will remember my promise!" he said, raising his voice. "But you will help yourselves first! You have luxuries here you do not need. Rings, jewellery, the pictures on these walls, your best clothes. There are people who will take them in Galway for money or food."

"A son of mine suggests I should bargain with the gombeen man! It is . . . I could not have heard you correctly. And you in the comfort of Eagle Lodge!"

"There is little comfort at Eagle Lodge; I can assure you of that. We get by, is all. There are no rents coming in; the roof is leaking and no money to repair it. Anthony – Mr Altarnun –

talks of selling the furniture we do not use; *he* is not too proud to go to the gombeen man! He has already pawned some rings his mother left him in her will. Sold two of his horses. Mrs Keliher and the baby have been sick; the medicines were expensive. *He* paid for them, and, if Dr Lenehan gets no money, how can he continue his practice? We would all die of fever *before* we go hungry."

"He would help some unwashed peasant woman but not the family of his slave-of-all-work! He is a strange man. Strange indeed!"

"Mother, you disgust me," Michael said.

"We are in the hands of the Lord now." She looked down at her own hands, rubbing again at her wedding ring. She wriggled it off her finger, then gave it to Michael. "See how much you can get for that," she said. "I cannot go myself. Will you do it for me?"

"Are you sure?" he asked.

She nodded. "Before you leave, I will give you . . . There are dresses I do not wear, a cameo brooch, some silver." She glanced up at him. "I don't want you to feel disgust for your mother."

"I do not. I shouldn't have said so. I'm sorry."

Mr Tangney came in with Michael's clothes, now dry. He put them down on a chair. "Well?" he asked. The three of them looked at him in silence. "I see," he muttered, then turned and limped out of the room. He is a broken man, Michael said to himself, and felt moved; he wanted to run after his father and kiss him, but the blacksmith would have been even more demoralized by a gesture so unmanly.

"I remember a story of my childhood," Margaret said. "An old woman nearing death is visited every night by a ghostly horse and his rider. The neighbours are out of their wits with fear, so they send for the priest, who comes and keeps watch. At midnight the phantom arrives. 'Who are you?' the priest demands. 'Beelzebub,' the horseman says. 'This old woman received Holy Communion in a state of mortal sin. I have come for her soul.' The priest tells the old woman to spit up the sacred host, and when he takes it from her mouth he says 'Get thee behind me, Satan. Her soul is pure now.' Then there is a deafening roll of thunder, and the phantom vanishes with a terrible shriek."

She turned to Michael and Madge. Madge was wondering what

moral she would derive from this absurd story; Michael was putting his trousers on. "It is said," Mrs Tangney continued, "that whosoever receives the body and blood of Christ unworthily is *guilty* of the body and blood of Christ. I would not want that. Tomorrow is Sunday, and I shall take Communion, may it please God, though first I must ask Father Quinlan to hear my confession. I am guilty of many sins – pride, setting myself above others, lack of charity to the poor. Michael, will you come with me to the altar and take Communion too?"

He stared out of the window to avoid her gaze. "I cannot do that," he said.

"Ah . . . why not?"

"I have my reasons."

"What do you do at that house that is so wicked you will not go to the altar rails once in four years?"

"Mother . . ."

"Yes?"

"Whether I go to Mass at all is no one's business but my own."

"I hope you are not thinking to stay away from Mass! It is a mortal sin!"

He was, as it happened, considering it. The books Anthony lent him, particularly the Blake, made him seriously doubt, for the first time, that God existed. And the destruction of the potato was not God's handiwork, he was sure; here he was in agreement with Mr Peacock, though the famine did not raise any questions about the Deity in the minister's mind. Michael's thinking was that if there was a God He would not allow so much suffering.

From Blake he learned ideas quite heretical to Catholic doctrine; that man has no body distinct from his soul, that he who desires but acts not breeds pestilence, that brothels are built with the bricks of religion. 'Know that in a former time Love! Sweet Love! was thought a crime' was a statement that found an echo in his own experience; abstinence sowing sand all over the ruddy limbs and flaming hair, but desire gratified planting fruits of life and beauty there, was the authority he was searching for. However, if he came to believe that religion was nothing more than superstitious mumbo-jumbo, was convinced that every chimney-sweeper's cry was created by the blackening Church, it would be difficult to apostatize in Clasheen. It would cause too much comment.

Mrs Tangney went upstairs to find the possessions she wanted Michael to sell. Madge, alone with him, could now say what she did not wish her mother to hear. "I shall be able to help them," she said. "Soon there will be one less to feed."

He frowned. "What have you in mind?"

"Dan and I are to marry. Next week."

The news astonished him. "Are you quite off your head? Now, of all times? How will you live?"

"The Leahys are tenants at Eagle Lodge. So we won't go hungry."

"You are thinking of moving into their cabin? It has one room and seven people in it, not to mention a pig. It is hardly the way to begin married life. Are you wanting to make love in front of the whole family?"

"The pig has been killed and eaten. And . . . we won't be living with them."

"There are no empty cabins, and Mr Altarnun's brother would surely not let another be built."

"The Leahys are not tenants-at-will; they are forty-shilling freeholders. They can do what they like with that ground. You know that."

"Madge, you talked earlier of improvidence! This is – "

"What have we to lose? I may stay here and starve, or be with Dan and we starve together. The choice to take is obvious."

Michael had no reply for that; what she said was true. He remembered his own words to Anthony: "then we'll go hungry together." Why shouldn't Madge also do as she wanted?

She was being no more improvident than thousands of Irish girls of her time. To marry late or not at all is a curse of modern Ireland, a bequest of the Famine years; but until the 1840s people frequently got married at the age of sixteen or seventeen. The main reason why people married so young was the appallingly low standards of Irish life. As Madge said, they had nothing to lose. They did not need money: to erect a cabin required only willingness and muscles. A few yards of earth for growing potatoes could be subleased from one or other of the families; a spade, a cooking pot, a chair, even — what luxury! — a bed could be scrounged somehow.

"Which day next week?" Michael asked.

"Thursday. At Kilgarrin; Father Coakley, the curate there, will perform the ceremony. It could not be in Clasheen — Father Quinlan would insist that my parents be told. I shall tell them when . . . no, I will write them a letter."

"And I shall come with you to give you to Dan and to sign as a witness."

"Thank you." She stood up, put her arms round Michael, and kissed him. "I love him to distraction, but . . . I admit . . . I'm more worried than I appear. It is a step down in the world."

"I know something about love, too."

"Who is she, Michael? Some flinty creature who has broken your heart: *that* is the explanation!"

"Of what?"

"Why you never have eyes for a girl!"

"I kissed that red-haired colleen when I took you out dancing."

"Is it her? The O'Donovan twins never knew a good man when they saw one!"

"It isn't her." He laughed, then he said, still holding her close, "Perhaps I will tell you one day. When we have lived to see better times. One evening, round the fire, when Dan is not there; just you and me."

"Why shouldn't my husband be there? Has this . . . something to do with why you will not go to Communion?"

He smiled, then placed a finger on her lips. "No more questions," he said. He pulled her arms from his shoulders, then walked across to the window. It was beginning to snow again. "What will Dan wear for the wedding?" he asked.

"I am not marrying him for his clothes!"

"Hmmm. I will ask Mr Altarnun to look out a suit, a shirt and a neck-tie. And shoes. They are the same height, the same build. Would it worry you if Mr Altarnun knows?"

"He will not tell my father?"

"Not if I say he should not."

"Thank you. Again. Michael, I love you."

"I'm envious," he said.

"Why?"

He did not have to answer that, for his mother came back into the room. "I've filled a box with clothes," she said, "and trinkets and . . . it's heavy. How will you manage and it snowing again? Perhaps you should stay here tonight."

"Himself would worry."

"Ah, he will surely know where you are!"

"Mother, a full glass of whiskey to warm me up, and I'll get there as right as rain."

"There is no whiskey."

"Oh . . . yes." He felt embarrassed; he had forgotten for a moment that nearly all the provisions in the house had gone. "I suppose there is still a dreg or two in Flanagan's Bar. A potato shortage doesn't put every poteen-maker out of business." He picked up the box, and said "You see I am strong," then stepped out into the blizzard. It was late in the afternoon and the light was beginning to fade. The sky was ash-coloured, thick, as if it had vast quantities of snow still to let fall, and the wind was rising.

"God keep you and don't stay too long over there," Mrs Tangney said. "We will not want to see a petrified corpse on the Clifden road tomorrow."

"It is Eagle Lodge I am going to," he answered. "Not the South Pole."

They watched him walk up the street; before he reached the bar he was white with snow.

CHAPTER FIVE

THE few miles took him hours: it was dark; the driving snow was blowing down his neck, under his hat, and into his trousers which were soon as wet as when he had arrived at the forge. The box, though not heavy, was a cumbersome nuisance. He was only half-way to Eagle Lodge when he began to think he might not get there, that perhaps his mother's joke about a petrified corpse would turn out to be true. His strength was beginning to fail, and he felt light-headed: his body temperature was falling rapidly. His confident stride became a stagger, and he wasn't even sure if he was going in the right direction; was he walking round and round in circles?

Somebody else was staggering along beside him, he thought, a man of grey shadows. But there was no one there. I am going to die, he told himself, quite calmly and without any sense of panic at all; how is it a man can be taken so easily? It is strange.

Eventually he sat down in the snow. The man of grey shadows seemed to be sitting next to him. "It is like this at the South Pole," Michael said. "We are at the South Pole."

Anthony, worried he might be lost in the blizzard, came looking, and found him in the nick of time. Michael was dragged back to Eagle Lodge, still convinced of the third man's presence. Death, he said to himself; the man of grey shadows is Death. He hasn't come for me. It's Anthony he wants.

The following morning he had a touch of flu, but, surprisingly, no frost-bite, no other ill-effects. He stayed in bed for a few days, recovering in time for the wedding. He whiled away the hours reading Disraeli's *Sybil*: "Two nations; between whom there is no intercourse, and no sympathy; who are as ignorant of each other's habits, thoughts, and feelings, as if they were dwellers in different zones, or inhabitants of different planets; who are formed by a different breeding, are fed by a different food, are ordered by different manners, and are governed by the same laws."

He was surprised to find – as Disraeli had intended – that the two nations were not England and Ireland, but the rich and the poor. Did the author think the Irish and the English working classes were alike? They were not: the English were not dying of starvation because they had been forced for centuries to live on nothing but potatoes.

The Leahys did not come to the wedding; they were too embarrassed that they had nothing to wear. Once every member of the family had possessed a decent set of clothes, but, despite the hanging of the rent, they had had to sell suits and dresses to buy next year's seed. Only five people came to the church – Madge and Dan, Michael and Anthony, and Jim, the eldest Sullivan boy, Dan's closest friend. Madge was grateful for Anthony's kindness: he had insisted that some sort of celebration after the service be held at Eagle Lodge rather than in the Leahys' overcrowded cabin. Also, he was giving her a wedding present.

"What do they need most?" he asked Michael.

"A bed," Michael replied. "Could they not have one we don't use?"

Anthony laughed. "You would think of essentials! But . . . are you suggesting I should give them a piece of my brother's property?"

"You told me the other day you were thinking of selling a bed."

"I am."

"Have Leahys ever slept in a bed?"

"The parents. They share it with as many of their children as can climb into it." Anthony came to a decision. "We might as well be hanged for a sheep. Richard will throw us out for what we've done already; it makes no difference. They can have it."

The bed, for the time being, was to stay at Eagle Lodge as the cabin Dan was to build had not yet been started; it was impossible to do so in such severe weather. The ground was iron with frost, and thick snow still covered it. Where they were to live meanwhile Michael could not find out. "We have a place," Madge said, but she would not tell him what it was, nor where. It wasn't, she insisted, a corner of the Leahys' floor. Were friends in town taking them in, Michael wondered. Perhaps. But he feared Madge's "place" could be on some estate nearby, a tumbled cabin from which the tenants had been evicted, a scalpeen, a hole made in the ruins. Or worse, a scalp – a hole dug in a field, roofed with sticks and slabs of turf.

The wedding celebrations were a needed relief, not only to Michael and Anthony, but to all the guests. Every tenant had been invited, but the Cronins did not come; they were not friends of the Leahys, and, as Patrick O'Callaghan had said, they didn't care "to traipse in and out of the Lodge." There was little to celebrate with – no special foods, no wedding cake – but each family brought some poteen. Not enough to get drunk on; nobody could afford that, but it was sufficient for people to think that times could be worse, that the potato next autumn would surely prove a superb crop, that even the Government might relent and do something. The furniture had been cleared from the parlour, and in the light of dozens of candles the guests danced to Patrick O'Callaghan's violin.

Anthony produced from the cellar a bottle of champagne that had been there for years. The principal actors in the drama should have it, the tenants insisted, and, besides, they didn't know, they said, what such peculiar foreign waters would taste like. "It would do me great harm," the Widow O'Gorman said. "Poison!"

Anthony, glass in hand, surveyed the scene; the dancers, the poteen drinkers, old men with pipes – they were smoking dead leaves, not tobacco – and Patrick by the fire, playing fast and furious music on his fiddle. "If Richard walked in now," he said, "imagine the expression on his face! I would like to see it."

"I wouldn't," Michael answered. "In two minutes he'd have us all put out in the snow."

"He would need half a regiment of men to do that."

"He'd find them." He watched Madge dancing with Dan. The other dancers stopped and looked too; here was a performance superior to anything they could stage, a rhythm, a co-ordination that was perfect. As if they were not two people, Michael said to himself, but one . . . one what? He couldn't think of the right word. They were very much in love: very *physically* in love. He was still jealous, and surprised and annoyed that he was jealous. He had everything he could possibly wish for with Anthony, yet . . . he would like Dan to make love to him. The suit Anthony had loaned fitted perfectly, though Michael found himself wanting Dan in his usual rags: more of his body would be visible; legs, chest, arm muscles. "It's a crying shame they cannot spend tonight of all nights," he said, "in the bed you have given them."

Anthony refilled his glass. "What are you saying? That we should let them sleep here?"

"I wasn't. But . . ."

"It would be a kindness," Anthony said. "Well, ask them if you wish. If they do, you must sleep in your own room."

Michael was much intrigued by this suggestion. Did he want to lie awake and listen to what would be happening on the other side of the wall, the creaking bed springs? He did. I don't much care for myself at the moment, he said as the dance finished and he walked up to Dan. Ty Keliher was gazing at him. Ty no longer looked so innocent: solemn, Michael thought; he had big, solemn eyes that knew more than they should. But what did they know that was so special? Anthony and me? Rubbish! Ty was not quite right in the head, people gossiped. A lanky, loose-limbed boy of seventeen; a solitary who liked to wander by himself all over the countryside. The village idiot.

Dan was happy with the invitation. "But I'll have to ask my wife," he said. Michael watched them speak, but in the shouts and laughter of the guests he could not hear their words. Madge shook her head; she did not want to. Dan returned. "It is good of you, but she would rather we were in our own place," he told Michael.

They left soon after. It was the end of the ceilidh; the crowd began to drift off into the night. "We can clear this up tomorrow," Anthony said, looking at the empty glasses, ash on the floor from pipes, the guttering candles. In bed Michael was much more passionate than he had been for weeks: he was imagining Anthony was Dan. What was Dan like, his touch, his mouth, the way he made love? Oh, he would know how to make

72

love! As well as he could dance. "Hey, hey, what is this?" Anthony said. "Though don't think for a second I'm grumbling!"

Michael felt drained, exhausted. "Protect me from myself," he said.

AT the blacksmith's house a rather different scene was taking place. Madge's letter to her parents, telling all, had been discovered that afternoon. "As she says, it's a mouth less to feed," said Mr Tangney, in tones of disgust. Margaret was in hysterics. Dr Lenehan was summoned; he gave her a sedative which calmed her down, though it did not send her to sleep.

"Will you go out for me again?" she asked, later. "I should like to talk to Father Quinlan. It would be a comfort."

"Oh, very well." Eugene was not anxious to venture out a second time in the frost and snow, but the presence of someone else would mean he did not have to spend the whole night alone with her discussing the subject. He had nothing to say, he realized. It was just one more blow on the head of a man who was already reeling. He was angry with his daughter, and shocked, obviously, but these sensations were covered, cushioned almost, by an overwhelming cloud of depression.

He was appalled that he had been unable to stop his perpetual craving for food. He loathed stealing from the family's supplies: he had created wretchedness for Margaret and Madge – and himself. Madge. Madge! Deserting, like a rat from a sinking ship, and wed to that oaf; what was Dan Leahy other than a big, brainless, human hulk? Married! Madge's decision, he knew, was the result of his own behaviour. And Margaret had sold possessions – her wedding ring! – in order that they should eat. He would never lift his head up again.

Nobody outside the family was aware of what had happened, but he felt an intense loss of status; the community would soon know the Tangneys' plight – you couldn't keep anything to yourself in a place as small as Clasheen. He had dragged his wife and family down to the level of evicted bog-trotters; they would starve to death or be forced to emigrate.

A headlong exodus from Ireland had already begun: ships were leaving Galway every week, packed with men, women and children bound for America and the chance to begin new lives. To abandon one's native earth! For him it was out of the question. But what else? He would sell the forge if he could, but there was nobody who had the money to buy it, and, in any case, it provided no work, no income now. He had resigned from the Relief Committee that afternoon and refused to give a reason. "Why?" Mr Peacock had asked, more than once. "Why? We *need* you!" He would have said, if he had not felt so ashamed, and if Mr Peacock had been able to understand, what Michael had once said to Margaret: *non sum dignus*. I am not worthy.

Father Quinlan was not only reading, Michael would have been surprised to hear, Anthony's copy of *The Rights of Man*, but agreeing with every word Tom Paine had to say. He really didn't want to go out in that evening's sub-zero temperature, particularly if it was to listen to more of Margaret's imaginary little sins, but it was urgent this time, Eugene said. "No rest for the wicked," the priest replied as he donned his coat. "What is the matter now?"

"If I tell you," the blacksmith said, "you will only have to put up with it again when you greet herself."

Very true, Father Quinlan thought, so he spent the five minutes walking to the forge asking why Mr Tangney had resigned so abruptly, and obtaining no satisfactory answers.

Mrs Tangney burst into tears once more as she read out the letter. Father Quinlan, the blacksmith suspected, might have been a party to Madge's plot, but the expressions on his face of astonishment and concern showed otherwise. "The Leahys are good people," he said, when Margaret had finished. "You may have no worries there. God-fearing, sober Catholics, honest and hard-working – when there is work to be found. Dan is on the road-building; we need men like him, strong as an ox."

"I never imagined a daughter of mine would stoop to marry a road-maker!"

"You must not think of him just as that," said the priest. He was using his official voice now – the tones he used in the confessional, pronouncing Acts of Contrition, Hail Marys and Our Fathers. (Mrs Tangney usually got the minimum quantity, three of each.) "He is your daughter's husband, your son-in-law, the father of your future grandchildren. And a decent man."

"The son of an Irish-speaking peasant!"

"Mrs Tangney, when you come to be judged before the Lord our God, as surely all of us will, your lack of charity – pardon me for saying it – will be your undoing. There is nothing in the Gospels to show that Jesus had such attitudes to the poor. The evidence is quite opposite, indeed and indeed."

"He didn't marry one of them," Eugene said.

Father Quinlan glared at him. "He told us that it is easier for a camel to pass through a needle's eye than for a rich man to gain the Kingdom of Heaven." He laughed. "I am thinking these days it will not be so hard for any of us to get tickets!"

Mrs Tangney thought for some moments about the priest's words. "Madge did it behind our backs," she said. "Some hole-in-the-corner affair. It is *not* right!"

"I agree it is not right. Every child has obligations to his parents. When he or she has become an adult as Madge surely has, it is no longer a question of blind obedience, but there are other duties – openness, consideration, honouring one's father and mother. I will talk to her about it."

"You will? Good."

"Not in anger, as you may wish. It is not my business to be angry with her."

"You can understand now, Father," Eugene said, "why I resigned from the committee."

"I do not understand it at all! What has the one thing to do with the other?"

"I can no longer hold up my head." But he did just that: looked up and stared Father Quinlan, several inches taller than he was, full in the face.

Father Quinlan sighed, and made for the door. "Learn to love your new son," he said, "and remember your children are all you will have in old age."

"We will not live to see old age. The hunger is upon us."

"Eugene, the worst sin you can commit is the sin of despair! I will preach on that one Sunday. Maybe the whole parish could be helped by a sermon on hope; Mr Peacock said so yesterday."

He went off into the night, wondering why people only saw trivialities as sinful – cross words, coveting their neighbours' goods, telling a few little fibs to extricate themselves from an awkward situation. Such burdens were not crushing enough to prevent souls passing through the eye of that needle. Real sins were legion, and went unrecognized. Refusal to accept the grace of God. Refusal to love God, and the consequence of it: the inability to love others.

The Tangneys were not his only parishioners in this way defective; the quarrels between the Sullivans and the O'Learys and the Leahys and the Cronins, so ancient the present generations did not know the causes, were evil too – petty jealousies and spites destroying charity. The most Christian person he knew was, ironically, the atheist, Anthony Altarnun. Yet even in that man there was something short of one hundred per cent; Michael's decision not to receive Communion for – for five years it was now – had, he guessed, some connection with Anthony. He would dearly like to know: it was his duty to bring an erring soul to God; but he hadn't any idea, he admitted to himself, what that connection could be.

Well, we are all black sinners, he said aloud as he paused in the snow by Flanagan's Bar, and fingered a coin in his pocket. He had not drunk a glass of poteen in weeks. If Madge's wedding had not been so clandestine he would have officiated, attended the reception, imbibed more than one glass. The Leahys for years had been able to put their hands on a most potent, smooth concoction; an uncle of theirs out in the bogs distilled it. It's time too, he said to himself, I asked how poor Flanagan is doing and his stout, red-faced wife; very little money would have passed over that counter in recent months. He went inside.

And saw, as he expected, that he was the only customer, and that Mrs Flanagan, though still red-faced, was no longer stout. They exchanged news of famished and ghastly living skeletons they had seen or heard of, babies sucking at breasts of mothers already lifeless, whole cabins of people dead and stiff for days, the stench intolerable, and no neighbour alive to bury them or send for help; the rush of people in droves to the ships, whole communities deserted – the houses abandoned, the fields untilled, the only living things a few starved crows and rats.

"The Committee has no food left," Father Quinlan said, as he began his second glass. "No food and no funds. But we have a ray of hope: Mr Peacock has a letter from Dublin; the Government is to invest money in soup kitchens. They will give the nation soup."

"There will not be enough soup in the whole wide world to feed such millions," Mrs Flanagan said. "May the good Lord save us!"

Father Quinlan did not mention a somewhat more ominous paragraph in the letter. The Government had decided to throw the whole cost of supporting the famine victims onto the Poor Law: the workhouse system. In doing so, it was turning a blind eye to the fact that workhouses were paid for out of the rates — rates that could not be collected in Ireland because people had no money to pay them. Many workhouses, as a result, were either bankrupt or closed and their inmates expelled, or so badly run that death and disease were more likely to flourish inside them than out.

As far as the soup was concerned, the Government would give half the money required to open kitchens and lend the rest; but once the transfer of Relief had passed to the Poor Law, the advance would have to be repaid — out of the rates. Furthermore, the public works would be stopped.

The transfer to the Poor Law was a scheme that could not function: it was designed not so much to help the destitute as to free the Government of its responsibilities — let *Ireland* save the Irish. "We must do all we can," said Charles Trevelyan, "and leave the rest to God." (A year later he became Sir Charles Trevelyan, K.C.B., an honour bestowed on him for his labours in the Famine.)

"Perhaps we could start up a soup kitchen here," Father Quinlan suggested.

Mrs Flanagan was surprised. "In a public house?"

"It is the centre of Clasheen. The place where people gather to talk."

"It was."

Father Quinlan finished his drink. "So what is your opinion?"

"At least it would give us something to do," Mrs Flanagan said.

"I will put it to the Committee, then."

ONE evening, a fortnight later, Anthony and Michael, playing chess in bed, were surprised by a ring at the doorbell. "At this hour?" Anthony exclaimed.

Michael went downstairs: it was Madge. She looked almost blue with cold, and was shivering uncontrollably. "I am throwing myself on your mercy," she said. "Michael! Please help us!" He took her into the kitchen and put some turf on the dying fire: she held out her hands to the heat, but could not stop trembling. "It isn't the hunger," she said. "Who is not hungry now? We get by — Dan has been out to sea, fishing. No. It's the cold."

There had been no break in the weather and there was none in sight. That morning snow had fallen for hours, and the icy east wind was still ferocious. "What is this 'place' of yours, Madge?" Michael asked.

She stared into the flames, and said "A scalp. If we didn't have one another for warmth we would have frozen to death!"

"A scalp," Michael repeated. Anthony appeared in the doorway.

She nodded. "A hole in the ground, four feet deep. During the day it is not so bad; Dan is out with the fish, and I am by his mother's fire. It is the nights: we lie against each other and shiver. It is impossible to sleep."

But possible, no doubt, to make love, Michael thought, the old jealousy returning. "Where is Dan now?" he asked.

"Here. In the garden. He would not come to the door."

"Bring him in at once!" Anthony said. "You may both stay here in your own bed, for as long as you like. A scalp! That Michael's sister should . . ." He glared at Michael, almost as if it was *his* fault. "Why didn't you tell me?"

"I did not know," Michael answered.

"Fish would be welcome. Perhaps tomorrow he will catch enough for the four of us. Bring him inside!"

Madge did so. "God bless all in this house," Dan said. Though still a strong, well-hewn figure, he did not look at this moment the hurling champion, the expert dancer. His self-confidence had been totally sapped. "I am not used to begging," he muttered. "I am so ashamed!"

Michael, for the first time in years in his own room, could not

78

sleep. Madge and Dan were talking on the other side of the wall. He could not distinguish many of their words, but he heard Madge laugh, then Dan say "Why not?" Silence, for a long while. Then the obvious sounds. I cannot put up with this, he said to himself. He got out of bed, tiptoed into Anthony's room, and slipped in beside his lover so noiselessly Anthony was not aware of his presence until he woke in the morning.

This charade went on, night after night.

Dan did not bring fish home every day, but he netted the occasional herring or mackerel. Often he could not go out because of the wind and the snow squalls, or the sea was too rough. "It is a horrible life," he said. "I would much rather build roads for eightpence a day! It is so wet and cold my teeth chatter for hours. But I am lucky, thank God; I have a friend who does loan me his curragh."

Why did the Irish, starving in their millions, not eat fish, particularly as there were immense shoals nearby in the Atlantic? They had virtually no tools for the job. The west of Ireland is peculiarly treeless; there was insufficient wood to build the kind of vessel that could travel the distances. The Irish went to sea in curraghs, little light boats made of wickerwork and animal hides that were only appropriate for inshore fishing. In heavy seas, gales and storms, the curragh was useless.

The rocky coast with its tremendous cliffs meant few harbours, and the rough terrain inland was not always accessible by road; so, selling the catch in any quantity was unprofitable. The fisherman, like everyone else, depended on potatoes. His job was not a way of life: his catch was only a variation in the staple diet. During the Famine most fishermen sold their curraghs and nets to buy Indian corn.

Aware that the number of fish he took home did not make up for the food they were eating from Anthony's supplies, Dan persuaded Madge to go to the soup kitchen that had opened in Clasheen. It was not located in Flanagan's Bar but in the Tangneys' forge, so Madge was obviously reluctant. Mr Peacock had gone purple in the face when he heard Father Quinlan's suggestion. "It is the most unsuitable, most objectionable idea I have ever listened to!" he said.

"Why?" Father Quinlan was puzzled.

"Temperance, sir, temperance! Or rather, *in*temperance! A soup kitchen in a public house! What is to stop a man exchanging his soup for a peg of whiskey? We shall have an orgy of drunkenness on our hands!" Mr Peacock did not care for whiskey himself, or any strong waters; a good bottle of wine was his preference.

"Oh, I do not think that will happen at all," Father Quinlan said.

Mr Peacock was adamant, and there was no way of getting round his embargo as the money for the soup kitchen – and the soup – was to come, until the Government loan arrived, almost entirely out of his own pocket. Dr Lenehan, Father Quinlan and Anthony had little to spare now and the Committee had nothing. Mrs Peacock fancied the idea of running a soup kitchen, that favourite activity of philanthropic women; she could be seen to be doing something for the deserving poor.

"Intoxicating liquors are the bane of Ireland," Mr Peacock said to Anthony. "Did you know that the first sermon I ever preached was to a congregation of members of the Irish Association for the Prevention of Drunkenness in the Lower Orders? It was very well received." Anthony found it difficult not to smile or laugh at these absurdities of Mr Peacock's. The existence of such a society was, he thought, as grotesque and improbable as a book on Irish gourmet cuisine.

Father Quinlan gave way. "In that case," he said, "I suggest we approach the Tangneys. Their house is convenient to everyone, and because of the forge is well-known. Mr Tangney has no work; the forge is idle. We could start up a soup kitchen in there."

Mr Peacock had no candidate of his own to put forward, but he was tired of Father Quinlan always dominating the proceedings. "What will the Tangneys say?" he asked. "It is not their usual line of business."

"I think they will like the idea . . . There are many reasons."

"What reasons?"

"Well . . . that is private," Father Quinlan said. Mr Peacock did not care for such an answer. He often suspected that the Romish abomination of the confessional gave Father Quinlan all sorts of holds over his parishioners that a Church of Ireland minister could not have over his. "I am sure Mrs Tangney would be more than grateful," Father Quinlan went on. "And she would do it well."

"I do not know that she could work with my wife."

"It will doubtless be welcomed by both of them," said Dr Lenehan, who was anxious to finish the discussion. Anthony agreed, so Mr Peacock found himself once again in a minority, though one he could not veto.

The two women, as it turned out, worked very well together. Both were conscious of status; making soup and serving it to the hungry emphasized that they were far from the foot of the ladder. It also made them feel satisfied: they had given up their time to help those less fortunate than themselves; calls of duty had been answered; good deeds had been done. If Adelaide Peacock was aware that Margaret Tangney was closer to being at the foot of the ladder than she was herself, she did not mention it.

Eugene was also happy with the soup kitchen. To lend his forge alleviated his depression and guilt somewhat; it was a small atonement. And if, at the end of the day, there was any soup left, and sometimes there was when the weather was so bad that the sick and the old could not make the journey from their cabins, he could eat it up. But it wasn't particularly appetising, he thought. Mrs Peacock was not exactly prodigal with her ingredients: the recipe consisted of a few scraps of oxtail, some turnips, carrots and leeks, Indian corn, salt, and a vast quantity of water. It cost her about a ha'penny a pint. Nourishment for the distressed she might think it was, but he found it distressing nourishment.

Mrs Tangney was no nearer to passing through the eye of the needle despite her efforts in the soup kitchen. "Learn to love your new son," Father Quinlan had said, but when Madge and Dan first appeared at the forge, she gave a little cry of "Oh!" and hurried into the house. She did not come out until they had gone. On subsequent occasions she managed a cold "Good morning" to Madge, and ignored Dan.

"It is utterly humiliating," Madge said. "I will not go there again!"

"It is more humiliating to eat the Altarnun's food," Dan replied, "and we do give him nothing in return."

"You bring him fish."

"One tiny herring is all I have caught this week."

Michael enjoyed having Madge at Eagle Lodge; it relieved what was becoming an almost suffocating boredom. He had not had anything worthwhile to do for months. There was no money to start repairs on the house, and the snow made digging the garden impossible. Anthony had more to occupy himself with, visiting the tenants, attending Committee meetings, and, when the weather allowed, walking for miles in the countryside. Michael joined him on these walks, but that, and going to Mass on Sundays, was almost his only activity out of doors.

Since the wedding he had been less often to his parents' house, and when he did go to see them he did not stay long. He admitted, under cross-examination from his mother, that he had been aware of Madge's plans and kept silent. "You are a grave disappointment to me," Mrs Tangney said. Whenever she spoke to him now she seemed to be constantly reminding him of that disappointment. He had always known he had failed to live up to Eugene's expectations, but he'd learned to live with that. Because both his parents now thought him less of a son than he should be, he felt he did not want to spend much time with them. Why should I always leave that house, he said to himself, feeling guilty? I have done nothing wrong. If they cannot accept me, then it is too bad.

He was looking out of the window one morning: a ship was sailing for the open sea. It was the end of March, and still the winter had not softened. February had been worse than December or January, with blizzards so severe nobody could recall their like. Abandoned carts littered the roads; the bodies of men and horses lay freezing in snowdrifts, and the deaths from hunger mounted – what starvation began the unprecedented cold finished off. A week before April the landscape was still white.

Madge came into the room. "Brother, I must talk to you. There are several things."

He turned, and said "You are going to have a baby."

"How could you guess that?"

"By your solemn, I-have-serious-matters-to-discuss voice. Madge, I am glad! And me – an uncle. *I* should feel solemn." He took her in his arms and kissed her.

"I am not so sure that *I* am glad. What kind of a world is this to bring babies into? Another mouth to feed, may God forgive me that I say it."

"We will cope," Michael said.

"No. It has made up our minds for us. It's a terrible thing surely to cross the water to a foreign land . . . but next week we shall be on a ship like that one out there."

"Madge! You can't!"

"We shall only die in Ireland. Look at Dan, the shape of him, the strength of him! Going to ruin when he could be earning us a fortune, and I in his house keeping it clean and making him good meals, *happy* to have his children."

"What will I do without you?"

"You have Anthony."

He tensed: the words were odd. "What do you mean?" he asked.

She frowned. "Michael . . . this is difficult . . ."

"I thought we hid no secrets, you and me."

"Oh, but we do, brother! We do! It is plain as a pikestaff to anybody who is at Eagle Lodge one minute that you and Anthony are not the ordinary servant and master. They may not guess why; it never entered my head, though nights I hear you leave your room and go into his, then you creeping back in the morning imagining we're not awake. I still thought nothing. Then Dan . . . hinted . . . and I . . . well, it is the only thing that makes sense." She was nervously pulling at her shawl. When she looked up and saw the shock and fear in his eyes she said "We shall not tell a living soul, I swear to God! Your secret is safe as a house!"

He did not answer for some time, but clenched his fist and banged it on the top of his skull. "I am sorry . . . to have upset you," he said at last. "I *have* upset you."

"I . . . I would like to see you married, that's so. A sister-in-law . . . children . . ."

"Like my mother and father, you are disappointed in me."

"It is not my business. Entirely yours."

"But what do you think?"

"Of what?"

"You think it wrong. Wicked and vile."

"Our religion teaches us that . . . what we do with our . . . is for continuing the human race. All activities outside wedlock must be sinful."

"Oh, Madge, are you thinking of babies when Dan is inside you at night? Don't tell me you do not love his body!" He paused. "It is a beautiful body."

"I was wondering . . . I was guessing you thought that. Michael, you *must* know it is sinful! It is why you will not take Holy Communion."

"I love Anthony. It is a marriage."

"I don't understand. Why, how . . . I think it right we are leaving soon. I do not want a rift with you! We could fall out over this. I . . . am sorry for you."

"I am not sorry for myself."

"To have to lead such a hidden life. To pretend every day. It is a burden, surely."

He analysed this conversation at great length with Anthony. Their secret would not be whispered to the world; that wasn't the question. But were Madge and Dan going because of what they had found out, or because of the baby? Because Dan did not like it that Michael fancied him? What did Madge think of them now? Sinners who knew they were in danger of hell, and yet continued to sin and enjoy it: that was her opinion. She had made it clear. She said, too, there would be a rift if she stayed, but there was already a rift.

Michael felt a great need to talk to her again, to clarify matters, but it was impossible. It would be too humiliating to reveal whole aspects of himself he had kept buried from everyone except Anthony so he avoided the leads she gave him, changed the subject, let the problem hang in the air, a real burden.

She saw this, and knew what to do. Alone with him three days later, she said "You are still the Michael I've always loved. And you always will be. It makes no difference at all. The time I didn't know you, didn't speak to you, I'd hate myself for ever."

There was no rift.

CHAPTER SIX

INTROIBO *ad altare Dei, ad Deum qui laetificat juventutem meam*: I will go in unto the altar of God, unto God who giveth joy to my youth. The opening words of the Mass, and as usual Michael was in church, standing with the other men. Families did not sit together; as is still the custom in the ceremonies of public life in rural Ireland, there was a strict segregation. Women and children occupied the pews, men stood at the back. No edict forbids the mingling of the sexes; it just happens. The cynical would say the men like to be near the door so they can nip out during the sermon to have a smoke.

Though the faithful must, on pain of mortal sin, attend Mass every Sunday and on holy days of obligation, there are neat, casuistic definitions of what exactly is the Mass. Some would argue that it is no sin to arrive as late as the end of the *Gloria*, and leave after the *Ite, missa est*; and the sermon, they would add, is not technically speaking part of the ancient words one is obliged to hear. Many men at Clasheen did go out for a breath of air during the sermon, so, it being in the mother-tongue and the Mass itself in Latin, they never listened to the one part of the proceedings they might have understood. Michael, however, being of a more inquiring mind than most, always stayed inside to hear Father Quinlan's commentaries on the world, the flesh, and the Devil.

The sermon was preceded by the notices, and, during the past year, these had been dominated by the announcement of the names of those who had died from hunger or the diseases that followed hunger. Patrick and Julia O'Riordan, little Eileen O'Riordan, Francis Cournane, Maggie Cournane: "O God," Father Quinlan intoned, "with a firm confidence we trust in Thee that Thou wilt grant them, through the merits of Jesus Christ, the assistance of Thy grace, and after keeping Thy commandments, wilt bestow on them life everlasting, according to Thy promises, who art almighty and whose word is truth."

The congregation was then begged to remember, in its prayers, Dan and Madge Leahy, who were departing from Clasheen on the morrow to begin a new life in the United States of America. Michael, at this point, glanced at his father who was standing across the church from him, but Mr Tangney's head remained bowed. Michael's eyes met Dan's: Dan was blushing; he hated attention being called to himself.

Father Quinlan had promised a sermon on hope some months before, but what optimism there was in his character seemed to go into his practical day-to-day work with the hungry. In this he was always encouraging, even if in private he nearly despaired. His Jansenist cast of mind made it difficult for him to preach on the subject of hope. Sin he found easier. "Let us conceive a great sorrow for having offended God," he said, and went on to urge his flock to examine their consciences in relation to hard-heartedness, disobedience, selfishness, injurious words, blasphemy, backbiting, lying, scandal, incitement to sin, neglect of mortification, and sensuality in looks, conversation and deeds.

He was not usually as gloomy as this – nor perhaps as petty – but during the week he had talked on several occasions with Madge about her duty to her parents, the social consequences of her hasty marriage, and the evil of not being open with one's family. Madge had a temper and invariably spoke her mind. She was confident that she had taken the only possible course of action in the circumstances, and, emboldened by the knowledge that within a few days she would never see Father Quinlan again, she ordered the priest in no uncertain terms to mind his own business and get back to matters of real importance, the dead and the dying in the scalps and the scalpeens.

"Good for you," said Michael, laughing, when she told him.

As he made notes for his sermon, Father Quinlan said to himself that it was very difficult to like *any* members of the Tangney family. They were too individualistic. Too proud. Then, with a flash of insight, he said: I am not a good preacher; I am better at works of charity. That morning he had been miles away in the glens, dealing with the dying Maggie Cournane and her husband, and in another cabin, Julia O'Riordan, near death also, in bed with the corpse of her husband, while a famished cat ripped at the body of their dead baby. He looked up at the crucifix on the wall of his room and said "I would love some cheese." Creamy, soft cheese, ripe, almost running. Then he added a few sentences to his text on the sin of gluttony.

The sermon over, the Mass continued in Latin. What does it all signify, Michael asked himself for the hundredth time. He knew the literal meaning of the words, of course, but did they contain any real meaning *now*? This constant arid repetition of syllables – the monotony had been going on for the best part of two thousand years – like the words of a spell. It wasn't so far removed from paganism or witchcraft. The supposedly purposive tropes said aloud – *Orate, fratres; Vere dignum et justum est, aequum et salutare; Agnus Dei, qui tollis peccata mundi* –were merely indicators pointing to sites of importance in the fifth century, villages long since vanished and buried in grass, the only token that they had existed a green mound or a dried-up ditch.

So, too, in a few years' time, the present villages of Ireland: signposts would direct the traveller down lanes of almost impenetrable branches to communities quite dead, the inhabitants now in America or entombed under the soil of neglected graveyards, the cabins heaps of mud, the churches piles of broken stone.

He pulled himself together. It was just before the Communion; Father Quinlan was raising the sacred host: *Ecce agnus Dei*. Where, Michael asked himself, did he now stand, coldly and logically, in relation to all this? He would examine his conscience, as the priest had suggested. The words of the Mass were hocus-pocus. He did not believe in the existence of a good and just God; there was too much inexplicable suffering and pain. Did that mean he believed in a vengeful God of retribution? No, though he took a while longer to dismiss that idea. If it caused no comment, no adverse reaction, would he come here at all? What would he do on a Sunday morning if he was in London or New York? Lie in bed in Anthony's arms.

That was all cold logic, but, like most of us, Michael did not act according to the dictates of his reason when it was in conflict with his feelings. He stayed till the end, not just because of the tongues that would clatter if he did not, but because he might be totally wrong. To attend Mass was an insurance policy. If he did not attend, there was still a chance that God could damn his immortal soul for disobedience, pride, and not fulfilling his Christian duty. But if God should now want to condemn him for the sexual nature of his relationship with Anthony, he would give the Almighty a short, sharp sermon on His inability to understand and to love. Even Father Quinlan had once said – admittedly codding over a glass of poteen – that the Jehovah of the Old Testament was somewhat deficient in Christian compassion.

Outside the church he greeted his parents. "Will you eat with us today?" Mr Tangney asked. "We have a chicken."

"Where in God's name have you found a chicken?"

"Galway market. I bought it . . . I have sold some of the tools from my forge."

Michael softened. He had wanted to make an excuse, though it would have been difficult. Anthony was not at Eagle Lodge waiting for him to return; he was lunching at the Peacocks' house. The minister needed advice with a letter he was sending to the authorities in Dublin, a request for help – food or money, however little – to keep the soup kitchen going. His own resources were trickling away, despite the stinginess of his wife's recipes.

"Very well," he said. "Is it a special occasion?"

"It is," said his mother.

Madge came out of the church, and went up to Dan. She saw the family group and turned away, but her father hurried across to her. Now what is going on, Michael asked himself. Eugene came back, Madge and Dan following. Madge looked pleased.

"I cannot let them sail to the other side of the earth without my blessing," Mr Tangney said, when he noticed the surprise on Michael's face. "They go tomorrow and I shall never see her again. To part in some form of friendship . . . it is a small consolation."

Father Quinlan, as he walked by, smiling and nodding at his parishioners, said "I am glad to see you reconciled." They stared at him, too embarrassed to answer.

Special occasion it was, but there was little warmth and ease; too much had happened. But they were all polite, assiduous in ensuring that everyone had enough on their plates. Dan, feeling very awkward, was totally silent, but, Mrs Tangney said to herself, he does have remarkably good table manners. She and Madge kept the conversation going; it was mostly about the baby. "To think I shall have a grandson born thousands of miles off! And I never to see him!" Mrs Tangney said.

"You may well see him," said Madge. "You may follow us."

"Ah . . . now that would be hard."

"We shall call him Michael. It is a most fortunate choice, for Dan's father and my grandfather have the archangel's name. And my quiet brother sitting over there, though he does not deserve it."

"What if he is a girl?" her mother asked.

"He will not be," Madge said.

Eugene belched, and said "Emigration will be the ruin of this country. The best of the men go, and the finest of the women."

"And the others are left here to rot," Margaret said. "This island is accursed. How will we sing our songs and hand down our stories when there are none to listen? The music is broken. The words are broken."

"We shall keep the customs in the new country," Madge answered. "We shall sing the songs in a strange land. No one will forget. The Irish have memories longer than the elephant's."

"Of catastrophes," her mother said. "Cromwell, King William, Wolfe Tone. Emmet."

"But remember the Races of Castlebar," Michael said. "There is surely no cheering you today at all. Nor my father."

"You are right; there is not. The Races of Castlebar was a French victory, not to do with us. This house is broken. Madge disappearing for ever! It is a death sentence. I sometimes think sorrow will finish us all before the hunger."

"This is no way to talk!" Madge said. "There is always hope."

"Hope! What hope have we? You are young enough to start again; we surely are not."

"The chicken is good," Michael said. "I have not eaten so well in weeks." That ended the conversation. It *is* a death sentence, he thought. I shall not see her again. What will I do without her?

When the time came for Madge and Dan to leave, it was scarcely possible to exchange good wishes, last words with her parents; there was too much emotion, too many tears. And I will have to go through a repetition of this tomorrow, Michael said to himself: he was travelling with them to Galway, as far as the quay where the ship was already at anchor, waiting.

"This is terrible," Dan said to him. "Terrible!"

Michael left at the same time, ignoring his mother's plea of "Don't go just yet! Stay with us!"

"I cannot," he said. He had an overwhelming desire to be alone. He walked a short distance with Madge and Dan, then turned up a path that led between fields towards the mountains. He wanted to put his back to the ocean, to his parents' house, to Clasheen. He too, he decided, would like to desert it all, to be gone for ever – with Anthony. Where? How? He was surprised to hear the noise of trickling water; had in fact heard it all the while since he had left the road, but he had not heeded it. He noticed green patches of grass, buds in the hedges. The thaw had begun. The Great Frost was melting. "O winter! Bar thine adamantine doors!" he shouted aloud.

And felt hope.

TY Keliher was not the village idiot Michael thought him. He wasn't mad, schizoid, retarded, autistic, brain-damaged: just slow and odd. He had no real friendships with his brothers and sisters or with any of Clasheen's young people. He liked his own company, and he was at his happiest wandering about the countryside, pretending to hunt not only prehistoric elks but any sort of animal. Including humans. He was proud of his ability to be silent, stealthy, and cunning. He frequently stalked his own parents, the O'Leary kids, Dr Lenehan, Dan Leahy, Mrs Peacock, Michael and Anthony: none of them had ever spotted him.

This successful espionage gave him all kinds of information that nobody else knew of: his father had a gold coin hidden in their thatched roof; the eldest Scannell boy was a thief; the Widow O'Gorman wore scarlet underwear and loved looking at herself in it. Ty lived through the Famine relatively unscathed and, when he reached adulthood, he emigrated to Canada where he became a fur trapper in the Yukon; he married, had two children and died during the First World

War. Old, frail, and sick, a stroke finished him when he heard that his only grandson, a soldier in the Canadian army, had been killed at Vimy Ridge.

Anthony and Michael he considered his prize catches. His curiosity had been aroused by the episode he had observed against the tree, and in the months afterwards he noticed similar occurrences – the two of them holding hands, or standing in the garden with their arms round each other. Several times he peered through the windows of Eagle Lodge, at dusk before the curtains were closed, but he found nothing more unusual than one of them reading a book, the other washing dishes or watering a potted plant.

Until the day – at first he thought they were wrestling – he saw them in front of the fire, making love. Two men. He was not the innocent now who could form no attitudes; he knew that what they were doing was supposed to be between a man and a woman. But he felt no horror, shame, or disgust. In fact, he was sexually aroused, and for the first time in his life he masturbated. As he made his way home he was more worried about what he had done than what he had seen. Playing with himself, now that really *was* wrong: the priest had said so.

Father Quinlan, listening to the confessions of adolescent boys – details of lies, fights, petty thefts – was in the habit, if the boy had not mentioned anything sexual, of asking questions about lewd thoughts and impure desires. He was not being prurient, not satisfying his own impure desires; it was his duty to warn teenagers of the evils of the flesh – particularly masturbation. He did not believe, as some Victorian tracts on the subject stated, that it caused warts to grow on the offending fingers, but he did believe like most of his contemporaries that it led to insanity or blindness, that it wasted the seed, made intercourse in marriage difficult, sapped bodily strength. Above all, it was a mortal sin, and it was incumbent on him to lead souls away from the dangers of hell-fire.

Father Quinlan had asked the usual questions, but Ty didn't understand what he was talking about. "Of course I do touch myself," he said.

"Whereabouts on the body?" the priest inquired.

"Well . . . my face, my arms . . ."

"No, no!" Father Quinlan was becoming impatient. "Lower down!"

"My legs?"

"No!" He thought for a moment. "*Between* the legs."

The penny dropped. "Father, you mean when it is stiff?"

"Yes . . . I do mean . . . that."

"I do touch it. What is so wrong?"

"What do you think about when you touch yourself . . . it?"

There was a long pause. "Nothing," Ty said. "Nothing I remember. It only feels . . . good."

"You do not think about girls at these moments? No impure desires?"

"With respect, Father, what are impure desires?"

It was useless, Father Quinlan decided, to go on with such questions. "It is very wrong, Timothy, to touch yourself there, however good it feels. It is a mortal sin. You know what a mortal sin is?"

"I would go to Hell, Father, when I die."

"If you have not confessed it, yes. The purpose of that part of the body is to make children when you are married. It is a sin, a most displeasing sin in the eyes of the Lord our God, to play with it in any way, in any kind of situation, before you are married. It can lead to madness."

"People do say I am not right in the head now, Father."

"I'm sure that has nothing to do with what we are talking about."

"But . . . if I touched it . . . would it make me more mad?"

"Yes. It certainly would."

Ty went off to say his five Hail Marys, petrified with fear. Was he crazier than he would have been because he had frequently touched it? How could he *avoid* touching it? For some time afterwards he didn't even hold his penis when he urinated.

Now he had seen two men touch, do a lot more than touch, and brought himself to orgasm, which, even if it was forbidden, was a marvellous sensation. Were Anthony and Michael mad, what they were doing a sign of madness? And he – was he less right in the head than half an hour ago? He couldn't tell.

His spying at Eagle Lodge increased after this, and he was disappointed not to observe his catches making love on any of these occasions. He masturbated from time to time now, and began to have what Father Quinlan would call lewd thoughts about girls. He confessed these sins to the priest, who, he was amazed to discover, did not blast him with a torrent of angry words. He was told, rather wearily, not to do it again, to feel sorry for what he had done, and to say as a penance five Our Fathers, just as if he had confessed to a commonplace lie or to punching somebody on the nose. He worried continually about madness, however, and the size of his organ, which, limp or erect, was of prodigious girth and length. It seemed, after he masturbated, to be always a little larger than it was before. If he played with it too often, he reasoned, it might become so big that everyone would notice it and be aware of what he had been doing.

Anthony and Michael were in no danger from him, direct danger that is. He never told anybody about his finds; they were his secrets, his captured animals, like those he was later to hunt in the New World. A girl wandering alone in the mountains might have been more at risk than were Anthony and Michael. Ty had his fantasies; would he or wouldn't he dare? He sometimes saw courting couples (a clandestine relationship between two members of those warring families, the Leahys and the Cronins, had come under his scrutiny), but he rarely saw a girl wandering alone in the mountains. When he did he was so tongue-tied and so awkward he would dash off after bidding her good morning.

Rape and attempted rape were virtually unheard of in Ireland. More than one female traveller of that period from England noted she could go anywhere and never be molested, quite the opposite of what could happen to her back home. Ty Keliher was a characteristic example of the repressed sexuality – and the diffident gentleness – of Irish men.

THE attachment of the people to their country, however dreadful the conditions of life, and the considerable expense involved in crossing the Atlantic, made emigration from Ireland before the Famine very unusual. But a passage to Canada or the United States had recently become a great deal cheaper; ships bringing cargoes of timber to Europe needed something to transport back, both as ballast and to make the journey profitable. The passenger trade began.

The United States at this time was not at all keen on opening its arms to hordes of poverty-stricken European immigrants, particularly the penniless, starving, fever-ridden Irish, so it raised the price of the fare, and imposed both a limit on the numbers of people a ship might carry and strict conditions concerning their health and comfort. But to travel in a British ship cost very little, and the few rules and regulations applying to numbers, health and comfort were almost universally ignored.

Emigrants were crammed between decks; the crew was often drunk or incompetent; food and water were below subsistence level; a doctor was not required; sanitation was sometimes non-existent. If there were passengers who already had the diseases that attacked the starving – typhus, dysentery, relapsing fever – everyone on board was at risk. In the Famine years thousands who left Ireland quite healthy became infected and died at sea or in the totally inadequate quarantine stations in Canada and the U.S.A.

The ships themselves were often so leaky and old that many sank, with immense loss of life. At Westport a ship sank before it reached the open sea; nearly everyone drowned, watched by an appalled multitude of friends and relatives who, less than an hour previously, had been saying good-bye to those who were now shrieking for help.

When Madge and Dan decided to leave, the exodus was at its height. They were unaware of the horrors the voyage might produce, and torn, sad, and distressed though they were to go, they kept themselves cheerful by thinking that once they arrived in America all would be well. "Why, you can have a plot there so big you have difficulty seeing its edges!" Dan said. "And you don't rent it; you buy it for next to nothing! Sometimes nothing at all. If nobody is living there you just claim it for yourself. We'll be rich in no time and sending the money back for the rest of the family to follow."

"I wouldn't be happy with the Indians," Michael said. "In the United States there is a different meaning to scalp."

"You are codding us, brother," said Madge. "It is a land of milk and honey. A land fit to have children in."

They had no knowledge of the conditions in America they would have to face; they were as naive as kids who think the streets of New York are paved with gold. Michael knew nothing either, and Anthony very little, so they had no one to dampen their enthusiasm or to prepare them for the shock of reality.

Their last night in Ireland was spent with Michael at the grocery shop in Galway where Noreen, the married sister, lived. As they went along the streets to the harbour, Michael said to himself: "Seaport views which landmen love to see." He had been reading Crabbe. But this seaport was not as he remembered it. Where once there were well-dressed men and women on their way to a fair or to buy produce at the market, thin, pinched beggars in rags, their faces grey and skeletal, now grubbed in gutters or heaps of rubbish for a scrap of food. Shops were closed and derelict. Crowds sat in the squares or on the steps of churches, doing nothing, seeing nothing; defeat and hopelessness in their eyes.

Everywhere there was filth, disease, squalor: it was as if the heart of the city was dead. A disgusting stench of decay drifted from all the courtyards and alleys. A few feet in front of them an old, tottering broomstick of a man fell down and did not get up. People tried to help him, but he waved them away. "The fever is upon me," he said, and they shrank back. "I may as well rot here," he mumbled, "as anywhere."

Only at the harbour was there activity with purpose other than the useless scavenging for something edible. It was crowded with ships, one nearly ready to sail, its anchors up, its ropes loosened from bollards; the gangplanks of others were down, and passengers carrying baskets or bundles containing a few essential possessions were handing over tickets, walking on board. These people, though as starved, many of them, as the silent, hopeless throngs in the squares and on the church steps, were alive: they talked, swore, even joked – and wept, often hysterically, as last goodbyes were said to parents, cousins, neighbours.

Some had been paid to go: landlords, and not the worst kind of landlord, had begged them to emigrate, bought their tickets for them, given five pounds to each family. A few even looked happy. The rest, who had scraped the price of a ticket together somehow, still had a gleam of hope, a determination to live, however gaunt, frail and hollow-eyed they were.

"That is our ship," said Dan. "The *Lord Kingston*." The crew was on board, but there were no passengers as yet, and none waiting. They were not due to embark till the following morning, at seven o'clock.

"Now that we know where it is," Madge said, "we can go to my sister's house."

They found Noreen, her husband John, and their young son, William, living in a state of siege. The grocery store was locked and barricaded as firmly as if an army was about to attack; Madge, Dan and Michael had to go in by the side door. On the counter John had erected wooden panels that reached to the ceiling with only one small opening through which he could talk to the customers. "To protect ourselves," Noreen explained. "So many came in who had the fever on them. Black fever. Yellow fever. We had them put their coins in a pot of vinegar."

She was speaking in the past tense, Michael noticed. "It looks, sister," he said, "as if you are shut till Tib's Eve."

"We are," she replied.

"Why is that? The people are starving, and there is food in here! A great deal of food." On the shelves there was tea, coffee, biscuit, raisins, dried fish, sugar, flour, Indian corn, salted meat, even vegetables and fruit.

"The price of it all is so dear," she said. "We had to buy dear, so we must sell dear or *we* starve. No one has the money to pay for it, to pay for *anything*! Particularly now the Government has stopped the public works. Two days back, a mob burst in screaming for food. A man pointed a gun through the opening at John, God save us! Little William was behind the counter playing with the cat; he was *terrified*! As luck would have it, the peelers were close; they arrested the ringleaders and clapped them in jail, and the others shuffled out. So we have locked ourselves up. We shall eat our own stores. We can last a while, even months I think. After that" – she made a gesture of despair – "only the good Lord decides. We may opt for a ticket on the boats, but I do not want to. None of us wants to."

Michael thought of what Anthony would have done if he had faced a starving mob screaming for food. "You should have given them something," he said.

"And ourselves go short? Michael, you were ever the unpractical one of the family! I can see if you owned a shop you'd

96

be bankrupt in a day!" She laughed. "Let us go into the kitchen and eat. I daresay you are all hungry."

Michael ate as little as possible. The food, he considered, was tainted. But he drank several cups of tea: he and Anthony loved tea; Eagle Lodge had run out of it a fortnight ago.

Next morning, he went with Madge and Dan to the harbour. It was just gone six o'clock; a dull, sullen dawn, rain in the wind, and chilly. The homeless and the starving were still trying to sleep – on garbage tips, under bushes – hunched, wet, shivering bundles of cold. The passengers of the *Lord Kingston* were going on board, and there were pathetic scenes like those of yesterday – the farewells and tears of close-knit families breaking up. "There is a power of people already," Michael said. "Is there room for more?"

"I think we shall be a huge gathering," said Dan.

"The ship looks old. Are her timbers good? You do not fear the weight of so many passengers will sink her?"

Dan laughed. "It is a lot more stout than the curragh I did use for the fishing!"

"Michael . . . I shall write as soon as we are there," said Madge. "Oh, Michael!" She had checked her feelings till now; but the moment had come. She threw herself into his arms and sobbed.

"Madge. Madge!" Dan said, gently.

"To think I shall never see you again!"

"You will write. And write often," Michael said. "I shall look for your hand. Every day. And I shall write what has happened here, to Anthony and me, to Noreen, to the Leahys, to our parents . . . It will be just as if I am in New York with you. As if you were by the fire at Eagle Lodge still."

Madge stiffened. The mention of Noreen stopped her tears; she had felt the same as Michael had about the food. "I read once in a city that was besieged and the inhabitants starving, the hoarders of food were taken out and shot! But *she* will get away with it; mark my words!"

"Come now," Dan said. "It is time."

"I will not wait," Michael said. "It would drag out the pain. I love you both dearly."

He turned away, and walked through the town, to the shop, not looking behind him once. He drank tea with Noreen, who, when he said there was no tea at home, insisted he should take some back with him. His will was not strong: he tried to refuse, but couldn't. He left there in the afternoon, feeling more depressed than he had felt in his whole life. As he walked the miles to Clasheen he hardly noticed the soft rain that was soaking him. Not to see her again, he said to himself. Not to see her again. Never, never, never. Never.

When he arrived at Eagle Lodge he found it almost devoid of furnishings; only the bare necessities remained. Carpets, curtains, and most of the chairs and tables had gone. The leak in the roof was now serious; the snow had hidden the problem, but as it was melting water dripped into their bedroom, splashing the floor, staining the ceiling beneath. It is a ruin, this house, he said to himself; soon it will collapse in a heap of stones, and then what is to become of us? "I thought it would all have to go in time," he said to Anthony, "but why have you sold everything at once?"

Anthony was in sombre mood. "We need the money," he said. "You will be cross with me."

"No. It is not my furniture."

"Nor mine, come to that. But . . . I've done several things without consulting you. Important things." He hesitated, then went on: "I've been to Galway, but I didn't find you. The ship had sailed, so I must have passed you on the road. I don't understand; you've arrived home after me."

"I went back to the shop. They have tea to drink; look – I have some for you. They have food in plenty. No one can afford to buy it, so they are eating themselves bankrupt."

"I've had . . . a letter from Richard. He's in London. He says – you may read it – he will be here at the end of May. I have no doubt at all that when he sees what has happened, he will evict us."

"And I was about to plant the garden for summer!"

"Yes, I know." He touched Michael's face. "This is not all. I loaded the furniture onto a cart; Ty Keliher and his father helped me. Then I drove into Galway and sold it. It didn't fetch a lot; no one wants to buy settees and tables now. I . . . have bought two tickets for a ship. One-way tickets."

Michael stared at him. "America?"

"Yes."

"When?"

"The thirty-first of May. I had to. Richard will – "

"I never thought to go to America. I never wanted to." He looked out of the window. The rain, still soft and gentle, pattered on the glass; rose bushes – they needed pruning – were shaking in the wind. Clouds scudded in from the west, American clouds. In the bay and moving towards the open sea was a ship. "I'll go with you," he said. "Anywhere on the earth, as I've always promised. I could never leave you. But it is hard to leave *here*."

Anthony came up behind him, put his arms round him, rubbed his cheek against Michael's. "What else can we do?"

"Did the tickets take all the money?" Michael asked.

"No. There is enough to buy food for now and the journey, and for what we need when we get there. Until we can both find work."

"What work will we do?"

"I don't know."

"You . . . a pauper!"

"One of the tickets is for a cabin. So we have a bed; we shan't be sleeping on the floor, as many will. But the ship may be packed like herrings in a barrel."

"We? You said *a* cabin."

"We share it. It won't look odd; with so many on board there'll be five or six people, whole families to one bed."

"It is hard to leave here," Michael said again.

"I . . . have given some of the money to Mr Peacock: without it the soup kitchen will close. His letter to Dublin is not worth the paper it's written on."

"Anthony! How could you!" Michael turned and faced him, then said "I never knew such goodness." He burst into tears, tears that wouldn't stop, as if he were weeping, he thought later, not just for himself or for Anthony or the end of their life at Eagle Lodge, but for the whole miserable, rotten, *fucking* world.

Anthony held him, letting him cry, and thought: as the Government has at last steeled itself to shut down all the public works, I have a present for Richard – a road to drive on. It is only of use to him, just Eagle Lodge to Clasheen. The benefits of public works! They were meant to be for the whole community.

CHAPTER SEVEN

THE Scannells, the most improvident of the tenants, now had nothing left to eat. The money they had had in reserve because they were not asked for the rent was all gone. They told Anthony that unless he could pay for their fares to America they would have to go to the workhouse. "We cannot survive on the soup, your honour," Mrs Scannell said. "It is vile. Not enough to keep body and soul together."

"What makes you think you would be better off in the poorhouse?" Anthony asked.

"The Guardians are obliged to feed us, sir; they have the money. They have the food."

"There is only soup. In an English workhouse you would be given tea, sugar, butter, meat, bread, milk, even potatoes. But this is Ireland." Protecting his tenants from starvation, Anthony realized, also protected them from exposure to truth. "I haven't the money," he said.

"Saving your presence, you paid for Dan and Madge Leahy to go."

Pay for one, he should pay for them all – is that what they thought? The Scannells, he felt, were taking him for granted. But Mr Scannell knew his wife had gone too far. "Excuse herself, your honour," he said, flopping down on his knees. "She is always after prying into business that is not her own."

Mrs Scannell glared at him. Anthony said "Get up. Get up!"

He returned to a standing position, and fidgeted with his rags. "We have nothing left, sir. Nothing."

"Do you know what is happening in the workhouses? Clifden is shut, the inmates put out to beg and survive as best they can. Some of those people now live in caves, or holes they have dug in the bogs, and there they starve to death. Other workhouses have twice, three times, even ten times as many paupers as they were built for; the Guardians have no money to foot the bills, so there is nothing to eat and no medicines. The people inside are famished or dying of typhus; some of them are crowded four to a bed, the diseased with the healthy, and often not a stitch of clothing to cover their bodies."

"We have heard such things, sir," Mrs Scannell said. "But we did not believe them."

Anthony grew impatient. "Well, you are at liberty to go and see for yourselves. And don't say you haven't been warned! I will get Michael to drive you there."

"Will you tumble the cabin when we are gone?"

"No. They will not take you in; there isn't the room. And even if there were, you'll think your cabin a palace when you see what a Poor Law institution is like now. You'll be back in your own place before dark; I would bet on it."

"Palace, cabin, workhouse, what is the difference and we starving? We have to go where the food may be."

Michael was not particularly thrilled with the job he was asked to do. Though it would not now bring on an asthma attack, he would have to handle a horse, and he still disliked the beasts. The Scannells he regarded with lofty contempt; their ignorance, selfishness, and want of forethought irritated him extremely. They appeared to have little or no gratitude for what had been done for them. They were beggars by nature and when their begging-bowls were empty they just shouted "More!" as if they had some divine right to be fed. So Michael thought.

"You are too harsh," said Anthony. "Just take them to Coolcaslig, let them see how it is, then bring them back again."

"I would rather dig the garden over."

"There is little point in that now!"

Coolcaslig was twelve miles away along the Clifden road – track would be a better description; it was all ruts, pot-holes, puddles and mud. Michael had to concentrate so hard on controlling the horse that he had little time, he was glad to discover, for exchanging words with the Scannells. They were six brooding creatures of professional discontent in his opinion: four boys with snotty noses, their toothless mother with her vacant grin, their father with spittle running into his beard. I should not think like this, he said to himself: but they drive me to it.

It was warm; the sun made the last patches of snow on the mountains dazzle. The bog colours, brown, green and grey, were vivid, wet. Nothing, he thought, was as green as Ireland. Or so he was told: he would find out the truth of that when he saw the greenness of America. The wind was fresh and pure; a great draft of Atlantic air. He sang:

"Many a green isle needs must be
In the deep wide sea of Misery,
Or the mariner, worn and wan,
Never thus could voyage on."

"Now that is sad," Mrs Scannell said.

"It is not," Michael answered. "You do not heed the words."

Words of hope vanished, however, when they arrived at the poorhouse; there was no hope here. A vast throng of people waited outside, but it was shut, securely barricaded like a fort. Not because it was empty; he could see men and women looking out of windows. It had been locked to prevent this great sea of humans rushing in and swamping it. It was full, he supposed, beyond bursting point. The Scannells got down from the cart and pushed through to the gates.

He had never seen such walking skeletons as the stupefied, hungry, sick people of this crowd. Their condition was worse than anything he had noticed in Galway, much worse than in Clasheen. He could have counted the knobs of their spines, the numbers of their ribs. Skin was withered, hanging, like pale parchment or the dewlaps of cows, the wattles of turkeys; eyes were so bulging it seemed impossible they did not explode. In some cases the flesh had literally disappeared, and what were once men and women were bones covered in something like a human outline made of ill-fitting paper. Heads were living skulls. Children were wrinkled nut-shells, bent, old, their faces resembling baboons.

The inertia was astonishing: no voices shouted for a scrap to eat, and there were no screams of pain or moans of despair; just an extraordinary patience. They were all, he realized, without exception near to death. There were signs of disease: scurvy – he noticed the bleeding mouths, the dark patches on limbs; and dropsy – some, instead of dwindling away to skeletons, had swollen to a grotesque size, were round as tubs, a series of bowls on legs. Every person was filthy, unwashed, in rags.

One or two people, seeing he was well-dressed, tottered over to where he sat in the cart. "I have nothing," he said. "Nothing." He hated himself: he did have a few coins. But if I give one man a single penny, he reasoned, I will have all of them on my back, demanding, demanding. This, he was aware, was the attitude of the Government: if they fed Ireland, they would have Ireland begging for ever, and in the process make Britain starve. It was not true, of course; Ireland could be fed properly and it would not make Britain starve. But if Anthony and I, he said to himself, gave all our worldly goods it would not help many; we would end up like this, and who would feed *us*? Anthony had been a saint, was already reduced to nothing; two tickets for a ship his sole hope left.

He looked up, and saw a woman at one of the workhouse windows. Her grey hair straggled in all directions like a twisted tree in winter; she was screaming, her face demented, her eyes on stalks. She was screaming at *him*. He could not hear a word because she was on the other side of the window and her efforts to get it open were in vain. Was she mad, he wondered, or at that point of starvation before the stupor, when the excruciating agony of hunger drove you to frenzied bouts of herculean energy? He shivered: it was a terrifying sight. Perhaps she was cursing because he wore decent clothes and did not look famished. Why have I worried about hell-fire, he asked himself. *This* is Hell.

He did not know it, but the section of the workhouse where the woman stood was the hospital. She was screaming for water. There was only one doctor and he had not been there for two days; he was ill himself, with the initial symptoms of typhus. The nurses had all left and no one could be found to replace them. There were not enough beds; many patients had been put on straw without blankets or any form of covering. The living lay next to the dead. There was no food, no one to remove the bodies of those who had died, no one to give water to the sick, who, because of the fever, were going mad with thirst.

The image of that tortured face remained with Michael for the rest of his life. It was the face of Ireland.

The Scannells returned to the cart, astonishment and fear in their eyes. "It is not a workhouse," Mrs Scannell said. "It is a death-house. A place of living graves."

"They would not open the doors," her husband said.

"You were told," said Michael, "but you would not listen."

"The Altarnun was right. We had better go home to our cabin."

Michael took all the coins out of his pocket and scattered them in a wide arc. The few people who could still walk hobbled after the money, falling on each coin like so many gulls greedy for bits of bread.

"Now why in God's name did you do that?" Mrs Scannell asked. She was amazed: her breath, she said to Mrs O'Leary that evening, was quite taken from her.

"Blood money," Michael answered.

"You could have given us sixpence!"

"You're not worth a ha'penny!" he shouted. "It would serve you right if I left you here!" But he pulled at the reins, clicked his tongue at the horse, and drove the Scannells back to Eagle Lodge.

"I SOMETIMES think this is the most canting, dissembling country of liars in the whole world," Michael said to Anthony. He was digging the garden, preparing it for summer. His favourite job: though it was as purposeless as painting a mural on a wall that is being knocked down; they would be in America before anything had grown to fruition. But, he said, it was rewarding to do after the long, frustrating months of winter; they could at least put right one part of the estate for Richard.

"I was in the soup kitchen this morning, talking to my mother, and an old woman complained that the stirabout was cold. I tasted it myself: cold as a stone it was. Mrs Peacock took a sip, sucked on it a moment, then said 'I wouldn't say it was cold. It's just not as hot as you would wish it.' "

Anthony laughed. "But it would be difficult to outdo the English for hypocrisy," he said.

"Then in the street I saw a man arguing with Dr Lenehan.

'You owe me three pounds,' the man says. 'I sent you the bill two months ago.' 'I am about due to pay it,' the doctor says, very loftily. 'No,' says the man. 'You were due to pay it when you received it.' 'That,' answers the doctor, 'depends on what you mean by due.' "

"You have a way with words," Anthony said. "You twist them very skilfully. But you don't protest, with every appearance of complete sincerity, that black is white when it patently is black. The British are the world's experts. They have deluded themselves into thinking there is no fever epidemic in Ireland. A minister of the Government is quoted in last week's *Mayo Telegraph* – 'The accounts given to the contrary are,' he says, 'to a very great extent undoubtedly inaccurate.' Inaccurate! Where is his evidence?"

Michael leaned on his spade. The soil was hard; under the surface, it was still frost-bound. "They could give me some seed to plant," he said, "but that will happen when pigs fly."

"It would interfere with the operation of natural causes; such would be their argument. They don't like to interfere with natural causes – particularly famine, disease, and death."

"They'd interfere with *us* if they found out. They'd say you and I are not caused by nature, though we are."

"As the doctor and his man were at odds over the meaning of 'due.' Nature is a word invented by someone to pinpoint something, but ten people might pinpoint that something in ten different ways."

"It is so," Michael agreed. Anthony walked up to the flower-beds by the house, and began to prune the roses. Soft spring weather. A warm sun that would quickly wake the few seeds Michael was about to plant: Richard, or the agent he might employ, would have the benefit of some vegetables this year. If Richard decided to leave the house empty, then the tenants could help themselves. Someone, in that case, would be kept from starving, and have a bunch of red roses to decorate his window-sill too.

Michael worked on in silence; he could feel in his legs and his back that he was working, and he was glad. In America they would, he was certain, have a plot as big as this, and he'd grow vegetables and flowers just for the two of them. Did fuschias, cone flowers and montbretias, bulbs like tulips and daffodils, trees such as the larches on this lawn, exist in the United States? Cone flowers did; they were brought from there in the first place. On the other side of the Atlantic there were oleanders. He did not know what an oleander looked like, but the name sounded good. He would also like a strawberry tree; an arbutus. There were strawberry trees in Ireland, but he had never seen one. They did not flourish in cold windy Galway; you had to go south to find them, to the wet sub-tropical woods of Kerry.

"My love is an arbutus," he sang. Anthony snorted: the idea was absurd. Yes, Michael said to himself, one of those clapboard houses you see in pictures, with a big veranda, and drinking wine on that veranda at sunset in weather that was warmer and less damp than here; a long day's work in the garden just finished. Me and him. Dan, Madge and the children on a nearby plot: going to their house for supper. Dan wearing good clothes. The children laughing, playing in the trees.

Travel broadened the mind, so people said. Anthony could hold Michael spellbound with stories of far-away places. The Taj Mahal by moonlight. A concert in Vienna, the theatre in London. St Peter's cathedral in Rome. How curious that Anthony was content to give it all up, was pleased to rot in this primitive backwater! Fulfilled in other ways: seeing the tenants through the hunger. Loving and being loved; that had not happened in India or Europe. "Don't you ever miss the plays and the concerts?" Michael asked. "The power of the grand people you saw there?"

"The grand people! They were not so grand as you like to think. The greater part of the audience at a concert doesn't even hear the music. They are, most of them, old ladies dressed in what once was fashionable – old ladies who want to be seen by their friends, who are bored to death by their humdrum lives. As soon as the overture begins, they fall fast asleep."

"What does the orchestra think of that?"

"Not much."

"I have never heard an orchestra. I should like to listen to the symphonies of Beethoven and Mozart, their piano concertos too." He had often said this, so Anthony had obtained the music of some of the Mozart concertos from a firm in Dublin. They were technically quite out of Michael's range, except for the slow movements; he could perform the piano part of these, tra-la-la-ing his way through the orchestral bits. The slow movement of the twenty-third was his favourite: its F sharp minor melancholy reminded him of the sadness of Irish songs. "I imagine there are concerts in New York," he said.

"I doubt it," Anthony replied. He had finished with the roses, and was now pulling up dandelions. "A blessing of this winter is the weeds have had little chance to grow. But my back, all the same! New York is a rough place. You would have more opportunity in Boston."

"Then why do we not go there?"

"The tickets are for New York. Few boats sail for Boston now; the quarantine regulations are so tight. In Boston ships full of starving people, the fever upon them, have been turned away and forced to go elsewhere, back to Ireland in some cases. Massachusetts thinks its commonwealth will be the cesspool of the civilized world if it allows in too many Irish paupers. The Irish in Ireland are helpless victims, but as soon as they arrive in America, they miraculously change into the dregs of society and a burden on the poor rates. More twisting of words."

These comments, however, did not alter Michael's belief in his vision of the wooden house and the garden with the strawberry tree. America was huge and most of it empty; he and Anthony would not have to live in either the rough cities or the snob cities. "I'll do without my orchestra," he said. "I'll settle for a piece of land in the wilds."

"You think we should become farmers?"

"Why not?"

"We know nothing of it."

"We can learn."

"I had imagined employment in some business," Anthony said. "In the offices of a respectable company. That would suit us. We can read, write, add figures a great deal better than most."

"And are there men in New York like us?"

"Would you want to meet them?"

Michael thought about that. "It would be interesting to hear their experiences. Are we . . . thousands? Or millions? Or just you and me and a few others? There is no way of knowing, I suppose. We are not visible, as if we had a black skin on us or a green face."

"Which is just as well," Anthony said. "Imagine what our lives would be like if people knew! We would not even be allowed to exist, perhaps; all men with green faces to be hanged, drawn and quartered."

"There. I have done." Ground had been turned over and levelled: he had sown carrots, onions, cabbage. He was satisfied, and knew how much more satisfied he would feel the day he was tilling land they both owned. It was not a childish dream, he thought; certainly they would have to struggle before they obtained what they wanted, begin as Anthony said by earning money in the city: but it was all possible. No hell on earth such as the scenes he had witnessed in Coolcaslig could exist in America: a man holding up a child, its stomach distended, its match-thin legs bent stalks – it had looked like a chicken, plucked and ready for the oven. The woman with the grey hair screaming noiselessly on the other side of the window. All there was in Ireland for him and Anthony was a similar fate.

Nevertheless, it was hard to leave.

He thought of his parents. They should come with us, he said to himself; I neglect them. It was out of the question, of course; he and Anthony with his parents! The secret would be impossible to hide. His mother's horror, his father's disgust: the proof the blacksmith always wanted that his son was a very imperfect paradigm of the Tangney original. Better his parents stayed in Clasheen, ignorant, short of food. He would write from America, send them money.

It was time Mr and Mrs Tangney were told they were going; he had been putting that off. It was bound to be distressful.

"Will you cook tonight, or shall I?" Anthony asked.

"What is there?"

"Carrots. Eggs. Bread. A little milk. Not a Parisian dinner."

"I will disguise it with herbs you brought back from Dublin. Fricasee Eagle Lodge."

Anthony smiled, a bit sadly. "I wish I could give you a better life," he said.

"I am happy enough," Michael answered.

TY Keliher, after many disappointments, was at last watching what he for so long had hoped to see. Though he resisted the temptation – possible insanity was still a worry – for a few minutes, he soon allowed his fingers to slip between his legs. His indulgence in two pleasures at once, what his eyes showed him and what his hand touched, led to his being taken off guard for the first time in his life. The spy was being spied on. Mrs Peacock, taking advantage of the superb weather, had been walking along the beach, and as she approached the gates of Eagle Lodge she thought she would call on Mr Altarnun to thank him for his generous gift to the running costs of the soup kitchen. Ty should have heard the footsteps on the gravel, but his back was to her, and he was far too engrossed.

Mrs Peacock paused, and wondered what on earth was happening. Then she decided to shout at this trespasser, a ragged boy who clearly had no business to be there. But before she could do so, some instinct whispered to Ty that all was not well; he turned, saw her, and fled. He ran round the house – an uncomfortable experience, as he was hugely erect and close to ejaculation – then disappeared down the garden and into the bushes. He didn't stop running until he reached the waterfall, where he judged he was sufficiently safe to stop and bring events with himself to a satisfactory conclusion. Mrs Peacock continued on up the drive as far as the front door. If she had not seen Ty Keliher she would not have acted as she did now. She would have rung the bell and waited for Anthony or Michael to answer it; she would probably have had to wait for some considerable time.

She was not in the habit of peering through people's windows, indeed would have thought it quite reprehensible; such had been her response to young Timothy doing just that. But Mrs Peacock was as frail as any of us, and if we are aware of something of interest on the far side of a window, we might all, if we imagine we will be undetected, take a quick peep. That is what she did. Her first thought was the same as Ty's had been on that other occasion: two men were wrestling. Then it occurred to her that they were both stark naked. They were Michael and Anthony. And she realized.

Although it had not dawned on her in her whole life that

persons of the same sex would do such a thing, she knew exactly what it was that she was witnessing; she was not wholly innocent or ignorant: she had noticed the brute beasts of the fields – colts and bullocks – doing or attempting to do this, and she had averted her eyes in disgust. What she felt now was disgust, but it was a great deal more than that – anger, incredulity, shame, outrage: it was as if she had been physically assaulted, hit round the head, battered. Her feelings were not unlike those of a woman who has just been raped.

There are always her opposites, of course – men and women who think that the sight of two people making love is aesthetically beautiful, erotically stimulating, enunciative of what is finest, most tender, most human in every one of us. But appreciation, arousal, and the sympathetic emotions are frequently blocked by a learned morality, and Mrs Peacock's morality was such that what others might have seen as beautiful she saw as despicably ugly. What they would consider erotic she found revolting, and what sympathetic identification they could experience with Michael and Anthony she labelled as squalid, odious, nauseous and bestial.

Mr Peacock was reading One Corinthians thirteen – love is not perverse, etcetera – when his wife rushed in on him. He banged his Bible to in mid-sentence as it was immediately obvious that something dreadful had happened to her. She was hysterical and incoherent, at one moment yelling, at another sobbing, so much so that he feared for a while that she *had* been physically assaulted. It was a good half hour of commotion before he could begin to piece together her tale; tea and laudanum had to be administered first, and Bridget was sent to find Dr Lenehan – he was to stop whatever he was doing, Mr Peacock said, and come at once: this was an emergency.

"Let me get this straight," he said. "They had no clothes on, and – "

"Yes! Don't keep reminding me of it!"

"I'm sorry. But I'm still not clear about what it was you saw."

"They . . . he . . . Mr Altarnun . . ."

"Yes?"

"Was . . . inserting . . ."

"What?"

"You surely cannot wish me to say it out loud! The filth of such an act! The vileness! The most wicked women on the streets of Dublin – "

"Never mind the women on the streets of Dublin! Was it . . . in the rear? Michael Tangney's. . . ?"

She shivered, then covered her face with her hands and wept again. Mr Peacock waited for the outburst to subside, then said "I cannot imagine . . . It is astonishing! A crime against nature!" He paced up and down. "A crime in the eyes of the law as well," he added. "Were they doing anything else?"

"Is not that enough?" she shouted.

"They were on the sofa, you say."

"Yes . . . they were . . . kissing. Can you think of anything more horrible? Stroking each other's . . . flesh." She shivered again, as if she had just touched rancid meat.

Mr Peacock sat down behind his desk. "My dear . . . I am deeply sorry, *deeply* sorry that you of all women should have been a witness to these . . . monstrous depravities!" One such depravity was that both men were nude. She had never before seen a naked adult body, male or female, not even her husband's. That side of their marriage had always been performed in discreet darkness, the pair of them in night-clothes. Mrs Peacock had never found it enjoyable, but she knew it was an affliction women had to endure, the nature of men being what it was.

The Reverend, fortunately, had stopped bothering her years ago, from which she concluded that men got over wanting to do that kind of thing quite quickly. Not that she asked her husband's opinion – one didn't discuss such topics with anybody. Now she had seen a man naked, two men naked, two men naked and erect! And what was perhaps more extraordinary than anything else, they seemed to be *enjoying* each other's and their own nakedness. When she thought about that, she also realized that Michael and Anthony seemed to be enjoying everything that they were doing. It was worse than the brute beasts of the fields: colts and bullocks could be absolved – they had no understanding. "But it explains it all," Mr Peacock said.

"How can you say it explains *anything*? It is *inexplicable*!"

"You said yourself there was something queer about him. The Shakespeare sonnet. The servant whom we know now for sure is not a servant . . . the insolent boy with his feet on the table . . . the fact that there *are* no servants. We always thought that odd, didn't we? There would have to be nobody else in the house for them to . . ."

Mrs Peacock stared. "You are quite right. Quite right. It is beginning to make sense."

"The question is . . . what do we do with this information?"

"Do with it? Why, they must be *ripped* out of the community! Denounced! Branded! Horse-whipping is too good for them! We cannot allow such corruption . . . such a stench . . . to remain! Here, in Clasheen! You should go to the peelers. Have them clapped in irons!"

Mr Peacock squirmed, just a little. His disgust was as strong as his wife's — he was all condemnation, ready to strike out against what he, too, would agree was odious, nauseous and bestial, but the vindictive harridan that was part of her nature was not part of his. "I do not think horse-whipping is appropriate," he said.

"It is a crime in the eyes of God! A sin that demands vengeance! You surely know what happened to Sodom and Gomorrah!"

Mr Peacock was nettled. "My dear, there is no need to teach the Bible to *me*! I am quite well aware of events in Sodom and Gomorrah. And do not you forget that Lot's wife was turned into a pillar of salt because she *looked*!"

"Now you are being ridiculous."

"I do not think it a matter for the peelers," he went on. "Though it may eventually become one. We should remember Mr Altarnun's many acts of kindness. Without his help, the soup kitchen would not be operating now and his tenants would be starving. Another man, and doubtless a practising Christian which he is not, would have thrown those families out and tumbled their cabins. He has spared no expense. He has saved people from the workhouse and the hospital, from death itself."

"Sops to a guilty conscience."

"I agree with you that something must be done. I think . . . I should consult Father Quinlan. The Tangney creature is Roman Catholic; Father Quinlan would want . . . I do not know precisely . . . Tangney's salvation is in his care."

They heard the sound of a horse's hooves, a man dismounting. "The doctor," Mrs Peacock said.

"We should say nothing to Dr Lenehan of this. Not yet. I will tell him you have had an awful fright, but I won't reveal its nature. I am sure he will respect our wish for privacy."

Mrs Peacock nodded. She had no urge to recount her tale to anyone. Not even the pleasure of seeing astonished faces, of announcing she had been the principal witness to a crime, and enjoying all the sympathy and attention the story would elicit, moved her in any way. She was feeling unclean, befouled, soiled, and all she wanted was to forget what she had experienced, to bury it out of sight. And her husband, she knew, wasn't being ridiculous: Lot's wife *had* been turned into a pillar of salt because she looked. People would wonder what her real motive was for staring in at that window.

Anthony and Michael, of course, had no idea of the pandemonium they had created. They lay in each other's arms afterwards, silent for a long while, listening to each other breathe, listening to the wind outside; until Michael's shoulders began to ache, and he shifted his position. "It is more comfortable in bed," he whispered. "I don't mean I did not enjoy it. It was . . ." He laughed, a little murmur of happiness. "I've told you before . . . like seeing God."

"Oh, that is nonsense," Anthony said. "I see you. Only you. Though I can see me now, reflected in your eyes."

"You have a beautiful body. I love you."

"I love you too."

CHAPTER EIGHT

FATHER Quinlan's reaction to the news was predictable, and he too thought it explained a great many discrepancies.

"I am concerned . . . very distressed . . . for your wife," he said. He was vigorously jabbing the coal on his fire with a poker.

"To have it . . . thrust in front of her." Mr Peacock shook his head, sadly. "Her face, as it were, rubbed in it . . ."

"I hope she will get over it."

"She is a woman of strong character, Father. Now . . . what do you intend to do? I feel, in this matter, I should defer to a celebrant of the older religion." Here he let himself smile, wanly.

"Because Michael is a Catholic? Yes." Father Quinlan frowned. "I shall speak to him. Reason with him; his immortal soul is in danger. And then I shall have a word with Mr Altarnun, or perhaps both of them together. I will let you know what passes."

"I think they should be made to leave the district. We cannot allow . . . Do you know if the brother can be reached?"

"He is in London. Mr Altarnun told me."

"It would be possible to find his address? To write to him?"

Father Quinlan poked the fire again. "First, let me see what they have to say for themselves." The two men of the cloth stared at each other, the one with the big head, the squint, and the more corpulent body; the other craggy-faced, with his rocky knob of a nose, lean, tough, energetic. Their expressions were grave, inquisitorial; the mood positively that of ecumenism. "In all my years as a pastor of souls," Father Quinlan went on, "I have never run into such a case. In the Middle Ages we burned people for . . ."

Mr Peacock twitched. "I do not think burning is the answer," he said.

"No indeed."

"My wife talked of horse whips. And branding. But she was hysterical, not herself."

"It is obviously not a matter for physical violence of any kind! But if they are unrepentant . . . then a letter to Mr Altarnun's brother would . . . and . . . public opinion might be allowed to run its course."

"We must not forget Mr Altarnun's many charities." Mr Peacock looked at his clean white hands, and pressed his finger-tips together. "I hope we shall remember him . . . and his . . . in our prayers . . . I do not think we should press for criminal charges, do you?"

"I have no idea whether it is a punishable crime or not. I have never given it a moment's consideration; it is . . . it is *unheard* of in a Christian country!" Anger made a vein in his temple throb.

"In the unedifying case of the Bishop of Clogher," Mr Peacock said, "the law took its course." He stood up, and reached for his hat and stick. "I must depart; I have other duties. More pleasant ones, though until today I should never have thought of them as pleasant. I mean the burial of the dead." He looked at the clock. "I have a funeral at noon."

"I shall wrestle with Michael Tangney's soul. That is the priority."

With that thought uppermost in his mind, Father Quinlan set out for Eagle Lodge. His errand he did not see as distasteful, as Mr Peacock would have done, or a burden; he felt almost exalted, like a doctor whose specialist knowledge has been asked for. The struggle for goodness, himself against Satan, was his purpose, and, as with medical men, he possessed a store of diagnostic procedures, purgatives, cures, even a bedside manner. He loved his calling, and this was a beloved errand. He was *eager*.

He found Michael alone, as he had hoped; Anthony was somewhere on the estate, at Patrick O'Callaghan's, Michael thought. The priest indulged in no respectful preliminaries. He dived straight in, and repeated what he had been told more or less exactly, though he omitted the identities of both his informer and the witness. Michael was terrified: what he and Anthony feared most was now happening. He felt so shocked that he found himself trembling; his heart was thumping uncomfortably against his chest, and there was a sensation like paralysis in his legs and spine. He sank down onto the sofa, rubbed his tongue against the roof of his mouth, and flicked his hands several times through his hair.

"Who saw it?" he said.

"It does not matter in the least who saw it. I assume . . . you do not deny it?"

"No."

"Was it . . . an isolated incident?" No answer. "Has it happened on other occasions?" Father Quinlan was becoming fidgety, as he did so often in the confessional.

I could lie, Michael thought, but he knew at once that that would be a devilish temptation. He thought of Peter denying Jesus. He glanced up, out of the window, and noticed – it was a bizarre coincidence – a cockerel pecking at the lawn. *Their* cockerel, his and Anthony's, with their last three hens. The others had all been eaten or given away: chewed up by hungry Scannells, Leahys and O'Learys.

"No. Not an isolated incident."

"My child," Father Quinlan murmured. "My poor child. You are quite bewildered."

"I am not." If that cockerel crows, he said to himself, I will wring its neck and put it in the oven tonight! Whose side is it on? But the cockerel continued to peck happily at whatever it was finding in the grass.

"You are the most intelligent person of your age in Clasheen. You read. You think. You are not some dumb wild creature out of the bogs. Which makes it all the more damnable; you *know* what you are doing! I said the word bewildered deliberately. You're surely aware of the Church's teaching on matters of . . . sexual licence? The use and abuse of the body?"

"I have . . . thought it all out. Yes."

"And you remain a Catholic. You do not receive Holy Communion, but you hear Holy Mass. So you have doubts still. You know you have sinned, and sinned repeatedly! Michael, the flesh is evil. It is transient; it withers and perishes. Our time-span compared with Eternity is less than the blink of an eye! God is not mocked. Michael, turn your back on all this; return to

God!" He leaned forward. "What does it profit a man to gain the whole world and lose his own soul?"

"He said judge not that ye be not judged." On biblical texts, Michael, too, was a specialist. "Why beholdest thou the mote that is in thy brother's eye, but considerest not the beam that is in thine own?"

Father Quinlan sat back in his chair. "We could bandy verses from the Bible all day and it would not get us anywhere! What you are doing, what you have been doing, is an abomination in the sight of the Lord! You *know* that. It is barren, wasteful, foul; can only lead to misery. It has the very stench of Sodom!"

"I love him. He and I are as married as my father is to my mother."

Father Quinlan sighed. "I am on stony ground," he said. He thought for a moment. "You know the punishment for hardened sinners?"

"A denunciation? I . . . should not like that."

"Then think on it."

Anthony came into the room, carrying a small parcel. "We are discovered," Michael said. "Seen. Caught in the act. I don't know who it was; Father Quinlan will not say."

Anthony did not look at all surprised. "Just let me put this in the kitchen," he said. "It's fresh cheese! Ty Keliher gave it to me. Wild horses wouldn't drag out of him where he got it from."

"What is the matter with him?" Father Quinlan was astonished. "Does he not understand the seriousness?"

Anthony returned. He was at his most English, the epitome of calm. "Ty Keliher has told me," he said. "How he watched us . . . peeped through windows . . . that he meant no ill will . . . that Mrs Peacock saw him . . . that she might have looked too . . . that the worthy lady might have informed others. Evidently she *has* informed others. I must say I don't think there is anything wrong with young Timothy's head! We have all mistaken him, I fear. The cheese: it was a present. He was unhappy that he could have been the cause of trouble. Father Quinlan, I hope you will say nothing of this to Ty."

A sudden shaft of sunlight through a window lit up his face and hair; the hair blazed gold. Michael said to himself: how beautiful he is.

Father Quinlan never found it easy to conceal anger, though he often prayed to be given that power. "You have no authority, sir, to forbid me to do anything I see as my duty! That you should . . . however . . . it is not my duty to question Timothy Keliher. I shall listen to whatever he says when he comes to confession, and that will of course remain secret."

"What kind of sin has he possibly committed?" Anthony asked. "He saw something through a window. Just as Mrs Peacock did."

"We are all black sinners," Father Quinlan said, not for the first time.

"There is far too much emphasis on sin this morning! The Roman Catholic Church in Ireland is obsessed with it."

"That is not for you to judge!" The priest controlled himself with some difficulty. He stood up. "I am wasting my time," he said. "I will speak to you both again when you've had a while to think. Meanwhile, I shall pray for your souls."

"Very thoughtful of you, Mr Quinlan. And thank you for calling on us."

The deliberate rudeness of "Mister" made Father Quinlan hesitate. "Mr Altarnun, I beg you . . ." He stopped, and they looked at one another, eye to eye, for a moment. "No. I can see it is of little use . . ."

Anthony grinned. "Father, would you like some cheese?"

Father Quinlan laughed, in amazement. "Man shall not live by bread alone. So Jesus said when he was tempted by Beelzebub."

"Can we leave Jesus and Beelzebub out of it? I know you're partial to cheese. Take it, in memory of a friendship. We respected each other. Liked each other. We worked well together on the Committee. I, of course, resign from the Committee as of now. I would be grateful if you would inform the Reverend Peacock."

The thought of cheese made the priest's mouth water. It was a ticklish dilemma: should he accept? Was this a temptation of the Devil's? "No," he said. "I could not." But Michael had already gone to the kitchen and cut a large slice which he pressed into Father Quinlan's hand. Father Quinlan laughed again, but nervously; he was now the one to be handicapped by the unanticipated move. He felt he had been lured into he didn't quite know what, something more than just a revelation of weakness, perhaps. "Thank you," he said, looking at the gift. It was rich, runny cottage cheese, exactly as he liked it best. "I cannot remember when I . . ."

He began to eat it before he got to the end of the drive. The cockerel looked at him as he passed, stretched its wings and flapped them twice, but it did not crow. As he munched, Father Quinlan said to himself that it would take a whole conclave of learned cardinals, even the full Inquisition or the Pope himself, to rule on whether he was committing a sin or not. However, he decided to say nothing to Mr Peacock on the subject of cheese.

"SO the Reformed Church still eats well," Father Quinlan said. He had been asked to stay to dinner. Salmon: a present from Mr Peacock's benefactor, Lord Smithers of Coolcaslig. Lord Smithers was an absentee, but Mr Peacock kept on good terms with his agent.

"We do not dine like this every day," the Protestant clergyman said. "If we did, it would stick in our throats; that is right, my dear, is it not?" Mrs Peacock did not answer. "But I think there is no wrong in doing so when we can. If the three of us starved to death, what would become of the soup kitchen? The poor and hungry would die."

Father Quinlan was not certain that this reasoning was without flaw, so he changed the subject. "I could get no sense from either of them," he said. "They seem to think their behaviour is normal, loving, and just! He said – Michael – that they had not asked to be the way they were, that it would surely be easier if they were as others; but, in the circumstances, it would be unnatural to suppress the affections – loving kindness, tenderness, everything that is customary between man and wife."

"Normal!" Mr Peacock exclaimed. "How can he think that? It is contrary to nature! Their actions are perversely and wilfully learned."

"It is so," Father Quinlan agreed.

"Everything that is customary between man and wife! Where

is the wife? Or – *which* is the wife? Whatever would our good Lord have said!"

"I think we can imagine."

"I have drafted a letter to his brother Richard," Mr Peacock went on, his mouth full of salmon and cream sauce. "I will show you after we have eaten. Do you have the address?"

"I did not ask. He would not have said, surely. But the London offices of the East India Company would find the man."

"May we talk of something else?" Mrs Peacock suggested. "It is so distasteful! Particularly at dinner."

"Of course, my dear," her husband said. "I'm sorry; it was tactless of me." He muttered to Father Quinlan, in a low voice, "She is still very distressed."

When the meal was finished, the clergymen retired to Mr Peacock's study. "It is monstrous how that poor woman has been made to suffer," Mr Peacock said. "Unforgivable! My own wife! Justice must be done, and be seen to be done!" He handed the letter to Father Quinlan.

"I suppose they will be evicted," the Catholic priest said, when he had perused it.

"They deserve no less."

"The community should know what it is harbouring, perhaps. I am not sure. I shall talk to them again, and if there is no change I may say a few words from my pulpit. My imaginary pulpit, that is . . . the proceeds of the Faith in Ireland do not run to fine buildings with real pulpits. Tin sheds are what we are mostly blessed with."

"Before Emancipation, not even those. You are lucky that your ministry is in a liberal age."

"The Church Temporalities Act of 1833," Father Quinlan said, "was supposed to allot stipends to Roman Catholic priests, but the money was spent on repairing the roofs of *your* churches."

"Do not speak of that Act! It is the unspeakable! 'The ruffian band come to reform, where ne'er they came to pray.' John Keble's words, and he was right. We lost two of our archbishoprics, Cashel and Tuam, and we only had four to start with. Eight bishoprics disappeared as well!"

"Until the time of Queen Elizabeth, they were *our* sees."

Discussion, more or less amicable, on a great variety of ecclesiastical subjects continued far into the night; points of doctrine and organization, the authority of the Pope, the strange character of the present incumbent of the Protestant archdiocese of Dublin, the use of vestments and incense, the veneration of images, what St Augustine said or did not say, and so on: a bottle of port was consumed. Father Quinlan, returning to his house at one o'clock in the morning, felt he had succumbed to many different temptations during the course of the day; the cheese, the dinner, and openly admitting once or twice to Mr Peacock that the Reformed argument had some points to be said for it. Tomorrow he would devote to prayer. Prayer, in particular, for light to shine on the darkness in which the inhabitants of Eagle Lodge walked.

Michael and Anthony, holding each other close in the darkness of their bedroom, were attempting to reassure themselves that things could have been worse. Ty Keliher was not a threat; the priest and the minister weren't gossips, and, though Mrs Peacock was an unknown quantity, it was unlikely that she would care to whisper *that* all round the neighbourhood. A public denunciation, too, was improbable: Father Quinlan would not rush into anything so drastic without weighing all the consequences.

"We are leaving soon," Anthony said.

"Yes. I would not like to be here if my parents were told. If they confronted me directly, I don't know how I should answer. To see their sorrowing faces!"

"I don't think that will happen."

"Anthony . . . you have such strength."

"From my years in the army."

"I meant of character. I lean on you more and more."

"That's just as true of yourself. If I lost you, I would have lost . . . my life."

THE O'Learys' fourteen-year-old son, Tom, was ill: with typhus. The disease was now epidemic throughout Ireland; most people thought it a natural result of starvation, but it wasn't. It was the way in which the majority of the population now lived that was exactly right for its spread. The sicknesses that starvation can cause, dropsy and scurvy, had already appeared in Clasheen, striking those whose physical condition was weakest; most of Dr Lenehan's patients were victims of these illnesses. More people died from them than from hunger itself. Typhus and yellow fever – which had also reached epidemic proportions – were spread by lice, but in the mid-nineteenth century this was not known, and thought by only a few medical men to be a possibility.

Typhus had not been found in Clasheen until Tom O'Leary went sick. Its organism lives in the excrement of lice, and it can enter the human body through the smallest of skin abrasions; or when the excrement has crumbled to a microscopic dust it can settle on the eyes or be inhaled. There were never so many louse-ridden bodies in Ireland as during the Famine. To heat water for washing was beyond the ability of the starving, and they were unable to change their clothes, as everything except a few basic rags had been sold.

Vast numbers of people were on the move as never before; evicted paupers and beggars, infested with lice, tramped the roads in search of work or food, bringing the disease with them. The cruel winter had led to people clinging to each other for warmth, and traditional Irish hospitality allowed friends, neighbours, even strangers, to sleep round the same turf fire. Tom caught typhus because the O'Learys let a man and his son, evicted from a cabin on Lord Smithers' estate, share their fire for three nights. One louse, riddled with the disease, transferred itself to Tom and bit him: he scratched the bite, and the organisms passed into his bloodstream.

The first symptom is a sudden rise in temperature – it can go up to one hundred and seven – which is followed by delirium, then the red blotches on the chest, abdomen, and wrists that gave typhus its ancient name, spotted fever. The blood circulation slows, which leads to facial swellings and a darkening of the complexion; hence the other old name, black fever. The victim raves, twitches, vomits and can develop gangrene, leading to the destruction of his toes and fingers, and he smells quite revolting – not the stench of blighted potatoes, but just as malodorous. Death, fortunately, is fairly rapid. Dr Lenehan took Tom to the fever hospital in Galway where he died a few days later, surrounded by people already dead or dying from the same disease.

Anthony was thinking he should visit the O'Learys, but Michael implored him not to. "You have done enough! Reduced yourself to penury! Are you looking for martyrdom as well? What kind of man do you think you are? Some latter-day saint?"

Anthony smiled. "I, persuaded by the Book of Mormon?"

"Don't evade the issue! You know perfectly well I was not talking of Mormons, ridiculous pagans! What will *I* do if you catch the black fever?"

"I shall not go so close; I'll ask the O'Learys to come outside. That way I shan't breathe the smell of their cabin, and I'll stand at a distance, six feet or more. Impossible for a lousy louse to jump six feet."

"Who says it is a louse? Who is it knows the germs aren't spread on the air? Like potato blight. Thousands and *thousands* of poor souls have the black fever; was it lice in every case?"

"I have read the medical journals, and in their pages a few of the more enlightened physicians argue that it may be lice. Dr Lenehan is of that opinion too."

"Anthony, don't go! If you love me at all you will not go!"

"This is absurd."

"I don't care what it is!" He was beside himself. "I shan't touch you again; I shan't allow you to make love to me! I won't be here when you come back!"

"Michael . . . be an adult." He left. Michael, furious and frustrated, hurled a saucer to the floor; it smashed in little pieces.

Two more of the O'Leary children – there were six living – now had symptoms of typhus. They were hot as an oven, Mrs O'Leary told Anthony, their eyes unnaturally bright, their poor little brains addled so that they raved like mad things, screaming for water to quench their thirst. "Oh, God! The hardest heart would melt to listen to them!" she said. "Mr O'Leary has gone for Dr Lenehan, though what good will that do? The doctor will send them to Galway just as he did with my darling Tom, and they'll die there as sure as if they stayed in the cabin. You only go to a hospital to die. It's not that we care for ourselves, me and my husband; you will understand that – it's for the other ones still sound."

From which Anthony deduced that she realized death was certain, and that, sensibly, she was trying to save what she could. Someone in the cabin began to scream. "Listen to him! And I with only a jug to fetch water. We need a pail, a huge pail!"

"I will bring you one from the house," Anthony said. "Immediately." He walked off, but a great commotion from the cabin made him stop and turn. A boy, perhaps ten years old, ran out, shrieking that he was burning alive, and, with the energy that only the overwhelming impulse to fly from the clutches of some appalling horror can give, he raced at extraordinary speed down to the stream and threw himself in it. Mrs O'Leary dashed after him.

Anthony hesitated: he felt he should go to her assistance, but he had promised Michael not to venture close. As he watched, it became obvious that Mrs O'Leary did not need help. She dragged her son out of the stream, his energy – he had achieved that coolness he wanted – utterly spent. He was half-pulled, half-propelled back to the cabin; limp and exhausted, soaked to the skin. Trails of wet lay in the dust where he tottered, like water splashed from a water cart.

When Anthony returned to the house, Michael ran up to him and embraced him. "I'm sorry!" he said. "It was selfish – but what *would* I do if you died?"

"You see I am living and uninfected," Anthony said, and kissed him. He removed Michael's arms. "I have to take the O'Learys a bucket."

"How are they?"

"Two more of the children have it now."

"Put the bucket outside the cabin, then come straight back home! Please!"

Anthony did not answer. At the cabin he found Dr Lenehan about to drive the two sick children to Galway. They already looked like corpses. Mr and Mrs O'Leary stared, speechless. The doctor's courage, Anthony said to himself, was a marvel, an example to everyone; *he* was not afraid to go close, to touch even: he was shifting the two little bodies on the waggon into a more comfortable position.

Dr Lenehan died a few months later from typhus. The death rate among physicians during the Famine, mostly of fever caught from their patients, was very high; in Connemara two thirds of all the doctors were victims. Their mortality was only equalled by clerics. Mr Peacock and Father Quinlan, however, survived to argue theology down the years; in Father Quinlan's case – and he was no more fearful than Dr Lenehan to touch the sick – it was, Mrs Peacock said, the luck of the Devil.

During the next few days more tenants of Anthony's contracted typhus: Mrs Scannell and her eldest son (the boy Ty Keliher knew for a thief), three of the Cronins and Dan Leahy's two sisters. The Kelihers escaped, as did the Sullivans, the Widow O'Gorman and Patrick O'Callaghan. The widow and the old man shut themselves up in their cabins and would not answer a knock, not even from the Altarnun himself; they only went out when they were absolutely sure there was nobody in the vicinity.

The Kelihers' and the Sullivans' survival was probably due to accepting Anthony's advice. He lent pails to all his tenants and told them to wash their clothes as often as possible, to heat water over their fires and keep themselves scrupulously clean; to search their bodies, constantly, for lice. With the Scannells, the Cronins and the Leahys, it was already too late, which brought Anthony near to despair. He had done everything he could to see them through till better times; now they were being struck down by an agent totally beyond his control. Famine he could fight, but disease was an invincible adversary.

His relationship with Michael, the one sure anchor in this long period of hell, was suffering too. The illnesses of the Scannells, the Cronins, the Leahys and the O'Learys were the cause of the problem; for Anthony refused to listen to pleas not to visit the tenants. He could cope when Michael begged or complained or shouted, but attempts to make love being rejected, sullen silences that went on for hours, or being told to sleep by himself, were intolerable. One night, awake and restless, he went into Michael's room and said "You know I can't sleep without you."

No answer.

"Would you prefer to go back to your father's house?"

"What in God's name should give you that idea?"

Anthony sighed. "Because you're unhappy," he said.

"I will never leave you. You know that. But I wonder at times, risking your life as you do, if you love me at all."

"I am *not* risking my life!"

"I read in the paper today of some great lord in Wicklow, a marquess it was; he has died of the black fever. Do you think he huddled up with his peasants in their cabins and caught their lice?"

"Perhaps he had a mistress. One of the girls in the house. Perhaps he seduced a dozen of them."

"Oh, that is nonsense and you know it!" Michael said. "If you died . . . I should go mad."

"That is nonsense too."

"What would you do if *I* died?"

"I wouldn't go mad."

"I am sure you would not! You would look about you for some other man."

"Maybe in time."

"Why don't you look for him *now*?"

"I'm going back to bed," Anthony said, crossly. "Standing here in the dark, not a stitch of clothes on . . . I'm freezing cold." He went out of the room.

Michael followed him a few minutes later. "Here I am, oh Lord High Hickory Dickory Dock," he said as he slipped under the sheets. "You may work your evil way with me." He threw his legs wide apart, hands holding his buttocks open. "One that converses more with the buttock of the night than with the forehead of the morning. Shakespeare. *Coriolanus.*"

"You feel like acting the whore?"

"Why not? When love has gone. It will cost you a shilling, sir. Cheap at twice the price. *Sir!*"

"I will punch your face in a moment."

"That will cost sixpence."

Anthony laughed, then grabbed hold of him. Michael struggled fiercely with fists and feet, and bashed Anthony about the head with a pillow. "You will not be touching me!" he shouted, several times.

"I will. I am!"

Michael could not win; his lover was much too strong. Soon Anthony's legs were wrapped round his, rendering them

126

powerless, and the thicker, more muscular pair of arms had his twisted up behind his shoulder-blades. "I won't give in!" Michael cried.

"Then I will." But Anthony didn't slacken his grip. "I'll take more precautions. I'll only see the tenants in cases of dire emergency. Will that satisfy you?"

"It will have to," Michael said, after he had thought about it. "Anthony, my anxiety has not been so unreasonable."

"I understand it."

"Will you let me go now? My legs are bruised and my arms almost dislocating themselves out of their sockets."

"I'm enjoying myself."

"You enjoy inflicting pain on me? How very typical of a man that is!"

Anthony freed him. "You're no less of a man," he said.

"I'm aware of that. I've asked myself would I be happier being a woman? Never is the reply to that question. I would not wish to wear their clothes, have babies . . . be a housekeeper. I don't know why I am the way I am, but I've ceased to worry about it. I do know that I haven't been put in the wrong body."

"I think we should stop talking and make love."

"Can you spare a poor girl one shilling, kind sir? It's cold and wet and I'm . . . aaagh!" He could not continue, for Anthony was kissing him.

Afterwards, Michael said "You've given me what I required."

"What we've just done?"

"Your promise to be more cautious."

But word came to Anthony at breakfast that Mr Scannell had been taken seriously ill during the night. When he had finished eating, he walked down to the infected cabin.

CHAPTER NINE

A WARM, wet, blustery day three weeks after Easter, dull columns of rain smudging the land. Mountains were lost in cloud. Out at sea a black storm loomed. Grass was so wet and emerald it looked new-made, as if it had just been put there. I shall miss all this, Michael said to himself as he walked into Clasheen, to Mass. The third Sunday after Christ had risen; in a fortnight Pentecost, the celebration of the tongues of fire. The Church's seasons, the land's seasons: the same on another shore? He presumed they were.

He had thought little recently about America; events had blotted it from his mind: it was just a date to come. But he would tell his parents after Mass that he and Anthony were going. Too much of the here and now had been holding his attention: the discovery, disease, Mr Scannell's death, worries that Anthony, who had taken more precautions, had not taken enough.

He enjoyed the wet on his skin, the soft needles. This could only be in Ireland, he felt sure. Rain in New York would be different. No vivid greenness, no freshness of colour. These fields, now uncultivated and barren, stretched up a mountain that looked, with the cloud swirling above its summit, remarkably like a volcano: there would be nothing like this in Ohio or New Jersey, or wherever it was they would settle. New York would be buildings. As Dublin was? No. Nor Galway. But famine, typhus, dependence on potatoes, unfeeling brothers to evict their next of kin; that would all be left in a far country.

Introibo ad altare Dei, ad Deum qui laetificat juventutem meum. The ancient words flowed by him as usual, a chant, a spring bubbling: sheep blethering. The Epistle was from chapter two of the first Epistle of St Peter. "Dearly beloved, I beseech you as strangers and pilgrims, abstain from fleshly lusts, which war against the soul; having your conversation honest among the Gentiles: that, whereas they speak against you as evil-doers, they may by your good works, which they shall behold, glorify God in the day of visitation." And so on. The notices: remember in your prayers the soul of our dear brother, Roger Scannell.

A few men slipped out when the sermon began, but most stayed; last Sunday Father Quinlan had said that this habit, though not unlawful, was irreverent. "By your good works, which they shall behold." He liked to preface his homilies with a text from the day's Epistle or Gospel. "We have all of us seen his good works," he went on, "and it would be unpardonable not to remember them. Indeed there are people here present who will not forget, for the rest of their lives, the good he has done." (What on earth, or rather, *who* on earth is he talking about, Michael asked himself. He rambles more and more every week: is above the heads of most of us. It is his age. Or the hunger.)

"The apostle Peter, as you have heard, said we were to honour all men, and to love the brotherhood. In saying so, he emphasizes that he does not mean love in a carnal sense. 'Abstain from fleshly lusts, which war against the soul,' he writes. 'I *beseech* you.' Brethren, when these two things, the pursuit of right action and the pursuit of fleshly lusts, join together in a man, then the good is undone: his soul is no more saved than if he were the greediest, most grasping, most tyrannical of landlords!"

Michael began to feel uncomfortable.

"When there is evil in the community it must be destroyed. Brethren, if there is an abomination in the eyes of the Lord so vile that it cries out for punishment, we must pluck it from us! We may not notice it for years, not hear of it, meet it, smell it; but it may be there all the same. The fleshly lusts are wicked. The woman who sells her body, the man who takes a woman who is not his wife: such people are manifestly wicked. Not so manifest, but just as wicked, are lewd thoughts, salacious glances, impure desires; others may not see them, but God sees them all! All are sins of the mortal kind, which, if they are not confessed, will send the soul of the man or the woman who commits them straight to Hell!

"You may think these sins have the excuse, the explanation, of being natural. It is in us, you will say, to be as the beasts of the field. But this does not mitigate the sin, nor lessen the torment of the soul in the fires of Hell. It merely reminds us that we can understand the sinner, that there, but for the grace of God, go we."

Tension in Michael slackened; Anthony did not seem to be the object of Father Quinlan's invective. But who was this sinner? He looked about him, as did several other members of the congregation, for the guilty person. There were too many candidates – men mostly – gazing defiantly ahead, not meeting anyor.'s eye, and some who were staring hard at the ground or the ceiling. Ty Keliher, he noticed, was fidgeting in a torture of embarrassment.

"Worse and much more offensive to God, dearly beloved, than those sins I have called natural, are sins *unnatural*. There are crimes against nature so horrifying that we hardly ever think of them – the crime of the man who fornicates with his own daughter, the mother who seduces her own son. But most heinous of all – and for these sinners the hottest fires of Hell, the most exquisite agonies, are reserved – are the men and women who pursue with lust their own kind! I am speaking of the sin of Sodom and Gomorrah, which so angered the Lord our God that he rained down brimstone and destroyed those cities in the twinkling of an eye."

Nothing in Genesis about the twinkling of an eye, Michael said to himself as he looked at his shoes, and felt the scarlet rise in his face. I must not seem guilty. I must stop myself shaking. The pit of his stomach lurched, and his heart banged more painfully than on the morning Father Quinlan told him he had been found out. I can get through this, just, if he does not name names, if Anthony Altarnun and Michael Tangney are not words left floating on the air like black ravens! He would not, *could* not name names! Dear God, give me strength! He *must* not!

"There are two men in our parish who have committed the sin of Sodom. Not just once in a guilty moment of sudden lust, but repeatedly over the years; who know it for a sin and who love and relish that sin, who are without shame or repentance, who indeed have every intention of continuing in their practice of that sin! It behoves me to perform a very solemn duty, one that in my twenty-five years as an ordained priest of God I have never had to perform. But I would be shirking my responsibilities if I did not do it. I have to denounce these men in order that you should know who they are. I am speaking of Anthony Altarnun and Michael Tangney."

Inhalation, exhalation of breath. Mutterings, murmurs. Michael looked up and saw his father's appalled face. Then a slight commotion in the pews: Mrs Tangney had fainted. He turned, and the men stepped back, parted, leaving an avenue to the door, as the sea for Israel. As he walked unsteadily between the lines of hostile male bodies, each man, he felt, wanted to hit him, stab him. Someone said "Whore!"; another said "Girl!"; a third said "Bastard!". But Ty Keliher's face was fellow-feeling, sympathy, almost torment. Ty moved his hands half an inch in Michael's direction, then withdrew them. Pontius Pilate, Michael thought; then, no, no, no, I'm not being fair.

He reached the door and walked out, past the few men who had decided to give the sermon a miss as usual, who were unaware of what had happened. He walked on into the street, then up the Clifden road, out of town, towards Eagle Lodge. The rain washed him, cleaned him a little, cooled his hot face. The clouds still rushed in from the sea; the fields were still that extraordinary wet green. They should be different, he said to himself; should register their shame too, their hate. Why are they not red?

There is Anthony. America. We must leave at once.

He did not look back. This was the first time, except for days when he was ill, that he had not heard Mass to its end. He never went to Mass again, anywhere.

A shout came from behind him. The first stone? He recognized the voice, and stopped.

Eugene Tangney was out of breath. "Did you not once think of the dishonour and sorrow," he panted, "that you would bring on your poor mother and me?"

"I . . . did not wish it." Michael's mouth was parched, his lips dry; the words came with great difficulty.

"You did not wish it. It did not make you think before you . . . We will never hold up our heads again!" Silence. "You are not my child. Not now." Silence. "You enjoy a man's instrument in . . . in the place of filth and disease. Or is it that you put yours in his? What . . . are you?"

"Your only beloved son."

"You may wander over the whole world, but you are not my only beloved son, not here nor anywhere! A girl in a man's body. What freak of nature did we fashion and bring to light? It is worse than deafness, a dumb tongue! It is a total deformity! You will not come near us again. Nor speak to us. Nor write letters." He raised his hands to the sky, and, looking out to sea as if the ship taking Madge to America was still there like an enigmatic word, said "Your poor sister is beyond the reach of us now, thank God, and the little one she will give birth to will never know."

He spat in Michael's face. The saliva hit the lashes of the left eye, then ran down the cheek to the mouth.

"So the first stone is from you," Michael said. "I should have guessed." He walked off, then stopped and turned. "May God keep you always," he said. Mr Tangney was walking in the opposite direction.

ON the way home Michael experienced an asthma attack, his first in ten years. It lasted only a few minutes, was mild, just an echo of what he had endured as a boy and an adolescent. But the inability to breathe, the fluttering of his heart as if it was fragile like a butterfly's wings, frightened him, was too much of a memento: those very real fears of death from asphyxiation.

AT Eagle Lodge his emotions overwhelmed him. He wept as much, was as hysterical as Mrs Peacock after she had witnessed the awful act. Anthony cradled him, rocked him as he would a tiny child. "We're together," he said. "We're safe."

"I'm not. *We're* not. We must leave. At once!"

"Our tickets are for five weeks' time.'

"Change them."

"Michael . . . I understand . . . I know what you've been through, but . . ."

"You *don't* understand! This is Ireland, not some civilized part of London, where people play out the game according to rules! They will . . . do things."

"What things? Not that I feel we should venture into the town just yet. If at all. But no one can hurt us in our own home. At Eagle Lodge!"

"Oh, how upper-class and British you are! The Englishman's home is his castle! The sanctity – the sanctuary – of private property!"

"What are you afraid of?" This was all mere reaction, Anthony thought. They would leave Eagle Lodge in their own good time, and with dignity. Ostracized, cut dead, yes – but not physically assaulted. People might loathe what they had been told; nevertheless they would not organize some skirmish, some affray. Impossible!

"I remember, when I was young, nine or ten . . . I wasn't supposed to look; I disobeyed my parents . . . who does not? . . . A woman, Maggie Lynch, not so old as I am now. The girl who never said no; they are rare in Ireland but exist they surely do. She was a thing of the gypsies and tinkers, the men from the bogs; it was said they all fucked her. When she found she was pregnant she accused some man of the town, a man of standing. I don't remember who it was. Father Quinlan preached a sermon on the text of the woman taken in adultery, but he did not denounce her; he did not name her from the altar as he did us. One night her hair was cut off and she was stripped nearly naked. She was left in the street, her hands tied to a post, a placard around her neck, until Father Quinlan, the doctor, and some others were told what was happening. They untied her, gave her clothes to wear, and bundled her off, out of Clasheen."

"I hardly think the same would be done to us!"

"It might be worse."

"What worse?"

"I don't know. Not cut off our *hair* . . ."

"Oh, nonsense!" Anthony scoffed. "That is too wild! Your imagination!"

However, to reassure Michael he checked that all the doors and windows of the house were fastened at night, and he kept a loaded pistol beside their bed. They lived in a state of siege. Michael tiptoed about, listening to every unexplained noise. Nothing happened. Nobody came to the house, not even the tenants, though Anthony saw Ty Keliher once, standing in the garden. Ty let himself be seen, and waved. Anthony waved back.

Nothing happened.

"IT is not unknown to medical science," Dr Lenehan said to his wife, "but I haven't come across a case of it myself. In rural Ireland, we . . . I doubt if the cause is known. Or a cure, come to that. Now, the Ancient Greeks – "

"We are not in Ancient Greece!" Mrs Lenehan answered. "Which is just as well, is it not? The decline of the Greeks, indeed the fall of the Roman Empire, is attributed to that . . . grossness."

Dr Lenehan was surprised. "What do you know of such things?" he asked.

"I can read, husband. Gibbon was recommended as suitable in my school."

"An expurgated edition, no doubt."

"Yes. So I went to the trouble of finding the complete work." The doctor laughed. "With what result?"

"I was . . . somewhat shocked by Caligula," Mrs Lenehan admitted.

In no other household in Clasheen was such a risqué conversation taking place that Sunday afternoon. The doctor, though he was born in County Galway, had not lived there all his life. He had attended medical school in Dublin, and practised in the capital for some years afterwards, until the appeal of roots pulled him back home. Mrs Lenehan was a Dubliner. She had travelled with her husband, seen London, Paris, Madrid. She was on the whole content with her lot; it was a happy marriage.

"I wish Father Quinlan had not spoken of it at all," the doctor said. "A denunciation, the naming of names . . . it is all barbaric, in my opinion. People should be left to themselves. If they indulge in their own choice of imperfection in the privacy of their homes, what hurt is done to others? The Bishop of Clogher was removed from his see because he was caught in such an act; it was said at the time that the scandal drove Lord Castlereagh to commit suicide: he was being blackmailed for something similar. Why should such men be made to suffer? However distasteful you or I might think it, it harms neither party nor anyone else. A little girl stopped me in the street, just now before lunch; she asked me what was the sin of Sodom. Can you imagine *that*? I was most embarrassed . . . in the street too . . . Father Quinlan has put ideas into people's heads that would never have lodged there in a whole month of Sundays! All of it at Mass, in front of children and babies! It is not right."

"I sometimes think he is ashamed of his own Christian goodness," Mrs Lenehan said. "As if the Old Testament and the New were at war in him. He works his fingers to the bone for the starving; speaks volumes of encouragement to them which he probably realizes are false. Then he makes amends to himself by preaching brimstone and hellfire."

"Typhus, scurvy, yellow fever, and what the Government is not doing to feed the country are much greater obscenities than anything that may go on at Eagle Lodge." Dr Lenehan stood up and put on his coat. "Where is my hat?"

"On your head."

"I have to visit the workhouse in Coolcaslig now; their doctor is still sick. Perhaps I shall call in at Eagle Lodge on my way, and offer my . . . condolences." He did not do so, however: as he neared the end of the new, paved section of the road he decided against it. I would not know what to say, he thought. But the real reason was that if one of those lesser obscenities was being enacted he did not want, any more than Mrs Peacock had wanted, to be aware of it.

Two miles further on he met Mr Peacock. The Protestant clergyman had, of course, been holding his own service at the time Father Quinlan was fulminating, so his knowledge of what had been said was entirely second-hand. Both men, when they saw each other, reined in their horses. "Is it true?" Mr Peacock asked.

"If you mean the drama at Mass this morning," the doctor replied, "then, yes, it is true."

"It is no more than they deserve, don't you think?"

Dr Lenehan patted his horse's neck. "As a medical man, I have no view on the case, sir. It is outside my province."

"But as a private man?"

"As a private man, I keep my view private."

Such an effective trump annoyed Mr Peacock; he was not

always so easily outwitted. "I have heard rumours," he said, "that some kind of physical attack may be contemplated on the persons or the property of Mr Altarnun and his . . . his . . ."

"That," said the doctor, "must be stopped!"

"I would not interfere myself; it is none of my business. But an assault on Eagle Lodge would be an outrage!"

"I do not catch your drift, sir. Assailing the man you would let pass, but aggression against his property you would condemn." He frowned. "You are eccentric."

"Private property is sacrosanct!" Mr Peacock said, raising his voice. "It cannot be touched with impunity! That is one of the fundamental laws on which our whole civilization is founded!"

"To whose civilization do you allude? That law has been the blight of this country since the English conquered us in the twelfth century! A fig to your private property, that is what I say, sir, and a fig to you, sir, as well!" Dr Lenehan galloped off, annoyed and amused; Mr Peacock, he thought, was such a ridiculous little ass. The cleric was left staring after him, quite astonished. Such an outburst was remarkable, Mr Peacock said to himself, unheard of! Perhaps he had some sorrow, some grave problem at home. His wife? Mrs Lenehan had been saying to Mrs Peacock only the other day that she felt like a widow since the onset of the fever; she hardly saw her husband now. She was not a happy woman, Mrs Peacock decided.

THE wind that had blown the cloud and drizzle in from the sea that morning was driving itself into a tremendous gale. It howled round corners, rattled windows and doors, lifted carpets and rugs. Mr Tangney, looking up from his armchair, saw a woman in the street, her head covered in a piece of cloth to keep out the wet, being thrust along as if by a hand. But she had a second, nevertheless, in which to glance at the house, as if, he said to himself, she were saying "*That* is the place where the bum-boy was born."

"There is, in every barrel, a rotten apple," he said to Margaret, who was sitting at the parlour table.

"I don't know what you mean," she replied.

"It is not our fault."

"I try to think so. Dear God, I do try! I have been mulling it over, again and again . . . when he was a baby, then his first tiny steps . . . teaching him . . . I don't have the words, but you surely know what I am saying."

"I do not," Eugene said, wishing his wife would not talk in riddles.

"The . . . functions of his body."

"Oh."

"My mother said . . . I can see her now, in a white dress, standing in this room. 'You are too hard on him,' she warned me. 'You will do that child a great mischief. Let him learn in his own sweet time.' A good woman, my mother was. I worshipped the ground she walked on."

A long silence followed this. Eugene drummed his fingers and sighed; Margaret sniffed, blew her nose, then rubbed her face, which was swollen from hours of crying. "I do not see what the Devil that has to do with it," he said, at last. "I am telling you it is not our fault! It does not come from *us*. His sisters were reared in the same way as he, and there is nothing the matter with them. That man corrupted him."

"What man?"

"Altarnun, of course! Oh, I could blast his head off! I would too . . . if I thought I could get away with it. He has seduced Michael with . . . I don't know what . . . the promise of a fortune, a life of luxury, a gentleman's existence. That is it; you may depend on it."

"Michael would never fall to such lures. He knows right from wrong; why, he nearly became a priest!"

"No, he did not. That is your imagination. And he *did* fall, as you put it, to such lures. We heard it today . . . at Holy Mass! Oh, the *shame* of it! My heart will break!"

"I am thinking . . . with yourself so busy in the forge and he with no liking for horses and having no brothers. Growing up in a household of women."

"Prut, Margaret! Dr Lenehan had nothing but sisters and a widowed mother, old Mr Lenehan being killed in that accident on the Castlebar road, and the boy kept in skirts till he was nine years of age. It did not cause *him* to be niminy-piminy."

"I cannot believe," Margaret said, "that Michael is entirely to blame."

"Of course he is not. *Altarnun* is to blame! I shall go to Galway tomorrow, to consult Mr Hanrahan, the attorney."

"Is it punishable by law?"

"If it is not, why, dammit to God, it should be!"

"Then, Eugene, you will have the law down so on Michael's head."

This argument reduced the blacksmith to silence. Eventually he stood up, and walked over to the window. "This gale will bring down chimney pots," he muttered.

"Perhaps we should have encouraged him to take more interest in girls."

"Do young men need encouragement? They follow the scent, as dogs do bitches."

"You are not in the forge now with some conacre man!" Margaret said, wincing at the indelicacy.

"Isn't it so? When I was seventeen – "

"I do not want to listen to this!" She covered her ears, but when she saw Eugene begin to speak she removed her hands.

"All I have to say is we do not know what girls he may have had eyes for. A boy at seventeen, eighteen, dances at the cross-roads on Saturday nights. He comes home, he goes to bed, he does not say next morning where he has been, merely that he has enjoyed himself. His parents do not ask him prying questions. I did not; you did not. We wait for the day he tells us he is courting Kathleen or Maureen or Eileen, and wishes to bring her home. Because Michael said nothing does not mean Kathleen or Maureen or Eileen do not exist. They jilted him; to be sure they broke his poor heart."

"As he has broken ours."

Eugene nodded. "How do we talk to the people we have lived with all our lives? Hold up our heads?" On the mantelpiece was a miniature of his son, drawn when Michael was twenty. He turned it face down. "Shame and ruin! I never want to see him. Never."

She made a little gesture of hopelessness, and said "God will answer our prayers."

"God is not in the habit of answering prayers. Particularly Irish prayers."

"Eugene, that is blasphemous!"

"I shall not go outside this house again."

He did, but weeks later. Mrs Tangney also could not bear to look at her friends and neighbours, so she, too, stayed indoors. She sent a message to Mrs Peacock that she could not help in the soup kitchen; she was indisposed. The charitable Protestant lady found she had to deal with all the work herself. "I have become a domestic, a menial, a skivvy," she grumbled to her husband.

A LETTER from Richard was never welcome, but the most recent was even less welcome than usual. It was mailed from Dublin. "I have come to see conditions here," he wrote, "and it is obvious that reports reaching India, indeed London, to a very great extent gloss over the magnitude of the catastrophe that has overwhelmed Ireland."

"Yes, we do know," Anthony said.

"I have seen for myself," the letter went on, "the hordes of starving beggars on the pavements of this city; wretched scarecrows that were once men and women in the prime of life and health; children and babies with the faces of old hags, their stomachs grotesquely swollen, their limbs so thin one could break them with one's little finger. I have seen the ravages fever has caused, the darkened complexions, the hideous yellow skin, the agonized sufferings of innocent people, and I am moved more than words can say, more than tears can express. The crowds that throng the port are patient beyond belief as they line up for the Liverpool ships, though they must be desperate to abandon the stricken country before the Great Reaper mows them down with the scythes of hunger and disease."

"He is good with the florid phrase," Anthony said. "The purple metaphor."

"It's as if he thinks we know nothing," said Michael. "Does he imagine an island of surpluses here? Every tenant-at-will with his belly full of warm potatoes?"

"I have to ask myself this," Richard said. "How is it my brother succeeded in obtaining the entire rent for last year? He must have forced every cottier to surrender his last penny, thus, presumably, pushing whole families into the workhouse, or shovelling them onto the roads to beg their sad way round the countryside. Whatever has happened, he has sent them to an almost certain death from sickness or lack of food. I hope to God that this is not the case, but I am unable to see how it can be otherwise."

Much to Michael's astonishment, Anthony laughed. "If I did not," he said, "I would weep, rage, scream! The irony is . . . breathtaking!"

"The care I took composing those false figures!"

"The money I sent him out of my own pocket!"

"The letter he wrote saying you should tumble cabins for a grazing farm!"

"I have evidence that leads me to think I am correct in my surmise," Richard continued, "evidence, alas, which shows I have been utterly mistaken in my judgement of your character, which suggests that you are not only unfit to manage my estate, but should be barred from any career a man of position and breeding might normally pursue.

"I am referring, sir, to the repugnant and unnatural relationship between yourself and your so-called servant. I am not so far out of this world that I am ignorant of such behaviour, but I had always supposed it confined to bestial creatures, benighted Asiatics and Polynesians whose customs have not altered since the Stone Age. It had not occurred to me for one instant that an officer and a gentleman, British by birth and Christian in upbringing, a product of all that is civilized in the civilized nineteenth century, would harbour such lickerish tendencies, such lubricious proclivities . . ."

"His hand is beginning to shake," Anthony said. "See here! He has worked himself up into a fine old lather."

"What is lubricious?" Michael asked. "And lickerish?"

"I don't know."

"They roll off the tongue . . . like quicksilver."

"I order you," Richard said, "to dismiss this thing, this male strumpet immediately. I shall arrive at Eagle Lodge two days after you receive this letter, and I do not want to find any evidence whatsoever that this person has been on the premises. I shall expect you to pass over to me all the documents and moneys relating to the estate, together with the keys of the house and any bills that are unpaid. You will remove all your personal possessions forthwith. I intend to secure a qualified, trustworthy agent as manager. I shall not, of course, impart to my dear wife, or to any other members of the family, my knowledge of the character of one whom I was proud to call brother; but the dishonour and sorrow you have heaped upon me I shall bear with me to the grave."

"Strumpet," Michael said. He shivered. "How can people be so . . . unkind?"

"Inhuman," Anthony answered. "Dogs don't savage their own. Wolves don't. Rats don't. But men and women do. Christians are particularly good at it." He crumpled the letter into a ball, and kicked it across the room. "We will not be here when he arrives. We will leave tomorrow."

"Where can we go?"

"To Galway. To your sister Noreen; I imagine she has not yet heard. We can try to change our tickets for the first ship available. I don't care what destination, New York, Boston, Quebec, Montreal . . ."

Michael nodded. "I agree," he said.

"Come here."

They stood by the window, holding each other very tightly, not worrying now if anyone saw them; Anthony feeling that the only precious goodness in the world was the man he was embracing, Michael feeling that never had he needed this loving protection so much.

Ty Keliher, hidden in the larches, saw.

"I'm sorry," Anthony murmured, as he kissed Michael's hair. "I'm sorry . . ."

"For what?"

"That I've led you to this."

"You haven't led me. I was, I am, most willing. But . . . what is to become of us?"

"I don't know."

"I'm frightened. Afraid . . . for our very survival."

"They can't destroy that. They can't destroy *us*."

I shall be here to warn them, Ty said to himself.

NEWS of a calamity Michael would have considered far worse than the discovery, the denunciation, the scene with his father, or Richard's letter, was mentioned that week in *The Freeman's Journal*. Neither Anthony nor Michael saw this edition of the newspaper and nobody told them; it was half a year before Michael found out. If he had known at the time, it would have broken him utterly. Mr Peacock was the first to read of it; he thought he had better tell Father Quinlan. It was possible that any ship now sailing from Galway might be carrying some of the Catholic priest's congregation. The *Lord Kingston*, as it neared the American coast, had run into a terrible storm and had sunk; the entire crew and the three hundred and eighty-nine passengers had all drowned.

Father Quinlan knew the significance, and that it was his extremely painful task to break the news to Mr and Mrs Tangney, and to Mr and Mrs Leahy.

The Tangneys had not heard Mass at Clasheen since names were named. Their only trip out of doors was to the village of Kilgarrin, a five-mile walk up the Coolcaslig road, to hear Mass celebrated by Father Coakley, the shy, gentle curate who had married Dan and Madge, and whose sermons were quite the opposite of Father Quinlan's in substance and tone.

Father Quinlan thought this shift of loyalty was to be expected, considering what had happened. But it never occurred to him that he had caused immense and unnecessary suffering to two innocent people by speaking out, and he was therefore genuinely surprised by the coldness, indeed the hostility, which enveloped him when he arrived at the Tangneys' house. He was the bearer of tragic news, but the chill, unfriendly atmosphere was obvious before he spoke of the *Lord Kingston*. He was still puzzled when he left: such is the Jansenist mentality, that perceives the world only as very black and very white; mostly very black.

Disasters come in threes, he said to himself; the Tangneys had now had their three: the consumption of their supplies, Michael, Madge's death. Things could only improve from now on. This was not logical of Father Quinlan. In fact it could be called untypically superstitious, unless, of course, one chooses to think the whole paraphernalia of Roman Catholicism from first to last superstitious nonsense, and its priests the arch-purveyors of sublime irrationality.

Things did not improve for the Tangneys. They both came to believe that life was all predestined, that neither they nor anyone else had control over what happened to human beings, that people were straws blown helplessly hither and thither by the wind of an accursed history or a malevolent Fate. Such thinking, too, is Jansenist, though the Tangneys had never heard of the famous heresy. They were only trying to make sense of the colossal depression that now overwhelmed them.

The superb potato harvest of 1847 and the recurrence of blight, famine and disease the following year found them to a great extent immune to the joys of the former and the woes of the latter. They died, she a week before him, in January 1850, well before they should have died – they were only just older than the century – and their deaths were not caused by hunger or its consequent illnesses, nor indeed by any illness known to medical science. Dr Lenehan would have diagnosed it correctly, but the new man, Dr O'Hara, was baffled. They died simply because they had given up the will to live.

MR Peacock, after he had handed the paper to Father Quinlan, was about to mount his horse – he already had one foot in the stirrup – when voices in a nearby alley made him hesitate. What he heard incensed him, though he took no action other than galloping home instead of trotting. "I will not put up with this!" he shouted to his wife, who was sewing a new hem in one of her old dresses.

"What on earth has happened now?" she asked.

"The hobbledehoys and slubberdegullions of this God-forsaken town are planning an assault on Eagle Lodge! I shall stop it!"

"It is what those two . . . men . . . deserve, and it is nothing to do with us. You would be far better advised to let nature take its course."

"Nature? It is not nature we are concerned with here! Or are you thinking of the hopelessly evil nature of the Irish peasant? If private property is not protected against the mob, then this country is *ruined*!"

"These bees in your bonnet. I shall never understand you."

"And I shall never understand how *you* never understand. Though women always made ill-matched bedfellows with political thought."

"I should like to point out," Mrs Peacock said, positively stabbing her needle into her sewing, "that the present monarch, the head of state, the defender of the Protestant churches, is a *woman*. And Queen Victoria is a very *capable* woman."

"Where is my blunderbuss?"

"You are surely not going to carry fire-arms!"

"Not only that, my dear, but at ten o'clock tonight I fully expect to be using them to the utmost of my ability!"

CHAPTER TEN

TY Keliher arrived just after dark, breathless with haste.
"They are coming!" he shouted. Wide-eyed with fear and
excitement, he stood on one leg, on the kitchen door-step.
"They are *coming*! Do you understand? Look to yourselves!"

Michael stared at him, dumbfounded. Anthony came in from
the parlour and said "What is it?"

"The mob," Michael answered.

"There is a power of men," Ty said. "They have sticks and
stones!"

" 'If you want to throw a stone, every lane will furnish one',"
Anthony said. "Dean Swift. The gates are locked, but they'll climb
over the wall, just as you do, Ty." Ty blushed, and grinned.
"There are shutters for the downstairs windows, which won't
prevent them being smashed, but it will minimize the damage to
the rooms. The upstairs windows . . . well, there's no defence.
We'll close the shutters now." Michael ran to do so; Ty made to
follow, then stopped. He did not know if he was wanted. "You
may help if you wish," Anthony said. Ty smiled from ear to ear,
immensely glad to join in; it was a great game: nothing as thrilling
as this had ever happened. "Are you sure that what you've told us
is true?" Anthony asked.

"I am sure I am sure," Ty said, pulling at one of the shutters.
"But never tell my father I am here. He will *kill* me!"

"Is he one of the mob?"

"No, he is not! Nor any of your tenants; they are all at home by
their fires."

"Why are you doing this?"

Ty scratched his head. Because he thought it more evil than
what he had observed through the window, Michael wanted to

ask, but he did not put the question; such delicate balancing of moral problems would be beyond Ty's reasoning faculties. Ty, however, gave him part of the answer. "Neither of you has hurt anyone," he said.

When the shutters were closed, the doors locked, and the lights extinguished all over the house, they went upstairs to the master bedroom and waited. Anthony held his pistol. "If I have to fire it," he said, "I hope to God I won't hit anyone."

Ty was disappointed. "It would help," he said. "They would scatter like leaves in a great wind."

Michael laughed. "You would make an excellent soldier, Ty. Have you ever thought of joining the army?"

"I have not. The army! Pooh!"

"Sssh!" Anthony said. "I hear them."

A foot kicking a stone. A body creeping stealthily through the vegetation. Michael's eyes had grown accustomed to the dark: out on the lawn were the dim outlines of men. A dozen, fifteen, perhaps twenty still shapes. The night was black: no moon, but not so much cloud as to obscure the starlight entirely. His heartbeat quickened, and his body was full of tension. Anthony's too, and Ty's: he could hear them breathe more rapidly than normal. Anthony was touching him, searching for his hand; kissed him, and said "Don't be afraid."

"I am *terrified*!" He was trembling, uncontrollably.

"Michael Tangney, come out!" someone shouted. "We know you are there!"

"Don't move," Anthony whispered.

"It is the Flanagans' Maurice," Ty said. "He is the leader. May he boil in Hell!"

A long silence. Everyone, outside and in, was a statue. "Michael Tangney! Michael Tangney! We want you!" a voice called. This was followed by a few laughs, some jeers, and several obscenities. A third voice cried "You thought you would like to be a woman? We will show you what it is to be a woman!" Loud guffaws. "We'll put you in a pretty dress," mocked a fourth voice. "And paint your face," said Maurice Flanagan. "And give you the pleasuring of your life!" the second man shouted. "A score of us are here, and we are *men*!" They all hooted with laughter at this.

A stone was thrown. Glass splintered, crashed to the ground.

146

"We have nice things for you." It was the man who had called him a bastard. "You don't think we'd use you as we would our wives, surely? We have clubs instead. Long, thick wooden clubs, Michael!" "The necks of broken bottles!" another yelled. "You did not want to be a boy, Michael? Well, you need not have that worry any more. We can grant you your wish!" "All the handsome fine lads of Dublin will kiss your sweet arse, Molly Michael Tangney!" The shouts and obscenities rose to a crescendo, then stopped, leaving one cry: "It's so easy, Michael! One swift cut and you're changed for ever, Michael!"

"Why *me*? Why not *you*?" Michael hissed.

"You are one of them. One of us," Ty said. "*He* is English."

Michael collapsed. Ty pulled him away from the window; the noise alerted the crowd: "They are in that bedroom!"

"Where?"

"Upstairs! Third window from the right!" Another stone smashed the glass in the room next to the one Anthony, Michael and Ty were in. Anthony pointed his gun out of the window, which he had left ajar, and fired, repeatedly.

"I hope I have murdered a man with every shot!" he cried. He was shaking with anger; it had been difficult to hold the pistol steady. "They are *animals*. No, not animals! Filth that must be . . . *ripped* out of the world!"

The men had scattered, but they had not run off. No one had been hurt. They came back, singly, in twos and threes, pressed themselves against the wall of the house, where they thought they would be safe from the gun. They started to demolish all the downstairs windows. Some of them were hammering on the kitchen door: if the lock does not hold, Anthony said to himself, what then? A running battle in the rooms and corridors, in pitch darkness? Three against twenty, even if one of us is armed; they can still get what they want: Michael.

Ty was kneeling, Michael's head resting on his legs. Michael had come to, and was sobbing, whimpering. Ty did not know how to restore him to his senses; he just held him and stroked him as he stroked the wounded birds he sometimes found on the estate. "I'd be glad if you would not kill any of them," he said to Anthony. "I do not want to see you hang. Now a nice bloody gash in the flesh would be another thing altogether."

Anthony did not reply. He felt his way out of the room, and groped along the landing. On the stairs smashed glass crunched under his feet. He found the front door, threw it open, and fired into the night. At almost the same second a gun went off near the gates: two men leaped their horses over the wall and galloped up to the house. Someone, by the larch trees, was screaming with pain. The mob now ran away in earnest, not, as Ty had hoped, like leaves in a great wind, but as fast and as desperately as any scared gang of humans might disperse and disappear. The horsemen arrived at the door. "Mr Altarnun! Is that you? Is anything damaged?" The voice was the Reverend Peacock's.

"Come inside," Anthony said. "And light one of the lamps, please. My hands are shaking too much." He laughed. "I am out of practice. We never shot at Afghans after sunset; they played to the rules, as we did. Daylight firing only."

Mr Peacock did as he was requested, and, when the lamp was lit, Anthony saw who the other horseman was: Father Quinlan.

"There is some damage," Mr Peacock said, as he looked around in the downstairs rooms.

Anthony ignored him. "The Church Militant in strength," he said to Father Quinlan. He subsided into a chair, still holding the pistol.

"Sarcasm is not appropriate," the Catholic priest said.

"Mr Quinlan, has it ever occurred to you that your zeal for rooting out sin might cause you to transgress far more gravely than the blackest sheep in your entire flock?"

"I do not understand you. I do not wish to hear – "

"I hope your soul burns in the warmest fires of Hell. Inciting a mob to commit violence against two men who do nothing other than mind their own business *I* would call a mortal sin."

"It is not for you to – "

"Do you know what I would like to do with this pistol, sir? Point it straight at your head and pull the trigger." He raised the gun and aimed it. Father Quinlan ducked. "If I thought I could avoid the consequences, I would fire!"

Mr Peacock attempted to intervene. "Mr Altarnun, your emotions are understandable, but – "

Anthony did not let him finish. "You sir," he said, "are a sanctimonious old humbug! Not as evil as the Vatican edition here, but almost so!" Ty came into the room, supporting Michael, who could hardly stand upright. His knees sagged, his arms twitched as if they were not in his control, his eyes were puffy, and he was breathing with immense difficulty. It was as severe an attack of asthma as any he had experienced.

"Are you pleased?" Anthony cried. "You think you've broken him?" He stood up, walked across to Ty, and took Michael from him. He held Michael, kissed him. Then he turned to the clergymen and said "Get out of my house."

They left. The door shut after them: they climbed into their saddles; the hoof-beats of their horses faded away in the distance. The only sounds were the wind, the murmur of the lamp, and Michael's strangled gasps as he struggled for air.

"I should go," Ty said, but he seemed reluctant to move.

"Stay here tonight if you wish," Anthony said.

Ty looked pleased. "I will be slaughtered already for not being at home. But I can tell them I have been at my aunt's, out in the bogs. Now . . . where would I sleep?"

"In Michael's room. There is a bed."

"I have never slept in a bed! Oh, I have always wanted that! But . . . how do I do it?"

Anthony laughed. "We'll let you work that out for yourself." He carried Michael to a chair, and sat him down. "Michael. Michael! In the morning we leave. For ever. Leave all this . . . Think of the ship. America."

Michael nodded. He could hardly speak, but he managed, with great difficulty to whisper: "A dress . . . one swift cut . . ."

"Clear it out of your mind. Forget it all. It didn't happen."

"I shall . . . never forget."

"No," Anthony said. "I imagine not."

After an hour, the air passages in Michael's throat and lungs became less constricted, but Anthony had been nearly as frightened as Michael; he had not seen an asthma attack before. He sent Ty for Dr Lenehan, who, late though it was, came out at once. Michael was just beginning to breathe more normally when the doctor arrived; only a sedative was necessary.

"What caused it?" Dr Lenehan asked. "He has not been like this in years."

Anthony waved an arm. "Look about you," he said.

"I am sorry." He had noticed the smashed glass. "Very sorry. Father Quinlan has this on his conscience I would like to think. The . . . denunciation . . . was a gross indecency, in my opinion. At Mass! I . . . wish you both well. And every happiness in America. I hope you will not conclude, sir, that all men in this district are barbarians."

"I do not. Thank you."

When he had gone, Michael said "They would never have broken me. They never will break me!"

TY had slipped out before Anthony and Michael were up. "I wanted to say goodbye," Anthony said. "And give him the keys of the house. I don't feel like talking to the other tenants." Apart from the embarrassment it entailed, he wasn't well. "Only yesterday night's antics. Nothing more. A cold, perhaps."

"I'm exhausted," Michael answered. "I'm still a bit . . . shocked." It had been a great effort to drag himself out of bed, but otherwise he was more or less his usual self, physically.

Slowly and wearily they collected up their possessions, and packed them. More than most emigrants at that time were taking; books, Anthony's souvenirs of India, bedding, crockery, cooking utensils, all their clothes, Michael's music, a stockpile of food, and a bag filled with earth from the garden: Irish earth. They loaded everything onto a cart which they would pull as far as Galway. In the city the cart would be sold. They had some money too; not an enormous amount, but sufficient.

"Will they let all this on the boat?" Michael asked, as he surveyed the trunks and cases. "There is enough of it!"

"If they object, I shall be at my most English," Anthony said. "Upper class superiority. That will do the trick."

Michael shrugged. "I shall turn the other way and pretend I do not know you." He looked at the debris that was the consequence of last night. "Should we sweep this up?"

"No. It will give my dear sibling a little work to occupy himself with. Or perhaps he'll employ one of the tenants: somebody could earn a shilling or two."

"Ty, I would hope."

It was another grey, damp morning; a thin drizzle, though not much of it, in the wind. Cloud shrouded the summits: I shall never see them again, Michael said to himself; I had wanted a final look. But he was happier than he had ever imagined that Ireland was soon to be lost in the past. There was more than one good reason for emigration: the prospect of starving was not the prime motive for him and Anthony. Hunger and fever had avoided them; their experience of the Famine years wasn't that of most of the nation: but they were not as other men, and Ireland did not tolerate men who were different.

If we ever did throw out the British, he wondered, would the people really be free? He doubted it. You would have to be a peasant, a Catholic, and marry a nice girl if you wanted to enjoy that almost illusory society, an independent Ireland. We are a race too stubborn and intransigent. Our kings died; our bards died; we are fed on legends: chew the remains of a deceased culture. We know nothing of the real world, which is more than a broken harp string.

Just as Anthony was about to look for Patrick O'Callaghan to give him the keys, Ty reappeared. He was out of breath with running, as he had been yesterday evening. "Oh, I am so glad you are not gone yet!" he panted. "I have something for you." He was holding a gold sovereign.

"Where did that come from?" Anthony asked.

"A coin my father is keeping in the thatch for . . . oh, all my life."

"Does he know you've taken it?"

"He does not!" Ty was indignant at the suggestion.

"I cannot accept it, Ty. It's stealing."

"It's not worth much. We do not think of such coins to buy things with. It's there because it is a . . . lucky charm. To deliver us from evil."

"But the food this would bring you all!" Anthony exclaimed. "It's ridiculous! Do . . . most of my tenants have coins like this?"

"Oh, yes! I thought my father the only one, but I have seen them now at the Cronins, the O'Learys and the Sullivans. The Widow O'Gorman has two! But she is always greedy, people say."

Anthony looked at Michael in amazement, then he laughed. "I have never heard such a story," he said.

"I have," said Michael. "But I did not credit it."

"Take the coin," Ty urged. "I had such trouble finding a

moment when everyone was out of the cabin, and I am thinking you surely need it now much more than we do."

"Then I will take it," Anthony said. "Thank you." He was moved by the kindness, wanted to hold the boy in his arms and kiss him: a natural, spontaneous gesture of affection. But, he thought, it might produce fear or disgust. "Tell me one thing, Ty. You're the only person who has helped us. Why is that? Are you . . . as we are?"

"As you are?" Ty was puzzled.

"I mean . . . would you . . . prefer a boy to a girl?"

"Oh, no! No, I would not!" He looked indignant again. "Though I haven't yet found a girl who is preferring me."

"Then why?"

He scratched his head vigorously, something he always did, Anthony realized, when he was trying to concentrate. "What I saw through the window everyone says is wrong, the priest at Mass . . . so it is so. But it isn't the shameful, horrible thing they think it is; my father, he . . . It excited me. It was . . . I have not the words . . . beautiful, I want to say." This speech had cost much effort: Ty was blushing and stammering.

Anthony found he did not have words, either; he could think of nothing to answer that. Perhaps Ty was able to see through a glass less darkly than he could, or the Peacocks, Father Quinlan, the Tangneys, even Dr Lenehan, all cluttered with complex acres of learned responses that were used as measures to judge people and events.

"We must go now," he said. He gave Ty the keys. "Hand them over to my brother when he arrives tomorrow. I'd be grateful. And if you want to earn some money, ask him could you sweep up this mess, tidy the house, dig the garden for him. He should pay you at least a shilling."

Ty nodded, then stood by the front door as if, he said to himself, he was the new owner, and watched what he would always think of as his prize catches pull their cart through the gates and along the road to Clasheen. They did not look back. He watched until they disappeared from view, then let himself into the house. I will sleep in their bed tonight, he decided, as he walked up the stairs and peered at the forlorn, damp, empty rooms. And imagine a girl. The thought aroused him: it. He was no longer worried its growth would be so huge everybody would see; that was a nonsense, a childish thing.

THE drizzle, the warm day, the colours: it is perfect for a stroll in the countryside, Michael thought. Not rainy enough to soak you, not so hot you would sweat. For the first time in weeks he sang aloud. It was a reaction to last night, a wild lurch to optimism from despair. But the wet was not good for Anthony, who sneezed more than once and blew his nose. He was listless, and when it was his turn to pull the cart their pace was a crawl.

As the outskirts of Clasheen appeared, Michael's good spirits sank. He did not want even a glimpse of his parents, but the road led past the forge: if they were standing outside . . . Other people did not matter. They were, with very few exceptions, no longer people to him; the nameless, mindless thugs of yesterday were what Clasheen now meant. He would walk through, head high, not looking in any direction other than the town's end. If stones were cast, he would not flinch. But he doubted stones would be in evidence; even if ill-feeling remained, the desire for violence had probably burned to ash. Some of those men might have been drinking to crank themselves up, might now be ashamed of what they had done. It wasn't certain: some human beings were irredeemably evil.

He looked at Anthony. English, an army officer, wealthy by any Irish standards: now reduced to pulling a cart. Why had he let himself? Some people had irresistible grace.

"What is going on here?" he said.

At almost every doorway in the long straggle of the main street, men, women and children stood, unsmiling and silent. Their black rags of poverty suited the grim expressions on their faces. Is it for us, Michael wondered, and he felt an echo of last night's fear. But they surely could not know we would be leaving today; or, even if they did, that we would be passing through now, at this minute.

The people, however, only spared Anthony and Michael a momentary glance, the occasional whisper: he imagined the words – "They fornicated with *each other*!" "Their sin is so wicked you cannot *name* it!" Which one had wanted to use a broken bottle? Which of them would have cut. . . ? Panic began to seize him: being here was like imprisonment in an airless room; he had to get out, breathe . . .

"Be calm," Anthony said. "They are not here for us. It's a funeral."

Ahead of them a group of people was following another cart, on which, Michael thought, was a body. It was difficult to tell because so many heads were in the way. But if it was a body, why wasn't it in a coffin? So poor was the family they could not afford a coffin? Or with so many dead now there was no wood to make one? The gap between him and the crowd behind the funeral cart narrowed; the body was a girl's. He did not know who she was.

In a doorway near Flanagan's two women wept into their shawls. Outside the bar stood Maurice: "And paint your face." Michael hoped the loathing he felt, and also the pride he had in being who and what he was, were painted on his face for the leader of the assault to come to terms with. Maurice seemed to recognize: and acknowledged the detestation – and the dignity – by looking down at his shoes.

"Don't go so fast," Anthony said. "We shall find ourselves mixed up with the mourners."

Michael slowed; he hadn't realized he was almost cantering through the town, so eager was he to leave it. He remembered his ordeal in the winter, staggering in the snow-drifts; the man of grey shadows. How different was his stride now! They reached the forge; his parents, thank God, had not come out to watch the funeral. But Mrs Peacock was there, taking a moment from her duties in the soup kitchen. She saw them, made an agitated gesture, then hurried inside.

"Evil-minded bitch," Michael said.

The procession turned up the street to the church, which was near enough for him to catch a sight, the last he would ever have, of Father Quinlan, on the steps in a black cassock, holding his missal.

> And priests in black gowns were walking their rounds,
> And binding with briars my joys and desires.

Nevermore, he said to himself. Nevermore! The road ahead was clear. Only a few cabins, then the town's end; beyond it the open road: sky, sea, moorland. This was his last picture of Clasheen, a huddle of grey, graceless streets; the smoke of turf fires: tight-lipped staring men and women in black. He was filled with exhilaration, a sense of joy like flickering, fluttering larks' wings. He was free.

ON their journey to Galway they stopped to help a woman bury her husband. He was naked and missing an arm. The woman, too ill to do much, had dragged him into a field and covered him with stones; a pack of famished dogs had found him, torn off the arm and eaten it. Anthony and Michael dug a proper grave.

"He is decent now, may God reward you," she said. "But the Church rites will have to be foregone." She sat down against a stone wall. "It is terrible how we are hit. So many bodies, and no one to bury them. No coffins. The priest is seven miles away. Whole families are dead, and their neighbours not having the strength to move them. Some tinkers came by last week and tumbled the empty cabins over the corpses. At least that prevents the dogs. I am not well myself." She keeled over sideways: then fell flat on the grass. She, too, was dead. Anthony and Michael dug a second grave.

That was their worst experience, but everywhere they saw appalling distress. In most towns and villages the devastation was much greater than at Clasheen: ghost streets with no one left alive, others inhabited only by the dying; and in every one where people still lived they were accosted by ragged beggars who saw their good clothes, the quantity of their luggage. These places had not had a Dr Lenehan ministering tirelessly to the sick, an Anthony to hang rents, a Mrs Peacock to open a soup kitchen, a Mr Peacock or a Father Quinlan to form a committee that raised money and employed men on public works. In Clasheen there was always hope, however small.

Anthony hated to do it, but he now refused the beggars. If he gave to one, he would have to give to all, and that "all" would be endless; the news would travel so fast that the cousins and brothers and neighbours and friends of the recipient would be on him, beseeching: he would arrive at the ship with nothing. One man he refused said "You must live to tell the tale, your honour. If we all die, then the world will never know. When you've crossed the ocean, just say that in the village of Coolies in Ireland you met

Thomas Maher, a dying man who told you, please God, it *must* not go unrecorded!"

Whole districts of Galway seemed abandoned now; there were streets where every house was derelict and shut up, not even a cat hunting in the garbage. Leaves and bits of dirty paper eddied in the wind, the only movement. The stench of typhus drifted on the air. But the port was busy, crowded with people. Some were attempting to sell possessions they could not take – a cart, a bed, a cow – but nobody wanted to buy. Some quarrelled with brokers about the price of tickets; others, who had never seen the city, stared at the buildings; still more foraged in gutters and rubbish dumps for a scrap to eat. The happiest were those already boarding a ship. Soon everyone who had an ounce of strength would have unpeopled Ireland, Michael said to himself; it was becoming a desert to be inhabited only by forgotten sagas and bones.

Anthony secured a cabin on a ship called *The Cedar of Lebanon*, from a man and his wife who had changed their minds because they could not bear to leave. It was bound for New York, and there were two days to wait before it sailed. Their original tickets Anthony sold to a broker. They then went to the grocery store: Noreen and John were still living as if they expected an attacking army; it was some time before they would even answer the knock.

Noreen was surprised to see who it was; Michael had not sent to warn her they were coming. But he and Anthony were very welcome to stay two nights: evidently she had no suspicion that Anthony was other than the friend and employer Michael said he was. Michael was relieved. He had feared she would have heard the news, but there had been no contact: she had not had a message from her parents for some time, and was puzzled by this. "And no word from Madge yet." Noreen, too, had not seen yesterday's newspaper. "Poor Madge! And she so gaily walking out of this house and down to the ships. It is terrible and I do not think I shall ever get over it."

She shed a few tears as she embraced Michael. "Everybody has lost somebody, I know, and whole families dying of the hunger. But it hurts when your own flesh and blood has to cross the water." She wiped her eyes, then sat, staring at nothing. "It is not good to brood," she said. "I tell myself that each day. The rest of us here live on and do what we can. You are to sail now, and you will have all the luck, please God, she is now having."

"I will," Michael said. "I will."

"And how are my parents? Madge and yourself leaving . . . they have taken it badly?"

He nodded. "Yes. Badly."

"It is as I thought, then. I will go next week to ask do they want for anything."

"They . . . would like that."

"It is a bitter blow for them."

"It is. It is."

"And Dan, one of the handsomest men I ever set eyes on."

"He is indeed. He is indeed."

"But you will be a joy to the American girls, brother. You may take your pick of the best, and give me nephews and nieces and gladden our dear mother's heart. And our dear father's heart too."

"Well . . . we will . . ."

If he were talking to Madge, Michael thought, how much more comfortable the conversation would be! No necessity to tell lies. And codding, or sharing sorrow, would have genuine affection. Noreen, somehow, never sounded sincere. Perhaps she *was* sincere; perhaps she did feel deeply. But her words and the tone of her voice were always artificial. He should not judge: maybe she was merely awkward. But Anthony noticed too. "She is not the woman Madge is," he said, when they were alone.

Anthony's cold was worse. "I think I have a touch of fever," he said, then, seeing the horror on Michael's face, he laughed. "I don't mean *that* fever. If I'm black or yellow the looking-glass is lying. I'm hot . . . my temperature isn't what it should be; that is all." He slept fitfully, tossing and turning. Noreen, of course, had put them in separate bedrooms, and not having his lover wrapped round him meant Michael didn't sleep well, either. He heard Anthony go downstairs twice, for a cup of water. On the morning of their departure Anthony was very pale and completely without energy. "I'm not sure I'm well enough to travel," he said.

"What shall we do?"

"Make the best of it. There's no going back now."

"And if the doctor will not let you on board?"

"Oh, he will," Noreen said. "He sits in a little booth with a tiny window, and as you pass by he only wants to see your tongue. It is not right I'm thinking; that way so many people already half dead with the fever slip through and infect every other passenger." She saw the alarm this remark was causing, and said "You needn't be anxious. *The Cedar of Lebanon* is a big ship, stoutly made, in much better trim than some of the leaky old coffins that have sailed out of here. I looked at it myself, yesterday; there will be people of substance on that ship. A mountain of baggage, all of good quality, was piled on the quay for loading. Why, I heard some desperate, starving family in rags complain of the price of the tickets: much dearer, they said, than other boats, out of their reach. There won't be fever aboard; you may depend on it. God is good."

Despite Anthony's condition it was a relief to be going. The two days at the shop had been like living in suspended animation, not of one time and existence or any other. Noreen was all easy talk on the surface but nothing below, and her husband was worse, a fat, florid, silent man with mean eyes; Michael felt the cost of every mouthful he ate was being added up in John's mental till. Nor was William an attractive child – a plump, sulky creature with the same eyes as his father's. He was totally without the Tangney good looks and tall slimness.

Noreen came down to the ship, threw herself on her brother's neck and wept the statutory tears. "You will write and tell us everything!" she said, between sobs. "Two hands to watch for now, Madge's and yours. Oh, you will meet over there, and it will be the most joyous celebration and reunion New York has seen!"

On the ship they leaned against the rail and looked back. I'm not in Ireland now, Michael said to himself.

They continued to look as the ship parted from the harbour wall, as the grey slot of water grew into a yawning gap, as they progressed out into the bay and the city slowly blurred to an indistinct smudge. Then there was Clasheen, sharp and close to, and Eagle Lodge: on the drive was a carriage, a man walking from it to the house. "Richard," Anthony said.

"Richard!" Michael yelled, waving his arms madly. "Richard!! We are *here*!!!"

158

"Idiot," Anthony said, laughing.

Another figure was bent over a flower-bed, picking up broken glass perhaps. "It's Ty! I'm sure it's Ty!"

Anthony stared. "It is. Good! Now may we go and find our cabin? I shall catch my death if I'm up here too long, warm though it is."

A mild, dull summer day, and the sea calm as the surface of a lake. It augured well.

AT the grocery shop, John said "I think it very fishy. A prosperous Irishman may sail for America with his possessions in a few trunks, but an Englishman! *I* would appear to have more money than he. There is a story behind it, I am telling you. He will be wanted by the peelers."

"The story behind it," Noreen said, "is that he has beggared himself by giving all his wealth to the sick and the starving."

"God would not want me to think it, but that only happens in little books about the lives of saints. *People* don't do that."

"It is peculiar," Noreen agreed.

"He and Michael are not master and servant. They are friends. They are in some cahoots together."

"My brother Michael? He is too innocent for that."

"They have done some wrong thing and are vanishing. It will out, and we shall hear of it."

They did hear of it, before the day was over. Noreen started to read the newspapers; she had previously been too busy to find the time with Anthony and Michael in the house. She saw the paragraph on the *Lord Kingston*, and decided to go to Clasheen at once. Her parents told her of the wrong thing her brother had done, and she, realizing they still thought he was at Eagle Lodge, told them he had sailed that morning for the United States. It was a complex plot – sex, sudden death, flight, scandal and grief – that she relayed to her husband when she returned.

CHAPTER ELEVEN

THERE were passengers and passengers, they discovered. Noreen was right in saying *The Cedar of Lebanon* was a superior class of ship, that it was carrying a number of well-to-do emigrants, and that its ticket prices were expensive. But she had not seen the crowds of starving ill-clad paupers, some of whom had the fever and knew they had it, stuffed into the hold. These were the tenants of two great estates that had been cleared, every person evicted and their cabins pulled down, their passage to America paid for by the owners.

The conditions they had to endure were dreadful: flimsy beds for some, but most slept on the floor. They had no food with them and were relying on the weekly seven pounds of provisions that the captain was legally obliged to give to each person. Their world was darkness, filth and stench. It was very different for Michael and Anthony: they were cabin passengers, among people with means and in good health, who supplemented the wretched seven pounds with their own food, and who had access to proper sanitary arrangements. Their world was the daylight, reasonable cleanliness, and fresh air.

The ship was overcrowded, but whether dangerously or not would depend on the weather, the adequacy of the provisions and the water supply. As Anthony had thought, two men in one berth produced no comment; even in the cabins whole families were sharing a bed. Overcrowding meant he and Michael at least could sleep as they always had done. And the weather remained calm. The gentle rocking motion of the ship soothed; the creak of timbers reassured.

On that first day their anxiety was water, which was strictly rationed to six pints per person, an allowance that had to suffice for washing and cooking as well as drinking. Some people had their own casks, so were able, for a while, to enjoy more than the daily six pints, but Anthony and Michael had not thought to bring one. Anthony was feverish still, and thirsty. Michael gave him a large share of his own ration. If the voyage took longer than expected, there would be problems: some of the ship's casks had once contained wine; they had not been properly cleaned, and the water in them was found to be undrinkable.

Cooking was done on deck, on a big makeshift stove the size of a double bed – it was a wooden box lined with bricks, the coals in the centre, the top iron bars. It worked efficiently; its heat was adequate. But the overcrowding meant waiting one's turn for ages; it was constantly surrounded by hordes of people from both worlds of passengers, squabbling and arguing. One family took too long, another pushed in, a third left a terrible mess. Fights broke out, and often the precious food was spilled, or stolen by those who could not bear the endless wait. Many people abandoned the idea of using the stove, and swallowed their dinner raw.

Michael, on that first evening, did not. He was in too good a mood to become impatient, and as Anthony was not at all hungry he decided to leave cooking until the crowd had dispersed a little. His meal – a lamb chop Noreen had given him, and carrots from the garden at Eagle Lodge – was, he thought, worth waiting for. It was the envy of those who watched him eat it. More than one man begged for a share. Michael refused, and was met with black looks. He would have to be on his guard, he realized; it would be easy to get involved in a brawl, or discover his supplies had mysteriously vanished.

Why are they begging, he asked himself. They had all got out of Ireland; starvation was behind them: there *was* food on board. It had not occurred to him, yet, how terrible was the plight of the steerage passenger living on the seven pounds a week ration. This was doled out each day by members of the crew, a pound per person. All it consisted of was Indian corn, not enough to prevent people feeling very hungry indeed.

Anthony did not stay up late. "My mother used to tell me to nurse a cold," he said. "So . . . I will nurse it."

"You have more than a cold," Michael answered.

161

"Yes. A touch of influenza. Don't worry! It will need more than that to kill me."

Michael was reassured; Anthony was probably right: it didn't seem to be anything dangerous. He was too excited to go to bed himself, too awake, so he set off to explore those parts of the ship he had not yet seen. A few moments looking into the hold disgusted him. It was the black hole of Calcutta. The smell was already sickening. A swarm of grey, ragged, emaciated bodies was eating, quarrelling, vomiting, defecating into buckets, trying to sleep. Perhaps in some dark corner even trying to make love. Not an inch of privacy between one human shape and another. Conditions on slave ships transporting negroes from Africa could not be worse. The only difference was these men and women had no chains, at least not visible ones, though it could hardly be said they were here of their own free will. And the blacks were given better food.

He went up on deck, and though he was unable to scrub the hold from his mind, he could not, at the moment, feel depressed. Ireland had disappeared from sight: the ship was in the centre of a perfect circle of calm sea. It was the one disturbance wrinkling an endlessly flat surface, a question mark on a blank page. On the water jellyfish drifted. The crew bustled about; industrious, sober men, confident in their ship and their tasks, Michael thought. The grey dull day had gone; the sky was blue, and sunset was beginning to redden the horizon. He leaned on the rail, and sang:

"When first her gentle bosom knows
Love's flame, it wanders never,
Deep in her heart the passion glows;
She loves, and loves forever."

"When the candles are out all women are fair," said a voice beside him. One of the crew: Michael had noticed him earlier. A little older than he was, a sunburnt lined face, long blond hair; in physique, massive, built like a bull.

"And who said so?"

"I don't remember," the man answered. "It's just a saying. Tell me now, are you one of the gentlemen in cabin number three?" The blue eyes searched him up and down. Michael shivered inwardly; he felt he was being stripped naked, and it was not at all pleasant to be stared at, nude, by this hulk of a stranger.

"Who are you that you want to know?" Michael asked.

"The other gentleman isn't well. Is the fever upon him?"

"It is not."

"If it is, why, you may want my services." He smiled, but it was a mirthless smile, like that of a predatory animal gauging its evening meal.

"You don't look to me like a doctor."

The sailor laughed. "No, I am not a doctor," he said. "Well . . . you will find out." He walked off. Michael watched him go, and thought there couldn't possibly be any services anyone would need from *him*. He stayed on deck, looking at the sun sink and the scarlet ribbons that stained the sky afterwards like a scribbled message. The colour began to pale to a delicate flush, then a faint glimmer in the west, a hint that the United States, still far below the horizon, had lit a beacon to summon him.

It was turning cold, so he went to the cabin and climbed in with Anthony, who was sleeping soundly, a deep, heavy sleep unlike the restlessness of the last two nights. The sickness is over, Michael thought; he is better, even if his body is as hot as a furnace. He wriggled himself into his usual position, on his side, curled like a question mark, the skin of his back and the back of his legs touched by and protected by the bigger question mark. Well, I shan't be frozen tonight, he said to himself as Anthony's heat began to make him sweat. He was not long awake, and his sleep was filled with sweet dreams of New York, of Madge and Dan, of little children and himself climbing the branches of green trees in a plot where lilac bloomed.

IN the morning when he woke Michael wondered, for a minute, where on earth he could be: then he remembered. And felt happy.

He shifted slightly and stared at Anthony. "I'm deucedly ill," Anthony said. "I think you'll have to fetch a doctor. But don't worry! It's not the fever." For Michael was already out of bed and putting on his clothes. Anthony's face was as white as a blank piece of paper, and sweat poured from him.

There was a doctor, unusual at that time on a passenger ship: he had been paid for by one of the landlords whose evicted tenants were part of the misery in the hold. And the man in the next cabin was a well-known Galway physician, Dr Coffey, who had not wanted to emigrate at all, but his wife had pestered him to distraction – "for the sake of our dear children's lives!" – ever since the first potato rot nearly two years previously. Michael found both men. They removed the bedding so they could see Anthony's skin; they felt his pulse, looked at his tongue, then said they couldn't be sure what the matter was. "He doesn't have any obvious signs of typhus," was Dr Coffey's conclusion. "No rash on the chest, no darkening of the face. He has not vomited, you say?"

"No," Michael said. Annoying, he thought, that the question was directed to him; it was as if Anthony was no longer a human being, but an object incapable of speaking up for himself.

"Then I doubt it is the relapsing fever, either," Dr Coffey said. "Though we cannot rule it out at this stage. He is certainly sweating too much."

"A severe dose of influenza," declared the ship's doctor.

"Has he lice? I do not see any."

"No!" The suggestion made Michael very indignant. But, in order that they should not imagine his knowledge to be questionably intimate, he said "As far as I am aware."

Anthony smiled. "I'm the one who knows if I am louse-ridden," he told them. "And I'm not."

"There is much argument in medical circles about the cause of both diseases," Dr Coffey explained. "I myself think they are spread by lice, and have no connection at all with the hunger. There is a prodigious quantity of lice on people's bodies at the moment. My learned friend here, Dr Moylan, would disagree, and I have to admit I have seen men and women who never harboured a louse die of one or the other sickness."

"We have lice always," Dr Moylan said. "But the yellow fever and the black fever we do not have always. These two follow starvation."

"I'm not starving," Anthony said.

"It is odd. Perhaps we will never know."

This discussion irritated Michael hugely; an intellectual analysis of the origins of typhus and relapsing fever seemed to be of more concern to the doctors than the health of the patient. "What are we going to do?" he demanded. "How are we to set about curing him?"

"We'll think of the cure," Dr Coffey said, "when we know the ailment. It is best that he should not eat much. Give him liquids. Water. Soup."

"I'm dying of thirst!" Anthony cried.

"The ration is only a little," Michael said. "But he can have mine as well as his own. I do not need to wash, and food is food, cooked or uncooked." He filled a glass with water and gave it to Anthony, who swallowed it greedily. "But what shall I do if that is not enough?"

Dr Moylan shrugged his shoulders. "You could ask people, perhaps. They might let you have some if you offered them a few pence." He then said Anthony should be taken to the steerage, a section of which had been earmarked as a ward for the sick; someone who was not ill could change places and share the cabin.

Michael was adamant in his refusal to allow this, particularly when Dr Moylan said five people from the hold had become feverish during the night and had already been transferred there. "Do you want to sentence him to death?"

"It is for your own good. Do *you* want to be close to a man who may have typhus?"

"I've paid for this berth," Anthony said, "and I will not be shifted from it! Unless my friend wishes me to go."

"I do not!!" Michael yelled.

"Stay then," Dr Moylan said. "Confined in this cabin you are not infecting anyone else. This is the love of David and Jonathan! Between an Irishman and an Englishman that is queer."

"If every Englishman and every Irishman were so well acquainted," Anthony said, "there would not have been a nation of paupers living on nettles and sea-weed. No famine and no fever."

"True for you," Dr Coffey said. "True for you! What sends you both to America? *You* are not paupers."

"We hope to buy a piece of land and farm it," Michael said.

"Well . . . may God grant you your wish. I will keep an eye on you."

"I'm thirsty," Anthony said. "I'm burning!"

Michael only left the cabin that day to fetch the water ration and to cook. I never thought I should be giving him stirabout, he said to himself as he concocted a soup on the communal stove. Already they were both wishing they were in New York. The voyage might have some attraction of novelty, but, as with the two days at Noreen's, it was a period outside time, between existences. They speculated at length on the future – how they would live in America – but Anthony was too fatigued to talk much. His skin was still very hot, and he was consuming vast quantities of water.

Michael read to him: Blake. " 'But first the notion that man has a body distinct from his soul is to be expunged; this I shall do by printing in the infernal method, by corrosives, which in Hell are salutary and medicinal, melting apparent surfaces away, and displaying the infinite which was hid. If the doors of perception were cleansed every thing would appear to man as it is, infinite. For man has closed himself up, till he sees all things through narrow chinks of his cavern.' "

"How true it is!" Anthony said. "The Peacocks, Father Quinlan, your parents . . . they see human behaviour through the narrow chinks of their caverns. They've closed themselves up."

"And Ty?"

"His doors of perception never needed to be cleansed. So the popular judgement is that he's not right in the head."

"I wish he was here with us."

"I do, too."

"Would you like to make love with him?" Michael asked.

"Wouldn't you be jealous?"

"No. I'd be doing it with you and him together."

Anthony began to laugh, but stopped; it hurt. "Blake says somewhere 'Let the priests of the ravens of dawn no longer, in deadly black, with hoarse note curse the sons of joy. Nor pale religious lechery call that virginity that wishes but acts not. For every thing that lives is holy.' "

"You can only wish where Ty is concerned," Michael said. He

was worried. Discussing Blake or their future in America was avoiding reality – Anthony's illness, though he did not think it was typhus: the doctors had reassured him a little. But Anthony had visited the O'Learys less than a week before; the last surviving members of that family were dying. If someone infected you, the symptoms soon appeared. A week gone, and you were safe. Nevertheless . . .

"Is there more water?"

"You have drunk every drop." Michael went to the door. "I'll see what I can find."

No one in the cabins or on the decks would let him have any. People looked at him as if he was mad; they laughed or swore, and told him to go to the Devil. The sailor who had spoken to him the previous night tapped him on the shoulder. "I'm watching you," he said. "You're after something. What is it?"

"Water."

"So . . . your friend with the fever has drunk his share?"

"Yes. And mine too."

"I could give you some."

Michael smiled, but he did not relax. This man, he was certain, was not to be trusted. "I would be grateful," he said.

"How much do you want?"

"A ration? Six pints."

"Now that's a lot. Though . . . it could be done. It would cost you."

"I have the money."

The sailor laughed. "I don't want your money. I'll tell you." He leaned forward, and whispered in Michael's ear. Michael drew back, furiously angry; he raised an arm as if to hit the man in the face, but thought better of it. "You'll come round to the idea," the sailor said.

Michael stared after him. The first he'd ever met other than Anthony: so the two of them were not unique. Of course they were not; there had been men he knew of in history, in literature, and Anthony had told him of those he had encountered in London and in India. But they had never seemed quite real to Michael, certainly not as real as himself and his lover, happily marooned on the isolated island of Eagle Lodge. Now he had seen one in the flesh.

He did not think, as Miranda did, "How beauteous mankind is! O brave new world, that has such people in't!" because to do what had been proposed would be the act of a whore, the use of his body for material gain – even if that gain was not for his but for Anthony's benefit. He was, however, surprised to find himself suddenly swept by a huge thrill of sexual desire, quite unlike anything he had ever felt for Anthony: it was much more basic, much more animal.

I am irredeemably wicked. Then: I am *not*! Self-loathing is as contemptible as self-satisfaction. He shook his head in disbelief. Water. There was no escaping it; he would have to go down into the hold and ask someone there.

What he could see was skin and rags, no scrap of room, no inch of the wood of the floor without heads, torsos, arms, thighs. It seethed, was in constant motion like maggots on rotting bacon, and the skin was the sickly yellowish white of candle wax. The smells – of stale food, bad breath, vomit, clothes and bodies unwashed for months, piss, shit – made him retch, was fouler even than the stink of slimy, putrefying potatoes in a blackened field. The babel: clanging tones of argument, whines of pain and suffering, cackles of laughter, squawks of recalcitrant children, shrieks, hoots, groans; all that soft, melodious Irish lilt stirred into a vile cacophony that pierced his ears, dizzied his head.

His sense of repulsion was almost hatred. No, he would never be an angel like Anthony washing the feet of the destitute; he was a faulty man with virtues and vices that were not outstanding, a snob like his mother. Did he hate them, or hate what had made them like this? He was not sure he could distinguish. What he longed for was never to go down into that hold, never to be of them.

But he went down.

And discovered the charity he couldn't find in the cabins. He begged a little here, a little there, and eventually secured six pints. "Don't ask us again for God's sake," they all told him. "We have not enough as it is. But . . . for the crust of a loaf we'd spare a few drops." He returned to the deck, humility in him now, not hatred, but still with an iron determination not to be of them, not to be reduced to *that*.

"You've been years," Anthony said. "I'm sorry to be ...
peevish. But I was imagining you'd gone for ever. I think ... I'm
delirious."

"It wasn't so easy to get," Michael answered. He dampened a
handkerchief, and wiped Anthony's face. Then kissed him. "I
love you," he said. "Imagining me gone for ever! The nonsense
of it!" Anthony drank a glass of water in seconds, then another.
This quietened him; he seemed drained rather than restless.

"I'm drowsy. I think I'll try to sleep."

"I'll stay here and watch you."

"No, no, you go and cook; you've only eaten soup today."

A sudden lunge of the ship sent Michael and the glass flying
across the cabin, and almost threw Anthony out of bed. The ship
slowly corrected itself, then lurched again.

"A storm?" Michael said.

"What is it like outside?"

He opened the door and stared: no reassuring sunset this
evening; dull, rushing clouds, black on the horizon. He was
pushed to the rail by the movement of the ship. He gazed down
at the sea, a cold deep green; it rose and fell alarmingly, sudden
yawning hollows, then horse-back hills of water. Spray dashed
into his face. Returning to the cabin was like heaving himself up
rocks.

"There's a bucket in one of the trunks, the large one over
there," Anthony said. "I think I'm going to vomit. I don't
understand; I sailed to India in a worse sea than this, and I
wasn't sick once."

"And all you've eaten is soup! There is nothing to bring up!"
He found the bucket and put it beside the bed.

"You must cook your dinner," said Anthony. "Do it now
before the storm makes it impossible."

Cooking was so difficult that many people had decided not to
bother, which at least meant Michael could get near the stove. It
was not easy to keep the pan steady on the iron bars, however,
and several times the lurching was so fierce he was almost flung
into the flames. He chewed his meal half-cooked, and ate his
vegetables raw. He felt unwell himself, but it wasn't fever, just
sea-sickness. The best thing to do, he decided, was to be still, so
he went back to the cabin and climbed into bed. Anthony was

asleep. Michael lay awake for hours, listening to the deluge of rain that was now lashing the ship. Fragile, helpless specks humans were, he thought; he and Anthony now just as fragile and helpless as the stinking crowds in the hold. His stomach churned.

THE storm lasted two days. No damage was done; no lives were lost. But for forty-eight hours Michael felt he had absolutely no control over his fate, nor any trust in those to whom he had, temporarily, surrendered that control, the captain and the crew. The ship was a frail, defenceless thing, a shell containing a few hundred terrified men, women and children who were just statistics, a list of the dead to readers of newspapers next month. It shook, veered, yawed, without sense, without pattern; impossible to know if it would lift, slide sideways, plunge – or split apart. Being thrust up an endless mountain of water was the least nerve-wracking kind of motion, the inevitable drop down the other side the worst.

The rain was torrential. Everything on the ship was wet, every person chilled to the bone. The one dry place was in bed. Cooking was out of the question, nor did he want to cook: he was too sea-sick. He ate a few dusty oatmeal cakes. His only ventures out of the cabin were to the latrines, and to find water for Anthony. On the first evening, a woman in the hold gave him some – a brackish liquid it turned out to be – but on the second nobody would give him or sell him any, or even exchange it for food.

Anthony's condition was worse. The vomiting was frequent now though he had swallowed nothing but water, and the fever was acute: he was delirious most of the time, imagining, as far as Michael could judge from what he was saying, that he was in India drinking in the officers' mess, or dodging bullets in some fracas in Afghanistan. Occasionally his limbs twitched violently, or he would leap out of bed and try to rush onto the deck: Michael had great difficulty in holding him, for, ill though he was, he was sometimes possessed by an almost demonic energy. They did not sleep together now; Michael spent the nights on one of the trunks, wrapped in a blanket.

The doctors still refused to give an opinion on what the

sickness was, or when Anthony would recover. To Michael's often asked question of "Is it typhus?" they said, wearily, that they could not tell yet.

No one would let him have any water on that second evening because a number of people had become ill, mostly in the hold, and every drop was therefore precious. "Ship fever," Dr Moylan called it, and when Michael asked how it differed from the black or the yellow varieties, the answer was vague in the extreme, as if the doctor didn't really know. There were too many cases now, he said, to move into the steerage; they would have to suffer where they were. He shrugged his shoulders, as if it was quite beyond his abilities.

"But they will infect many people who are not sick at all!" Michael protested.

"What can I do? Nothing!"

Michael climbed out of the hold, his water cask still empty. The storm had abated, and though the deck slid and slithered underfoot, it was more or less possible to move about the ship. People were beginning to emerge into the fresh air, to dry their clothes or cook an evening meal. A thin, pallid sun was trying to push through the grey banks of cloud. "Water," Anthony kept whispering. "Water! If you love me, water!" His lips were parched; his eyes blazed. His skin was as wet as if he had been swimming. What can I do, Michael said to himself, echoing Dr Moylan, but he did not add "nothing." He could try stealing. Or go to the sailor? He was tempted. He hesitated a long time before he came to a decision: no.

But the sailor came to him.

"Still looking for water?" Michael did not reply. "Your cask is empty." Silence. "If you meet me at the lifeboats in a quarter of an hour, I'll fill it for you." He grinned at the play on words, but it was lost on Michael.

Again he had the feeling that his destiny had been snatched from his hands. But it's not true! I have free will; there is no predestination of good and evil. His feet walked leadenly to the lifeboats; his mind ordered them to turn back. Then: it is for Anthony's sake; for my lover. Thirst is harrowing him beyond endurance.

"Where is the water?"

"Afterwards."

"Who are you?"

"You can call me Jack." The sailor did nothing for a while, then, when nobody was near enough to see, he took Michael into one of the boats, laid him down and ripped his clothes off. Michael willed himself not to be stirred, but he was overwhelmed with sexual excitement, with desire for this huge brute of a man, this gorilla. It was his first experience of sex without love. He shrank inside himself, shut his head off completely, indignantly refusing to kiss or to be kissed. But those great paws of hands fingering him all over, the teeth biting his nipples, the cock fucking him: the sensation thrilled him beyond anything he had ever dreamed of. Orgasm was an explosion of light.

As he returned to the cabin, his cask now full (Jack had stolen the water from the ship's supplies), Michael found he was shaking. Not with guilt, remorse, or disgust: just the shock of total animal arousal and satisfaction. What can I say of myself; what kind of a man am I? But the questions flew out of his head when he opened the cabin door. Dr Coffey was feeling Anthony's pulse. He drew the blankets back, baring the skin to below the hips. There were red blotches on the stomach and the chest. The face was swollen, purple in colour, the eyes now puffy. The doctor said "Typhus."

"No!" Michael screamed. "No! No, no, no! NO!!" His legs folded, and he sank down to the floor.

THEY slept a drugged sleep that night, Anthony heavily sedated, but Michael with a smaller dose, just enough to calm him. The hour before he slept his thoughts were clear and his body not tense. The implications of what kind of a man he was now seemed entirely different: could he survive at all? Was there existence after Anthony? Typhus was death. But himself alone was unimaginable; it had never, since he met Anthony, occurred to him as a possibility. Anthony-and-Michael had been the sole point and purpose. Whatever reason could there be for going on? The direction the ship was pursuing was of no consequence now; America, or back to Galway, Greenland, the South Pole: it didn't matter. It was just a ludicrous, long, long fools' errand.

Ironically, it answered the problems of what had happened in the lifeboat. Michael Tangney as a sentient, thinking being, a mature, sane, balanced human able to make choices, was not involved; merely some bit of Michael Tangney, animal, a part of himself as unnecessary as bits of the body from our antediluvian ancestors are unnecessary left-overs. If he needed to do it again to obtain water, he would; if he wanted to gratify an urge, he would. It was of the utmost insignificance. Everything significant was here in this room: this wonder of a man, whose like he would never see again, nearing a stupid, meaningless, very painful death.

I don't think I can continue, he said to himself. Do I have to? Nothing is important any longer. There are no priorities – except to alleviate his suffering, do everything that is required, be with him to the end.

Five days passed, all more or less exactly alike. The ship ploughed on in seas neither rough nor calm; it rained, and the sun shone or did not shine. The fever patients in the hold grew in number, and the smell from below decks contaminated the whole ship. Michael was aware of it, but took little notice. He earned his extra water at nightfall and took little notice of that, either; the usual sensations tingled him and orgasm followed. There was none of the previous excitement; he was merely enduring a function, one of the day's tasks, like going to the latrines.

People nursing a loved one in the terminal stages of illness sometimes experience a sense of detachment that causes a mountain of guilt, but which they cannot avoid: this man or woman is no longer central to their lives, is not a person now; he or she is too hideously changed. Is unrecognizable. Perhaps it is an inbuilt mechanism to help us cope with grief or loss, in a way the start of coming to terms with inevitable truth. So it was for Michael.

This Anthony *was* unrecognizable. The face became so swollen and so dark – the colour deepened from purple to bluish black, like ink – that it wasn't Anthony's face at all. The stench of the disease was utterly revolting. Michael thought of Anthony sweating after some bout of physical exercise, the very faint but pleasing odour that was his skin and no one else's, his smell just after making love; but he couldn't join these memories to this putrefying stink that was all the world's foetid hovels, prison cells and ships' holds concentrated together in this one little room. The voice, too, was altered beyond imagining: the male resonance that shouted or laughed, or just rose and fell in the duets of their conversations was a cracked, jangling gruffness. "Water!" was all it could croak.

There were no lengthy emotional scenes, no memorable last words. Anthony for most of the time was so intent on dealing with pain that he could not communicate at all, but there were a few lucid moments, and in one of them he asked Michael to read aloud. The choice of book – the Bible – came as a surprise and the book of the Bible equally so – not a homily to comfort a man at the point of death, but a love song, the Song of Solomon. " 'By night on my bed I sought him whom my soul loveth: I sought him, but I found him not. I will rise now, and go about the city in the streets, and in the broad ways I will seek him whom my soul loveth: I sought him, but I found him not. The watchmen that go about the city found me: to whom I said, saw ye whom my soul loveth? It was but a little I passed from them, and I found him whom my soul loveth: I found him, and would not let him go.' "

"My life's story," Anthony said. He searched for Michael's hand and gripped it. Michael sat there, tears streaming down his face.

On the fifth evening, when he returned from his duties in the lifeboat, his water cask full to overflowing, he found that Anthony was dead.

CHAPTER TWELVE

W<small>E</small> therefore commit his body to the deep, to be turned into corruption, looking for the resurrection of the body (when the sea shall give up her dead) and the life of the world to come, through our Lord Jesus Christ; who at his coming shall change our vile body that it may be like his glorious body, according to the mighty working whereby he is able to subdue all things to himself."

"It was always glorious," Michael whispered. "Never vile."

It was a Protestant burial, there being – remarkably – no Roman Catholic priest on board. Not that Michael was concerned. But the relatives of the six others who shared the same funeral obsequies felt it keenly. The deaths, from typhus, had occurred in the hold.

The long fool's errand continued – how could it be otherwise? – in calm seas and warm sunlight. Michael withdrew into himself, nursing his grief. As nothing mattered it didn't matter what he did, though he found he was choosing one course of action rather than another: to eat, walk round the ship, or stay in bed and mope. He angrily repelled Jack's advances, much to the sailor's bewilderment. "There is room for me in your cabin now," Jack said.

Michael struck him in the face. He could have been knocked unconscious to the deck by one blow of that massive fist, but Jack, looking confused, merely rubbed the place on his cheek where he had been hit.

Why haven't I caught it, Michael asked himself; why am I not dead too? It was a reasonable question. Anthony had contracted typhus by inhaling the dust of louse excrement when he visited the last dying O'Leary, though no one then had even guessed it was possible to catch the disease that way. Anthony had no lice on his body, and none, therefore, were passed on. Hence Michael's deliverance. But it seemed totally incomprehensible that one of them should have been singled out for death and not the other, unless it was some quirk of an inexplicably malevolent Fate. It was easy for him, his agnosticism being so recent, to think Jansenist thoughts.

He could have asked another passenger to share the cabin with him now, and thus liberated some poor creature from the miseries of the hold, but the idea did not occur to him. His offer would have been refused: a corner of the hold still free from disease, disgusting though it might be, was preferable to a place where typhus could lurk. Only Jack – stupid or reckless – was not worried on that score. Michael spent hours in the cabin, alone, reliving every memory of Anthony he could summon to mind: the afternoon they had met, the occasions they had quarrelled, laughed, been companionably silent together, strolled on the beach, drunk too much, praised each other's beauty and goodness, made love. He was mentally at Eagle Lodge much more than he was aware of himself on the ship, and America he gave no thought to.

Dr Coffey observed him, and tried to engage him in conversation, but Michael answered distractedly or not at all, as if other people did not exist, or were figments of his dreams. "He is like some widow mourning her lost husband," the doctor remarked to his wife. Michael's grief puzzled him. The reason for it did not enter his head as a possibility; he thought as the inhabitants of Clasheen did: Michael-and-Anthony was not one of the permutations human beings indulged in. Like Dr Lenehan, he would not have been greatly censorious had he been told; there would have been a little sympathy as well as scientific curiosity.

But Michael did not tell him, even though the chances presented themselves and he had reached the point where he needed to decant his pain onto somebody. That would have to wait, he decided. Madge was in New York; Madge would remove some of this intolerable burden.

He could not sleep without Anthony's touch. He would doze off at ten or eleven, then surface at two a.m.: he is not here, he would say to himself; then be wide awake for the rest of the night. It was the trauma of the death all over again; sleep had dulled the knowledge and waking brought back the full horror of it: himself alone. Sometimes he just lay there and cried, exhausting himself in the process, but not enough for sleep to return. Dr Coffey, who never slept well, and who found the rolling of the ship created almost total insomnia, heard him through the thin wall of the cabin.

At other times Michael would get up, dress, stand by the ship's rail, and stare at the moonlit water. One night, the doctor, thinking that a chat would help to relieve the boredom of sleeplessness, followed him.

"The pair of us surely have unquiet consciences," he said.

"No," Michael answered.

"Insomnia has causes."

"I just can't sleep, is all. And the tiredness is there the whole day. Is worse each day! I am a lump of lead on two legs. I wish I could collapse. Keel over like a weary plant."

"What is the problem?"

"It is obvious. I cannot sleep."

A peculiarly circular conversation, the doctor thought. "I could give you drugs," he said. "They might cure the symptoms, but they would not remove the reasons . . . whatever they may be."

"It would help. Thank you."

"I understand your requiem for him, but you are too hard on yourself. It was not your fault."

"No. It was not my fault."

"Then. . . ?"

Michael looked away, down at the sea. The water was dark green, the moon in it glittering gold, chill and uninviting. "That was then; this is now," he said, enigmatically.

Dr Coffey sighed. "I think I will take a walk round the deck. If you want some laudanum, come to my cabin before you turn in. May *you* rest in peace."

Drugged, Michael lay in bed listening to the sounds of the ship – snatches of talk from the watch, sea slapping wood, a man laughing, the timbers: creak-creak, creak-creak, creak-creak. It is rocking me, he said to himself, as if I were a baby.

DR Coffey was working from dawn till bedtime; the fever cases had grown to epidemic numbers. "Dr Moylan and I require some help," he said one afternoon. "Will you help us?" He thought work would take Michael's mind off whatever was troubling him. Michael agreed; if it led to catching typhus, then well and good. What he had to do, mostly, was to take water casks on deck and fill them, then return them to their owners, people too sick to climb up the few stairs into the daylight. But it was still difficult – even more difficult as conditions had worsened – to force himself down into the hold.

When the hatches were opened, it was not only the smell that was disgusting, but a cloud of dank air could be seen rising, thick like a fog; all the stale breath, effluvia, and germs of the diseased and starving. He covered his nose and mouth with a handkerchief, but, after a while groping about in the gloom, stumbling over limp, exhausted bodies, it was possible to breathe more freely; he got used to the noisome atmosphere.

It was surprising, though he didn't know why he should be surprised, to witness in the hold scenes of compassion and generosity. He had imagined human beings in this state of degradation were beyond the ability to feel for their fellow men, that it was each person for himself. He saw a grandmother gently cradling a howling child, women with stalk-like limbs and racked with fever trying to comfort their babies, old hollow-cheeked men close to death saying another day gone was another day nearer salvation, the good life in the Land of Liberty. It made him ashamed of his despair, though it did not diminish it, let alone drive it away. He still hoped contact with the hold would give him typhus.

Jack saw him with the water casks. "The angel of mercy, aren't you?" he sneered. "Why do you never come to me now? I miss you . . . I miss . . ."

"I would if I wanted to," Michael answered. "But I do not."

"Why?"

"If I had the desire, I'd come."

"The voyage is not over yet," Jack said, almost as if he were the soothsayer announcing that the Ides of March were not gone.

"I doubt I'll change my mind."

"I'm leaving the ship in New York; there are better ways of

earning a living than this drudgery. Why don't you and me go into partnership? America means opportunity. We could be rich!"

"Doing what?"

"A handsome fellow can make as much as a pretty girl."

"On the streets?"

"Yes."

Michael laughed, for the first time in days. Emigrating to New York to sell his body was a grotesque joke, about as distant from his thoughts as flying to the moon. The man was crazy! "I don't think we'd suit each other," he said. He laughed again, and was glad to do so: it released something.

He helped the doctors every day. The jobs began to involve more than just fetching water; people began to know him, to look out for him. He attempted to comfort the sick, not with medicines, for the supply was nearly gone, but with words: he was not good at it, but he did try. He wrote letters for those who could not read or write, who were determined that friends and family back in Ireland should hear of their sufferings; he even considered writing a letter about it himself. To whom? Noreen? There was little point. Richard? He should tell Richard of Anthony's death, but that could wait.

He helped to distribute the food supply. Indian corn was running low; it was supplemented by a little salted meat and salted fish. The quality of this was so bad and the salt so strong that it was inedible. Those who ate it were racked with thirst. Most of it was thrown away.

Dr Coffey, who was pleased with him and liked him, said "You told me you wanted to farm a piece of land in America."

"Alone?" Michael answered. "There would be no point in it."

"So what will you do?"

He thought for a while. Then shrugged his shoulders.

"I'm hoping to buy a practice in New York," the doctor said. "I need a reliable, honest assistant. There is always a quantity of pen-pushing . . . and I could teach you to mix drugs . . . What do you say?"

"Thank you. I . . . I don't know. Perhaps . . . I should try and find myself first. Find . . ."

"How to go on?"

"Yes."

Dr Coffey frowned, and said: "You should find yourself a wife." Very difficult to read this man, he thought. Servant and secretary to the manager of an estate, the dead Englishman; that was the only fact he was sure of. Why they had decided to emigrate he did not know, but the hunger, of course, had ruined landlords as well as peasants.

"I am not looking for a wife," Michael said. "Why does everyone tell me to get married? It is not the sole reason we exist."

"What *are* you looking for?"

He smiled. "Purpose," he said.

A very pleasant fellow, the doctor said to Mrs Coffey, hard-working, thoughtful, trustworthy, but a terrible queer fish: as well as being a grieving widow, he was a philosopher.

"Perhaps he has some guilty secret," she said. "Perhaps he is running away from some crime he has committed."

"A crime? Him? Nonsense!"

ANOTHER twenty-four hours and the New World would be visible. Miraculous, Michael thought — or was it a great pity? — that he had not been infected with any disease, not even the chronic diarrhoea that everyone in the hold had to live with. *The Cedar of Lebanon* had started the voyage with four hundred and forty-four passengers; one hundred and fifty were arriving in New York with fever, and one hundred and eight had died at sea. Michael had helped to shroud bodies in sail-cloth, and dragged some of them up to the deck for burial.

The food ran out on that last day, and, because of the wine-soaked casks, the water ration had been cut a week previously to a quart per person. Despite the conditions in the hold, the tenacity of people was astonishing. They still had hope: a day more to endure, then dry land. Some, even though near death, were jubilant.

Michael was not, but he was certainly looking forward to the end of the voyage. The ship was as enclosed as a prison; dreary, unchanging, a living Hell. The same words applied to himself: the utterly depressing loneliness after Anthony was a living Hell. There was Dr Coffey of course, and the passengers in the hold, but he always had to return to the cabin. It was filled with

Anthony – his books, his Indian souvenirs, a dried splash of his vomit that had not been washed off the wall, even the smell of him on the bedding. But no Anthony. Not a day passed without Michael just sitting for hours, eyes full of tears.

Jack did not disturb him again. Curious to know the reason, Michael kept watch: the sailor had found somebody else. Michael was glad, but a little part of him felt a prick of annoyance; though sexual activity was the last thing he wanted, he felt, in a way, rebuffed.

On that last morning the decks were crowded as they had not been since the passengers had waved goodbye to their relatives and loved ones on Galway quay. Only those too ill to move kept below; everyone else came up to see the United States of America. How long would it be now, they wondered; how long after that till they disembarked in New York? This was America – no landlords, no hunger, no fever, no British. The atmosphere was one of intense excitement. But the crowd was half the size it had been in Galway. The dead and the sick accounted for that; many of the rest had altered from the starving, emaciated, ragged scarecrows they were at the beginning of the voyage to even more ragged, colourless, spectre-like skeletons, feeble beyond belief.

When Michael saw the American coast on the horizon – a long, thin, grey thread much like his last view of the west of Ireland – he forgot for a moment, and turned to say "There it is!" But Anthony wasn't with him. He choked on his words, and the light in his eyes died.

An hour later *The Cedar of Lebanon* took on board the port physician of New York, who, on discovering that there were over a hundred cases of fever, directed the ship to Staten Island, where it would be held for a month's quarantine. The sick would be transferred to the hospital on the island; the rest could stay on board or disembark, but nobody was allowed to proceed into New York itself until thirty days had gone by. This was a staggering blow, almost devastating to people whose only wish was to be on the American mainland: a tiny island was as much of a prison as the hold they had travelled in. The excited atmosphere evaporated immediately, and the gloom increased when it was learned that there was nowhere for the healthy to stay at night; they would have to sleep on the ship.

Staten Island was a wholly unsuitable place for a quarantine station. It was so close to New York that a great number of people, who had no connection with the hospital, lived there and went by ferry into the city to work. They hated the presence of the hospital and the quarantined ships, and complained frequently of the risks they were subjected to. The stench blown on the wind from the holds, they said, was a hazard to their health; filthy, revolting garbage thrown overboard got washed up by the tide and spread disease.

But the real health hazard was caused by the ferry. Crowds of people came to see their relatives in quarantine, and there was little to prevent those who were ordered to stay on the island for the statutory month from returning with their families to the city, and therefore disappearing for good from the reach of the authorities. Typhus inevitably crossed the water. When *The Cedar of Lebanon* anchored, New York was suffering from an epidemic every bit as severe as that raging in Ireland.

Michael was determined to slip away on the ferry; like the other passengers he found little difference between being on the ship and being quarantined – both were intolerable checks on freedom. He was curious, now that he was so near, to explore New York, and his desire to find Madge was overwhelming. She, of course, would not be among the citizens coming over to look for relatives; she didn't know he was there. He had left Clasheen so soon after her that they had had no time to exchange letters. A letter, he thought, from Madge was probably even now waiting for him at Eagle Lodge, if Richard had not mailed it back or destroyed it. Eagle Lodge! It was so far distant and lost in the past; in another age. Another Michael.

Dr Coffey begged him not to leave for New York at once. He was himself needed at the quarantine station, he said; it was overcrowded and desperately short of medical staff. Michael could earn good money there, a great deal more than he had ever earned in Ireland; nurses, porters, and auxiliaries of every kind were wanted. Michael hesitated. What would happen to him, alone in New York? He did not have many skills to offer. He could read and write, which was more than most of the emigrants were able to do, but it wasn't much: New York might well have an abundance of literate employees. He went to the quarantine station and volunteered his services.

The pay *was* good, but what he saw at the hospital sickened him. Conditions were almost as bad as in the hold of *The Cedar of Lebanon*. The buildings were supposed to house four hundred patients, but there were three times that number, many of them herded together in flimsy wooden shacks that had been thrown up when the authorities grew alarmed by the size of the Irish influx. The roofs of all the buildings leaked, and sanitation was virtually non-existent. Proper beds were few; nearly everyone lay on iron grids thinly covered with straw, which, as their occupants were mostly skeletons of skin and bone, were as agonizing as the thirst the fever produced. The food was no better than on board ship, and the doctors and nurses more unsolicitous and ill-trained than Dr Moylan. At least he had not abused those in his care. Every single case of fever on Staten Island, Michael noticed, was an emigrant from Ireland.

Such was the welcome the victims of the Great Hunger found in the Land of the Free. Not that it made any of them wish to return; nothing could be as bad as that. But, Michael realized, Britain was not responsible for all famine and fever deaths; American dislike of being made the receiving ground for the sick and the impoverished contributed to the total. In 1847 "Give me the wretched refuse of your teeming shore" was not exactly a heart-felt sentiment in the United States.

An old woman, lying inert in the hospital, Michael thought he recognized. Her skin was yellow, and so loose he felt if he touched it it would peel off like the skin of a hot potato. She had long grey hair, as wild and twisted as a tree tormented by the wind in winter. He had last seen her screaming at him on the other side of a pane of glass.

"Surely you are from Coolcaslig?" he said. She nodded. "From the workhouse?"

"Yes."

"I remember."

"I remember a well-dressed, well-fed young fellow sitting on a cart. I took you for the gombeen man. And I on the rack with thirst, shrieking for water."

He hung his head, ashamed. "I could not help," he muttered.

"I know. It is what you stood for I hated. Why should some suffer the tortures of the damned and others grow fat?"

"I've thought of you often, since. You seemed to me to be yelling for . . . all of us. The whole disaster."

"I'm a poor widow. I buried my husband and all the five little ones. I may look an old hag of eighty, but I'm thirty-two. Cathleen McGillycuddy from Cahernane Cross. Not Cathleen ni Houlihan."

"Which ship did you come on?"

"*The Free Slave.* A good name, isn't it? But the crossing was worse than the worst weeks I spent in Coolcaslig poorhouse. Hell has no room like it."

"What happened?"

"The yellow fever. I nearly despaired each time I relapsed, but I fought it, fought it, and, please God, I am better now. There is purpose in everything. I have survived."

"You have beautiful hair." He touched it.

She laughed. "My husband never told me so," she said.

A nation other than the Irish, he thought, would have been extinguished utterly by the calamities of history, chance and the British, but we are the toughest people on earth. For the first time since Anthony's death, he began to think his own survival was of importance.

THE highways and byways of New York, he found, were no more paved with gold than those of anywhere else. It was a terrible place, corrupt, violent, and lawless. Wealth and poverty existed side by side on foul-smelling streets full of pigs, mad dogs, cattle and rats. There were no drains or sewers, no health authority, and the administration of the city was hopelessly inadequate. It was densely populated; people lived cheek by jowl with cemeteries, bone-boiling factories, glue works and slaughterhouses. There were some smart well-kept districts, but much of Manhattan Island was one big slum, and in the worst conditions in the worst part of the slum the Irish lived.

He set about looking for Madge and Dan. He had thought it would be easy, but he combed the city without success. It was these expeditions to the tenements and cellars that opened his eyes to the continued suffering of the majority of Irish immigrants. He discovered filthy rooms, verminous beds, men and women so nearly naked they could not go out of doors, people so ill-suited to life in another country – starving, or sick, or with no skills at all except how to use a spade for digging potatoes – that they would never find work, not even the lowest-paid drudgery no one else wanted to do.

He met families robbed of everything they possessed by crooks who promised jobs, by touts who sold counterfeit rail tickets, by the owners of private workhouses. He saw people who had been turned out of their rooms because they could no longer afford them, their money and their property grabbed by unscrupulous lodging-house keepers who charged exorbitant prices for food and a bed. The same families who had been evicted from their cabins in Ireland were now evicted all over again and forced to shelter in an American version of a scalp or a scalpeen – tiny, unventilated basements that were often without light, without food, that contained not a single stick of furniture, not even a box to sit on.

He saw a community demoralized by drink and fighting: alcohol was cheap, and an obvious way to escape, temporarily, from misery and disappointment. In some of these holes the only possessions were bottles of whiskey. It was as bad as Ireland, though no one would acknowledge that fact: the starvation continued, and the fever, and the white-haired old women and the little children begging in the streets. Just as bad, psychologically, was the shock of the new environment; beautiful Ireland, its mountains, shore-line, mists and colours had been exchanged for damp, rat-infested cellars in a dilapidated, dirty urban ghetto.

Dr Coffey had money and connections; he was able to buy a practice and a house with a large, tree-shaded garden in one of the more salubrious areas of the city. Michael lived in his house for some years, never really unpacking his things, always imagining it was a temporary arrangement, that he would move out and go west to seek his fortune. But when he did move out it was not to go west.

He began his working life in New York as Dr Coffey's secretary, though he spent two days every week at a nearby hospital as a porter and nurse. He earned good wages; his wants were few, and he saved money. In other matters he was not so blessed. The shadow of Anthony was too long; he could not think of another lover. There were male prostitutes in New York, as in any big city at any date, and he knew where to find them. Sometimes he did so. He did not see why he should be a sexual hermit.

He wrote two letters, to Noreen and Richard. Neither of them wrote back – Noreen no longer considered Michael a brother of hers, but a possible source of contamination to her young son, and Richard did not wish to communicate with a person he had called a male strumpet.

He could not find Madge and Dan. He wondered whether the *Lord Kingston* had been diverted from New York for some reason, and had anchored at Boston or another city up the coast. He began to fear the worst, that it had gone down at sea. It was Cathleen McGillycuddy who told him the truth. He met her one evening in a bar: she was still painfully thin, but brighter, happier, cured of her sickness, and living in a room near Trinity Church.

"My second cousin, Eileen, rents it; she crossed the water a year ago," she said. "A palace after what I have lived through. And how is yourself?"

He told her, then asked if she'd ever heard of the *Lord Kingston*.

She looked amazed. And upset. "The *Lord Kingston*," she repeated. "Yes. I certainly have heard of it. My uncle and his wife and all his family were on that ship. Did nobody tell you what happened? It sank in a fearful storm, and not one man, woman, boy, girl or baby was spared."

"Not *one*?"

"No." She saw the pain and horror in his face. "There were people on board . . . you knew?"

"My sister," he said. "And her husband. She was . . . pregnant." His voice rose to a cry. "I have no one left now! No one!" He buried his head in his hands. "Madge! Dear, darling Madge!" he sobbed. "*Drowned*! No one will ever hear my story now!"

She lifted his head, stroked his face, and whispered: "It isn't so. I'll listen."

"What is the point?" he said, wearily.

"There is purpose in everything. I told you that when I was in the hospital on Staten Island. Are you . . . quite alone in the world?"

"Yes. My . . . he . . . died of typhus. On the ship."

"He?"

"There isn't a name like husband, because the world doesn't admit such things exist. But I was as married to him as any man and his wife are to each other. You are shocked?"

"I'm not shocked. Nothing can shock me now. Tell me about him: what was his name?"

"Anthony."

Hours later, when he was too exhausted to say more, she said "There'll be another Anthony. I'm sure of it."

"You talked of purpose," Michael said. "I have to find that first."

"You will."

"I can only try. I promise you."

"Come and see me. Often." She smiled. "You also have beautiful hair. Do you know that?"

"Yes," he said. And smiled too.

ABOUT a million and a half people died during the Famine of hunger and its attendant diseases. Another million emigrated. Ireland lost almost a third of her population, and in the years that followed hundreds of thousands more joined their relatives in the United States, Canada, Britain and Australia. A nation that did not have enough room is now one that has too much to spare. No event or person in history, Cromwell, King William, the penal times, 1798, the Easter Rising, the Black and Tans, the Civil War, changed Ireland so much as the Famine. The pattern of early marriages was broken: no country in Europe now has so many elderly bachelors. An all-pervading melancholy seemed to replace the natural gaiety of the people, and it is still there.

Hatred of Britain and all things British was a child of the Famine. "We have subscribed, worked, visited, clothed, for the Irish," said Lord John Russell, "millions of money, years of debate, etc., etc., etc. The only return is rebellion and calumny. Let us not grant, lend, clothe, etc., any more, and see what that will do." The legacy of that attitude is the atrocities we live with now.

"I do not know how farms are to be consolidated if small farmers do not emigrate," Charles Trevelyan said, "and by acting for the purpose of keeping them at home, we should be defeating our own object. We must not complain of what we really want to obtain." The object the British really wanted to obtain was not total extinction, but it is difficult to see anything in Trevelyan's words other than a desire to reduce the population substantially. If that could be done, Ireland would be more malleable, less seditious, no longer a threat. If hunger, disease and flight were to be the weapons, well, so be it. More than a century later we are paying the interest on the Russell government's policies.

Several generations passed before those who left Ireland could take advantage of the opportunities of the New World. No emigrants were as unskilled, as poverty-stricken as the Irish; they were the children of the slums, exploited, disliked, feared and ignored. But times change. Even Presidents now search for a scrap of Irish lineage and they parade it proudly, like a banner.

Michael was one of the few to benefit from the opportunities. Six years after his arrival he had saved enough money to go to medical school. When he qualified as a doctor, he began to practise in New York's Irishtown, and he worked there for the next fifty years. He had learned, at last, to love the people of the one-roomed cabins, the ships' holds, the city ghettoes. He eventually found another man to love and to live with, an Irish doctor, whose apartment was two streets away from the Coffeys' house. It was not the same as it had been with Anthony; the intensity of that experience, its romantic passion and total commitment could not be repeated: it is for many of us only once in a lifetime, if that. He was fulfilled and relatively content, however; when he was dying he was able to think he had led a worthwhile, rewarding existence.

MY mother, on the occasions she has discussed her Irish ancestors, has talked of an incident that occurred at about the time of King Edward the Seventh's death, when she was eight. Someone, a great-uncle or a great-great-uncle, had emigrated to

America during the Famine. What happened to him there she doesn't know. The only facts in her memory are that he died at a very old age in 1910, that he never married, did not make a will, but left a considerable fortune. Attorneys acting for his estate asked for anybody who had a claim to it to come forward and prove that they were his relatives. About a hundred people did so, and nearly every one of them was found to have no connection at all with the family. Virtually the entire fortune disappeared into the pockets of the attorneys, whose expenses and fees for sorting out the muddle were vast. My grandmother eventually received twenty pounds, and her children five pounds each.

The only other piece of information my mother remembers is that the solicitor who finally sent the cheque was a Galway man named Moriarty, of the firm of Hanrahan and Moriarty. This stays in her head because, at the age of eight, it seemed a peculiar, amusing surname. Mr Moriarty died sixty years ago, and his papers and documents have long since been destroyed. So nothing of Michael Tangney's exists now.

Except for a silver spoon, which Mr Moriarty sent to my great-aunt Belinda; it has engraved on it the initials M.T. and this motto: *Hungry dogs will eat dirty puddings*. It is on my desk in front of me, as I write this.

also in this series:

Edward Lucie-Smith
THE DARK PAGEANT

In the confusion of fifteenth-century France, with the kingdom riven between the King of England, the Duke of Burgundy and the still uncrowned Dauphin, two romantic figures stand out: Joan of Arc, whose "voices" led her king to coronation and herself to flames and sainthood, and the glittering Gilles de Rais, Marshal of France, whose dark voices led him to the scaffold and hundreds of little victims to a ghastly death. Joan is still a heroine to France; Gilles has become a symbol of limitless evil.

Gilles' story is told here through the eyes of Raoul de Saumur, his childhood companion and lifelong comrade-in-arms, impelled by curiosity to fathom his friend's secret, yet terrified himself by what he might discover.

"An historical meditation on the paralysing fascination of evil" – *The Times.*

"The novel has to cope with this ghoul and with the enigma of Joan herself and does so with a solid sense of period" – *Guardian.*

ISBN 0 85449 006 X (paperback only)

GMP publish a diverse range of books, including art and photography, biography, fiction, health, history, humour, literature, poetry and politics. Our full catalogue is available on request from GMP Publishers Ltd, PO Box 247, London N15 6RW.